HIS TO PROTECT

DOROTHY MAILLET

CONTENTS

Chapter 1

I glanced over to see he was still asleep, I pulled the cover back off of me slowly trying desperately not to wake him. He didn't move so I held my breath as I scooted to the edge of the bed wincing as I moved my legs. They were aching bad today, I glanced over at Trey as I climbed out of the bed. Oh god please don't wake up! I gritted my teeth and tried desperately not to step on any squeaky floorboards as I tip toed over to the chair to grab my clothes and slipped into the hallway naked praying that none of his boys were up so early and would see me. That would be really bad for both me and them!

I pulled on my jeans and black vest top and made my way downstairs quickly grabbing a juice box and granola bar before heading to my car. He was gonna be mad that I left without saying goodbye but I really needed to go to classes today, I had a test coming up and I couldn't fail, not again, this was already a re-sit. I sped to off to school praying I wouldn't be late again, I really could do without another detention!

I met my best friend in the world in the car park. Melissa Porter was the best friend a girl could ask for, supportive, loyal, funny and kind. She was also gorgeous with poker straight blonde hair that hung just past her shoulders with the tips dyed a shocking cherry red. She had big blue eyes and was always smiling, she was around 5 foot 5 just a little shorter than me and was stick thin even though she ate like a horse. I on the other hand was about 5 foot 7 with a curvy figure which I hated, I had plain brown hair that was just above my shoulders and brown eyes and was totally average, well maybe not even that.

"Hey Brook" she said as she threw her arms around me happily, I winced as she touched my sore back but worked hard not to show it.

"Hey Mel" I said grinning.

"You stay at Trey's last night?" she asked curiously, I nodded and looked down at myself.

"That obvious huh?" I asked looking over my clothes that I had thrown on in less than a minute flat.

She laughed "You wore that yesterday, dirty stop out" she said teasingly as she linked her arm through mine and we started walking off to classes.

"So what, no one'll notice, who cares" I said shrugging.

She grinned, "Whatever tramp, guess what?" she said skipping along excitedly.

"What?" I asked grinning, what the hell is she so excited about? She only gets this excited about shopping, boys and oh no! "Not a party" I said grimacing.

She nodded happily, "My brothers best friend is having a party on Saturday and I scored us invites!" she said practically bouncing on the spot. I rolled my eyes, as if Trey would let me go to a party without him.

"I'm not going Mel" I said sternly.

She snorted "Yes you are! You need to have some fun without that asshole, and I know he's going away for the weekend" she said waving her hand dismissively.

I frowned "I can't, Trey would go crazy if he found out I went out when he wasn't here" I admitted. Mel knew all about Trey, how he was jealous and possessive and would beat me if I did anything wrong. God if I went to a party without him he would literally beat me senseless and I couldn't stand anymore pain, not yet, I was still recovering from the last beating he gave me for ruining his favourite shirt by putting it in the tumble dryer and shrinking it.

"You're going! This is gonna be the hottest party of the year, and besides, it's my birthday, I'm gonna be seventeen so you have to come with me, for my birthday" she said proudly thinking she'd cornered me.

I laughed "Your birthday's not for another two weeks" I said shaking my head, she is so sneaky.

She grinned "Yeah well think of it as a early present then, come on please, you're my best friend, you have to come with me, please Brook" she said giving me the puppy dog face. I sighed, I guess I could go for a couple of hours. I didn't know any of Mel's brothers friends so it shouldn't get back to Trey that I went.

"Oh for goodness sake fine! I'll go but ONLY if Trey definitely leaves for the weekend, there's some big deal going down and he said he needs to get it sorted before he can go" I said shrugging. Trey never really told me anything to do with his business and to be honest I just didn't want to know. She squealed and I smiled at how happy a simple party could make her. "Come on then, let's get to class" I said rolling my eyes. Hopefully I'd be able to go as long as Trey left town like he planned and I wouldn't have to let her down.

After school I made my way back to my house, Trey was already standing in my kitchen waiting for me as I walked through the door, "Hey boyfriend" I said smiling and trying to ignore the glare he was shooting me. He slammed his cup down onto the kitchen side smashing it and I held my breath.

"Where the fuck have you been Brook?" he shouted as he strode over and grabbed my arm digging his fingers into my skin. I tried not to flinch as he didn't like it when I was scared of him.

"I was at school" I said quietly looking at the floor not wanting to see the blow coming. I knew I shouldn't have crept out of the bed this morning.

He jerked my arm making me slam into his chest, "Why the fuck did you not say goodbye?" he shouted squeezing my arm tighter. Oh shit! Come on Brook think of something to make this better, I thought desperately of a reason but I couldn't come up with anything that would satisfy him at all. He slammed me back hard against the wall, I couldn't help the little yelp that came out as pain shot up my already bruised back. He put his hands on the wall either side of my head and leant his face into mine, "You think that's ok just to go fucking sneaking off without saying goodbye? Were you meeting another guy?" he asked angrily.

I gasped, holy shit this is bad! I wrapped my arms around him tight ignoring the ache in my upper arm where he gripped me so tight. "No hon, I swear, I went to school, I had a test in calculus and I didn't want to wake you so early I swear" I said honestly begging him to believe me with my eyes. His face softened slightly as he took a deep breath, he looked into my eyes for a minute before stepping back and running a hand through his short brown hair.

I felt my heart rate slowing back down again as he relaxed, he smiled his cocky smile and held his arms open for me. He looked really cute when he smiled, he didn't do it very often, not a real one anyway. I pushed away from the wall and went to him immediately wrapping my arms around him as he hugged me back kissing the side of my head. "I'm sorry baby, I just thought when I woke up and you weren't there that you'd left me, I've been calling you all day" he said as he held me tight.

I shook my head "No Trey, I wouldn't, I just needed to get to school, I had my phone off the battery was dead, I wouldn't leave you" I said wincing as his hand brushed over my bruised back.

"Good, because I woudn't let you leave me anyway" he said smiling but his eyes were hard, he meant it, this was a warning. I cupped his face in my hands and pulled his face to mine, swallowing my fear as I kissed him. He moaned in the back of his throat and pulled me closer as he kissed me deeply.

"Get on the counter" he said unbuttoning my jeans and pulling them down over my ass, he pushed me backwards to the kitchen counter. I gulped and lifted myself onto the counter, as soon as I was on he yanked my jeans the rest of the way off and ripped open his flies. He grabbed my legs yanking me to the edge of the counter as he ran his hands down my body looking at me lustfully. Oh please not again please! My heart started beating way too fast as I saw the passion in his eyes, this was gonna hurt, he wasn't interested in being gentle today.

He kissed me hard hurting my lips making me move my head back and bang my head on the cupboard behind me. He gripped my hips and thrust his shaft into me hard. I gritted my teeth as pain started to burn in my core, he wrapped my legs around his waist as he continued to pound into me. He kissed down my neck as his breathing sped up, oh God please hurry up!

He was moaning so I matched my moans to his and arranged my face to look like I was enjoying myself. He smiled as he pulled me closer to him gripping my hips tightly banging himself into me harder and deeper, I tried desperately not to wince as each thrust felt like being stabbed with a knife. "Fucking hell Brook, that's good, arch your back baby" he ordered, I did as he told me and he grunted breathlessly, a couple more thrusts and he climaxed digging his fingernails into my thighs.

I closed my eyes as he kissed over my face, "God that was good baby" he murmured against my lips.

I nodded "Yeah" I lied wrapping my legs round him pulling him closer to me, he pulled out of me and I breathed a sigh of relief.

"You'd better clean this shit up before your Mom gets home" he said nodding towards the smashed cup and the puddle of coffee on the side. He walked away zipping up his flies and went to sit on one of the kitchen stools watching me climb down from the counter. I grabbed my jeans and bent to put them on, "No, leave them off and do it" he said raising his eyebrow at me smirking.

I sighed and threw them back to the floor, God this was embarrassing! I grabbed a cloth and started mopping up his mess while he watched me with a small satisfied smile on his face. When I was done I looked at my jeans longingly and then back to him, he nodded so I grabbed them and put them on quickly before he changed his mind and wanted to fuck me again. I was still aching from his rough antics last night and that little episode didn't help at all!

"Come sit with me baby" he said patting his knee, I smiled and went to sit with him, "So I'm leaving tomorrow around one, so I guess I won't see you until Monday after school" he said running his hands down my back brushing my hair behind my ear. I nodded and hugged him, "Brook, why the hell are you wearing this shirt? You look like shit! Your too fucking fat to wear something this tight" he said sneering at me.

I gulped, and looked down feeling like a piece of shit, I knew I didn't have a perfect body, he reminded me everyday. I shook my head "I'm sorry Trey, I won't wear it anymore" I said fighting the tear that was trying to escape.

He smiled "Good, because it's fucking embarrassing, seeing you walk around with everything hanging out like that, you know everybody's laughing at you right?" he said smoothing my hair down. I felt sick, god everyone was laughing at me?

"Ok, thank you for telling me" I said quietly.

He smiled "You're welcome baby, now go change" he said happily easing me off of his lap.

I walked up the stairs and went straight over to the mirror looking at myself, I couldn't stop the tears from falling down my face, how the hell could I have gone to school looking like this all day? I looked like a fat ugly tramp. I ripped the top off of my head and threw it in the bin, I glanced back at myself in the mirror and brought my hands to my stomach gripping the skin there, I closed my eyes not able to look at myself anymore and grabbed a baggy t-shirt and quickly did fifty sit ups before heading back downstairs to see Trey.

My Mom was home now and her and Trey were sat around drinking tea in the lounge, as I walked in Trey smiled at me approvingly and patted the seat beside him.

"Hi Honey" my Mom said smiling at me.

"Hi Mom, good day?" I asked as I sat close to Trey leaning on him and folding my legs up resting my chin on my knees to hide my stomach from view even more.

She nodded smiling, "I had a great day, I was just telling Trey about this little boy who came into the hospital today, he was unconscious and" I couldn't listen to her anymore so I smiled and nodded pretending I was listening all the time wishing Trey would go home so I could go upstairs and crawl into bed and cry.

"Well I'm gonna go make dinner, you staying Trey?" my Mom asked a little while later standing up and heading to the kitchen.

"I'd love to Beth" he said politely, she nodded, my Mother adored Trey because whenever they would meet he would be the perfect boyfriend. I mean she had her reservations about him at first, he is seven years older than me. What mother likes being introduced to their thirteen year olds boyfriend who's twenty? I can't imagine many parents would be thrilled about it.

But we'd been together for four years now and he had some-how convinced her after about a year that he was worthy, that was around about the time that he first hit me, when I was fourteen, I forgave him then, but I should have just walked away. Now I was trapped, he wouldn't let me go. I tried to break it off once and he went crazy, broke my arm and three ribs, split my head open and told me that next time I tried to break it off with him he would kill my Mom. I lied to everyone about it, the only one that knew a slight part of the truth was Melissa, I told her that he hit me occasionally as she started to become suspicious about some bruises I had. I made her promise not to tell, and to this day she hasn't.

I sat watching TV with Trey in silence until dinner was ready then went into the kitchen to eat. I sat down at the table and my Mom put a big plate of cheesy chicken and chips in front of me. Shit this has a lot of calories in it! I glanced at Trey who looked at my plate and shook his head slightly meaning I shouldn't eat it. "Thanks Mom this looks great" I said honestly, it did look good.

"Yeah thanks Beth this is awesome" Trey said shovelling his food down his throat.

I picked up my knife and fork and began scraping the cheese from the chicken, I could eat a chicken breast right? I mean that's not too bad, I'd just leave the chips and the cheese. I finished the chicken and my Mom glanced at my plate, "You not eating the chips hon?" she asked curiously.

I shook my head "Sorry Mom, I had a big lunch today so I'm not too hungry" I said apologetically.

She smiled, my Mom was incredible, the best Mom a girl could have, so I couldn't let Trey hurt her. She was the only reason I put up with him, that and the fact that I didn't want to be on my own. I mean who the hell else would want to be with me? I can't go through life on my own, Trey always says he was doing me a favour being with me, he said he loved me and that's why he could put up with my flaws and my body.

"No problem honey, what did you have?" she asked happily.

I smiled "Mel and I went to the café down the road, I had lasagne" I lied. Actually I had hardly eaten at all today, I had been trying to cut down on the amount I ate for the last couple of weeks when Trey first told me I was starting to put on weight.

"That's nice hon" Mom said turning to Trey and starting a conversation about her car that was due to a service this month and wanted to know where the best place to take it was.

I tuned out and looked longingly at the pile of food that was still on my plate, I could feel my stomach hurting where I was so hungry. When everyone was done I excused myself from the chocolate cake desert and went to wash up while they ate.

After dinner we sat back in the lounge watching TV. At nine Trey turned to me and nodded towards the stairs, I smiled and took his hand, "We're gonna go listen to some music Mom" I said pulling Trey up from the couch. He smiled and followed me up the stairs eagerly, as soon as my door shut he grabbed me and pushed me towards the bed making me sit on the edge as he stood in front of me.

"I think you should give me a little going away present, show me how much your gonna miss me this weekend" he said smirking at me as he pulled his top off over his head. I nodded and reached to pull my top off but he caught my hand, "No baby, I don't want to see that, it'll turn me off" he said turning his nose up. I gulped ashamed of my body, wow I must be disgusting if he can't even look at me anymore! He unbuttoned his jeans pulling his shaft free and putting one hand on the back of my head guiding my mouth to his erection with a huge smile on his face.

When he finally left at about eleven I changed into some sweats and jumped on the treadmill running for ten miles then doing a hundred sit ups. I grabbed a piece of newspaper and taped it over my mirror inside my wardrobe covering it so I couldn't look at myself anymore. I couldn't see myself anymore, not if I was that repulsive. I climbed in the bed still sweaty and sticky from my work out and cried myself to sleep, how the hell did I let myself get like this?

CHAPTER 2

I was staying at Mel's for the weekend seen as Trey had left for Denver for three days. He text me and told me he'd left so I went straight to Mel's after school on Friday. I followed behind her in my car to her little house on the edge of the woods, I loved Mel's house, it was so cute and adorable. Her family were awesome too, and her brother, my god her brother was hot! I used to have a huge crush on Scott, he had blonde hair and big blue eyes like Mel, but he had a bad boy vibe going on. He wasn't a bad boy though, he was never in trouble or anything, he just had this badass attitude about him, I definitely wouldn't want to mess with him!

He was a college student so I hadn't seen him for almost a year, but he was back for the holidays today apparently so I was looking forward to seeing him. As I pulled up behind Mel I could see her waiting there for me excitedly, we were going to watch a movie tonight and have a girls night, she wanted to paint toenails and wax our legs all that type of girly crap and was ridiculously eager and excited about it! I skipped up to her pretending to be excited about it too.

"Come on then, I think Scott's home now" she said happily, Mel loved her brother and missed him like crazy. We walked inside and I saw a messy blonde head for a fraction of a second before he scooped Mel into a hug spinning her around in a circle making her laugh.

"Hey Scott!" she cried happily hugging him in the death grip.

"Hey Mel, missed you" he said just as happily. He glanced over to me and smiled his sexy little smile that always made me feel a little like I wasn't in control of myself. "Well hello Brooklyn, you've grown" he said smirking at me as he pulled me into a hug. I instantly regretted the choice of clothes, god even he said that I had put on weight!

I hugged him back uncomfortably "Hi Scott how's college?" I asked smiling.

He grinning his sexy smile at me, "Pretty good, not very many hot girls up there though, maybe I should come back here, what do you think?" he asked looking me over slowly making me feel so uncomfortable I wished the ground would open up and swallow me.

"Don't start hitting on my best friend already Scott come on!" Mel cried laughing as she grabbed my hand and pulled me towards the kitchen. Hitting on me? Why the hell would he hit on me? Scott followed us into the kitchen still raking his eyes over my body hungrily, I cleared my throat.

"So what courses you doing Scott?" I asked trying to get his attention off of my legs, he smiled and came to lean on the counter next to me his arm brushing against mine.

"Psychology and Sociology" he said smiling.

I nodded "Yeah I forgot you wanted to be a psychologist" I said frowning.

"Anything that'll get you on my couch" he said flirtily making me laugh, god I missed him!

I pushed him away "Go away slut, I'm not interested" I said teasingly, he pouted at me faking hurt.

"You still with that Asshole Trey?" he asked frowning a little annoyed about it.

I nodded "Yep still with him" I said trying to show I was happy about it.

He shook his head "I don't know what you see in that ass, you could do so much better" he said looking at me intently. I smiled sadly, yeah right.

"Yeah like who?" I asked jokingly not really expecting an answer.

He laughed "Um let me think, how about, anyone you set your sights on? Me maybe?" he said flirtily. I laughed yeah ok, like he would be interested in me, he's so damn hot!

"Whatever, want to come have a girlie night with us? We're painting toenails" I offered changing the subject.

"Hey why not, got any pink?" he asked jokingly looking at his nails.

"Sure whatever you want" I said laughing my ass off, he always was funny, I would love to have a brother like him, well actually I would just love to have a brother full stop. Someone to look after me and tell me it was ok, someone I could turn to for help instead of having to do everything on my own all the time.

"What if I want you?" he whispered in my ear making me shiver at how close he was, I swallowed suddenly really nervous.

I pushed him away slightly putting a little distance between us, "Well that's not on offer, sorry" I said rolling my eyes.

He sighed "Right, well then I definitely do not want a girlie night" he said faking hurt as he stormed out of the kitchen dramatically making me laugh again.

Mel rolled her eyes at him "God I though he was over it" she said shaking her head.

I frowned "Over what?" I asked confused, she laughed.

"His little crush on you" she said nodding to her brother who was now sitting watching TV with his feet on the coffee table. What the hell is that about?

"He doesn't have a crush on me! Don't be stupid Mel" I said laughing my ass off. God as if someone like him would have a crush on someone like me!

"Are you kidding? He's fancied you for years, I thought you knew" she said confused, I gasped and looked at her, she wasn't joking, this was serious, her brother had a crush on me for years? Mind you I guess when I used to hang out here a lot I was skinnier and prettier than I am now. There was no way he would still like me even if he did used to have a crush on me! She must have got the wrong end of the stick, Scott was just a flirt who liked to make me feel uncomfortable.

"Whatever, lets get a pizza tonight" I said starving hungry, I hadn't really eaten properly for days and I literally had an apple today and nothing else. She nodded eagerly and trotted off to get the phone to order it. Four hours later, after a huge amout of pizza, ice cream and popcorn and vodka I was laying on her bed while she painted my toes. Actually painted my toes, I don't think she was actually getting any on the actual nail! We were both giggling hysterically at nothing in particular.

I could hear people downstairs, Scott had some friends over but we were in Mel's bedroom so it didn't matter. "We need more alcohol!" I chirped swigging the last mouthful of vodka from the bottle frowning, where the hell did all that go?

Mel jumped up laughing and pulled me to my feet dragging me out of the room, "Let's go steal the boys drink" she said loudly in my ear, I winced as my ears started to ring. She shh'd me and crept down the hall but I couldn't stop laughing at her trying to be all stealthy as she crept along the wall like James Bond.

I trailed behind her giggling with my hand over my mouth, if I didn't stop laughing they were gonna hear us! "Shh" I whispered to myself and walked smack into a table knocking over a ornament. Quick as lightning Mel spun on the spot and caught it, "Fuck me that was awesome!" I cried impressed at how fast she had moved.

She looked at me shocked "I...I was" she stuttered looking uncomfortable.

I shook my head. "You should be on the netball team Mel that was fucking fast!" I said impressed, she grinned and put the ornament back grabbing my hand and pulling me into the kitchen.

Her brother and what looked like three friends were sitting in the lounge watching football, she grinned and pulled me over to the fridge, "If we get caught I'm gonna run, Scott'll give it to you but he won't give it to me" she whispered grabbing four bottles of beer and putting them in my hands as she grabbed another two.

"Mel you better not be stealing my beer" Scott called from the lounge.

She looked at me with wide eyes, "Flirt!" she said as she ran off towards the stairs just managing to get out of the room as Scott walked in.

He looked at me and smiled his sexy little smile as he leaned up against the door frame. "What's this then Brooklyn?" he asked looking me over, I suddenly became very aware that I was in a pair of short shorts and a vest top ready for bed. I blushed as he looked me over slowly making me wish I was about two sizes smaller.

"Um, I was wondering if I could have these beers" I said grimacing at how pathetic I sounded.

He smiled, "Right, and what's in it for me then, why should I give you my beers?" he asked as he took a couple of steps towards me, I gulped, ok what the hell is he looking at me like that for?

"I could pay you, I've got money in my bag" I offered looking around for my handbag, he laughed and shook his head.

"I don't want your money" he said taking another step towards me, he was looking at me really strangely and it was starting to scare me a little.

"Well what do you want then?" I asked confused, he smiled as he took the last step closing the distance so he was right in front of me.

"How about a dance tomorrow at the party?" he said raising one eyebrow, a dance? God I would have danced with him anyway so now I get the beers for nothing!

"Just a dance?" I asked checking there was no catch.

He smiled and nodded "Just a dance" he said nodding amused.

"Ok great, sure" I said happily.

He grinned and nodded over his shoulder "Go on then, don't throw up, I'm not clearing up after you" he said laughing.

I smiled "Thanks Scott, it really is good to see you you know" I said honestly.

He smiled "And it was definitely good to see you" he said looking me over slowly again making me blush.

I gripped the beers tightly and made my way out of the room heading towards the stairs. "Sorry guys, all the beer's gone" Scott said as he headed back into the lounge, I smiled, bless him he is so sweet!

"What? How can the beer be gone?" I heard a guy say, I stopped dead in my tracks. He had the sexiest voice I had ever heard in my life and my whole body was tingling with excitement for some reason. I wanted to hear it again, I wanted him to say my name.

I turned and was about to head in there to see who this voice belonged to when Mel grabbed the beers from my arms and laughed. "Come on, let's go" she said nodding for me to follow her up the stairs, it felt like I snapped out of some sort of trance. I could suddenly think again, what the hell was I about to do? Why the hell would I care who that voice belong to? I have a boyfriend who has no intention of letting me go. I shook my head and followed Mel up the stairs into her bedroom flopping on the bed. "Right then, let's watch another movie!" she said jumping up to choose one.

I woke in the morning and my head was pounding, I grimaced and buried my head in the pillow. Oh god I felt like shit! How the hell much did I drink last night? I lifted my head squinting through the too bright room to the alarm clock, it was almost nine in the morning. I groaned and rolled over to come face to face with Mel who was still asleep, I felt a little sick so I got up quietly and made my way to the bathroom for a shower grabbing my clothes on the way.

After a shower I felt much better and looked in to see Mel was still asleep so I crept downstairs to get something to drink. My tongue felt like sandpaper. "Good morning sunshine" Scott said grinning, I grimaced as my ears started to ring.

"Scott you have any painkillers?" I asked putting my throbbing head on the counter enjoying the cold of the granite on my forehead.

I heard him chuckle, "Here" he said putting two pills and a glass of water on the counter. I sighed as I swallowed them quickly drinking the whole glass of water, "Suffering after drinking all of my beers?" he asked teasingly.

I nodded and sat on the stool, "Yeah" I muttered closing my eyes, I heard him move and suddenly he was behind me rubbing my temples. I snapped my eyes open and pulled away, "What are you doing?" I asked confused.

He smiled "Making you headache go, I learnt about head massages in my class" he said shrugging and reaching for my head again.

"Seriously? I thought Psychology was about what's inside the mind not outside" I said sarcastically.

He rolled his eyes, "Fine, you don't want my help don't take it, suffer for all I care" he said shrugging, I sighed, my head was killing me, it wouldn't hurt to let him try.

"Ok, ok rub my head then" I said exasperated, he shook his head amused.

"Not if you ask like that" he said teasingly, I smiled, ok I guess I was a little rude.

"Scott will you please rub my head?" I asked stepping closer to him.

He laughed "Maybe I could ask you to return the favour later and rub my head" he said suggestively.

"Ew! Gross!" I said slapping his shoulder, he laughed and reached for me again, I pushed his hands away. "No way! I don't want to be owing you anything" I said honestly, there was no way I would be doing that later!

He grabbed my waist and spun me round to face him and moved his hands to my head massaging my temples in small circles making his way across my forehead and back again going down behind my ears making me moan at how good that actually felt. Someone cleared their throat behind me and Scott stopped "Finished seducing my friend?" Mel asked sarcastically.

Scott laughed "Actually no, can you give me ten more minutes?" he asked teasingly.

We all laughed and I stepped back, my head actually felt fine now. "Oh my God that did make my headache go!" I said excitedly.

He smiled and did a little bow "Told ya" he said winking at me.

Mel rolled her eyes, "Shopping!" she said excitedly, I groaned, oh shit I hated shopping!

"Do we have to?" I asked grimacing.

She nodded "Yes! You need to get something for tonight, your not wearing jeans so you need to buy something new, maybe a dress" she said happily.

I shook my head, "Come on, why can't I wear jeans?" I asked hating the fact that she would make me try on dresss and skirts.

She grabbed my bag and put it in my hands, "Come on, let's get something to eat on the way, I'm starving" she said dragging me towards the door.

"See you later Scott, thanks for the massage" I called as we headed out of the door.

After three shops of me refusing to try on anything that she picked out for me she finally had enough. She grabbed a black dress that looked absolutely killer on the hanger but on me would look absolutely hideous. It was tight and short and small! "Try this on Brook or I swear I'm gonna embarrass you in front of this whole store" she said warningly as she shook the dress in front of me.

I raised my eyebrows at her, what the hell is she gonna do to embarrass me? "Yeah?" I asked teasingly.

She nodded "Yeah I'm gonna start screaming and tell every-one that you just felt me up" she said grinning happily.

I laughed "Yeah ok, you do that" I said shaking my head at her amused.

She opened her mouth and screamed, shock shot through me and I jumped forward putting my hand over her mouth looking round to see everyone staring at us shocked and scared. "Shit, ok! Give me the damn dress!" I said angrily snatching it out of her hand.

She laughed "It's ok everyone, I'm sorry, I thought I saw a spider that's all" she said waving apologetically.

I laughed as she pushed towards the fitting rooms, "You are fucking crazy" I said as I stepped into the little curtain and started to strip out of my clothes being careful not to look at my almost naked body in the mirror. I grabbed the dress realising too late that she had picked up a size four, "Mel, damn it, you got me a four! Can you get me an eight or a ten?" I asked holding it outside of the curtain.

She laughed "A ten? Come on jeez try the damn thing on, fuck me, a ten yeah right!" she said laughing her ass off.

Oh for god sake! I pulled the dress over my head pulling it down to see it literally fitted where it touched. It was tight all over literally like a second skin. I looked like a fat ugly prostitute! The dress itself was beautiful though, made of silk and had thin straps, it was beautiful, well it would look beautiful on someone other than me.

"You have it on?" Mel called, I crossed my arms across my body.

"Mel, it's too tight, can you get me a bigger one?" I asked uncomfortably.

She wrenched the curtain open and gasped making me feel even worse. I closed my eyes not wanting to see the disgust at how fucking hideous I was, "Oh God Brook, this dress was made for you, you look so hot, I swear your gonna be fighting them off tonight" she said sounding a little jealous. I opened my eyes to see her looking me over proudly.

I frowned "It's awful Mel, seriously, I look like a fat tramp!" I hissed angrily.

She gasped again, "What? Fucking hell I would kill someone to have your body Brook, your cleavage, my god even I want to fuck you in that dress and I am most definitely straight" she said throwing her hair over her shoulder. I laughed and looked back in the mirror, I suppose it did make my cleavage look good, I dropped my hands slightly so I could look at my bust but still cover up my stomach, she wrenched my arms down to my sides.

"You're getting this dress" she said looking at me sternly, I grimaced.

"I can't wear this! Seriously Mel, come on get real" I said turning my nose up at myself.

She shook her head, "You're getting it, take it off, let's go get some new underwear to go with it, that dress deserves pretty underwear, oh and new shoes" she said clapping her hands.

"I'm not some damn Barbie doll!" I snapped making her laugh as she closed the curtain behind her.

After another hour and a half of shopping we made our way back to hers, I had bought some slutty black lacy underwear and a killer pair of heels to go with the way too tight, way too short dress that she made me buy. God I hated my life, but at least this party was at some friend of her brothers, I wouldn't know anyone there and they wouldn't be able to see me again to talk about my embarrassing show in a slutty dress designed for some runway model.

I showered and let her do my hair, blowdrying it straight and shaping it into a perfect bob, I applied my own makeup much to her disgust, I added a little mascara and some clear lipgloss, I never wore much makeup. Trey said it made me look cheap so I didn't even wear any when I was out with him. When I couldn't stall anymore she made me pull on the dress over the top of the lacy black slutty bra and thong. She was watching me the whole time with a proud little smile.

"I'm glad I've told Scott we'll meet him there, he is so gonna be drooling for you tonight, I bet he wouldn't let you leave the house" she said smirking at me. I rolled my eyes, yeah as if, the only one that would be drooling right now is Trey and he would be drooling with anger at how fucking embarrassing I looked right now!

Mel as usual looked beautiful, she added some soft curls to her poker straight hair and pulled on a gorgeous red dress that made her look super skinny and graceful. I was so jealous of her, god why the hell can't I look like that? I pulled on my shoes and she wrapped her arm around me, "Let's go break some hearts" she said winking at me making me chuckle. We walked to the car and made our way over to Scott's friends house on the other side of the woods.

As we approached I gasped, this place was gorgeous, like a log cabin with big green windows. It was so cute! Mel laughed and pulled me towards the banging music, "Right, let's get wasted!" she said happily as we got to the front door.

"Who's party is this anyway?" I shouted over the music as she led me through the house. It was really cute on the inside too, and much bigger than it seemed from outside, all open plan, the walls were all wood and looked really homey.

"It's Scott's best friend Jayden's, it's his birthday today" she shouted back pulling me over to the kitchen area. She grabbed two cups and went straight for the punch raising an eyebrow at me, oh crap there could be anything in there!

"Um maybe we should stick to bottles?" I said but it sounded more like a question.

"Don't worry, it'll be fine, Scott will look after us" she said ladling out two big cups of punch. I could feel everyone staring at me so I wrapped my arms around myself wishing I had on a pair of jeans and a hoodie to hide under.

Mel handed me a cup "Cheers" she said knocking our cups together, I took a big swig and almost spat it straight back out, it was fucking awful! There was so much alcohol in there it was just crazy!

"Ew!" I said turning my nose up, "This needs something" I said looking round for anything to put in the punch to take the kick away. I grabbed some orange juice and poured in half a carton before grabbing two apples and two oranges. "Find a knife, the fruit will soak up some of the alcohol" I said opening the nearest drawer.

"Here" Mel said sliding a knife across the counter, I chopped up the fruit and threw it in giving it a big stir with the ladle before serving up a little more into a fresh cup.

I took another mouthful and it was actually quite nice now, "Much better" I said handing my cup to Mel. She smiled and downed the cup nodding for some more, with our drinks in hand we made our way to the dance floor to find Scott.

"Hey, shit, wow" Scott said with wide eyes as he looked me over, why the hell is he looking at me like that? I blushed and dropped my eyes to the floor, I knew I shouldn't have worn this stupid dress!

CHAPTER 3

Jayden's POV

I dumped the last of the alcohol onto the kitchen counter looking it over to make sure we had enough, this party was gonna be awesome. I grinned as I counted the bottles, eight bottles of every single drink you could think of, people were supposed to bring something too so we should be fine. I grabbed the punch bowl and started mixing in shots of stuff, I had no idea how to make a cocktail or anything so I just threw in whatever I could get hold of first added some orange, apple and cranberry juices and mixed it up with the ladle thing. I spooned out a cup and took a big mouthful, fuck that was awful! I swallowed it grimacing as the alcohol burnt it's way down my throat. I grabbed some lemonade and poured some of that in too, after another test it still tasted like shit but the burn was gone so I downed the rest of the cup. I opened all of the snack stuff pouring them into big plastic bowls before heading upstairs to change.

It would be hot tonight and I was already running a temperature because of the moon so I pulled on a pair of low slung ripped jeans and a plain white t-shirt, screw it I'm not dressing up to go to a party in my own house. This party was arranged to celebrate my birthday, well that's what most people thought anyway, to my pack and family this was a coming of age party. It's kind of like a birthday party but it was special, today I was twenty. Which meant that I was now officially a full grown male shifter, it also meant that I had the right to challenge my father for Alpha of the pack seen as I was the next eldest male in the family.

My father had made it clear to me that he would not reject my challenge should I feel ready to face him, a challenge was not to be taken lightly though. If neither of us were willing to submit it would be a fight to the death, there was no way I was doing that. I didn't like my father, I mean he was never really a father to me, taking off just after my Mom died when I was five leaving me to be raised by my Aunt.

But he was still my father and I wouldn't fight him for something that I had no desire to be anyway, I mean why the hell would I want to be Alpha? I was twenty, in college, fucking anything that moved and generally having a good old time out of life. Who the hell would want to trade that for the responsibility of heading a pack of damn shifters? Not me, certainly not yet anyway, I hadn't ruled out challenging one day but not until it would suit me to do it.

I was the only one that had the right to challenge at the moment, it went on bloodlines, the Alpha had been in my bloodline for over two hundred years. The only time someone can challenge that is not of the bloodline is when the Alpha is either killed or wishes to resign as Alpha, in which case there is a fight amongst all male shifters over the age of twenty that want to compete. It's a fight into submission or to the death depending on how far you're willing to go for it. Basically it's a huge type of contest with the one left standing at the end being made the new Alpha, but like I say this hadn't happened for over two hundred years as the Alpha's had all bore son's to take over from them.

My father wouldn't give it to me easily, he would make me work for it and probably make me kill him just to test how far I would go. It seemed to me like I was always a disappointment to him, nothing I ever did was good enough so to be honest I just stopped trying to impress him. When my Aunt died last year she left me the house and a tidy sum to see me through college so I had been taking care of myself since then.

Once I was dressed I heard people arriving, pulling off the road about a mile away so I made my way down stairs. Scott, Anthony and Paul all let themselves in heading straight for the kitchen to dump the booze they had brought before slapping me a high five. "Wow man, coming of age! You excited?" Scott asked happily.

I shrugged "Same as yesterday man, nothing's changed" I said a little bored with the whole coming of age thing already, I just wanted to party and get laid.

"So you gonna make the challenge?" Anthony asked looking at me excitedly, I shook my head laughing.

"Nah, what the hell do I want all that responsibility for? It gonna get me any more girls?" I asked jokingly making them laugh.

"No more than you would get anyway" Anthony said rolling his eyes at me, I nudged Scott.

"Your sister coming?" I asked smiling knowing that it would wind him up me talking about fucking his little sister.

He looked at me warningly, "Don't even fucking think about it Jayden" he said angrily, his blue eyes getting a little darker making me smile.

"I was joking! What is she like twelve?" I asked laughing, I hadn't seen Mel for about a year since Scott and I went off to college, she was a nice girl but she just didn't do it for me, no one did.

"She's almost seventeen actually, she's bringing her friend with her tonight, Brooklyn" he said smiling. I frowned, watching his face, he liked this girl a lot, his little sisters friend I could tell.

"Yeah? The friend hot?" I asked wanting to wind him up again, his eyes darkened immediately as he stepped towards me. I could feel my wolf pushing to the surface, I didn't like to be challenged, even though I was teasing about the friend if he was gonna be stepping to me I needed to show him to back off.

I outranked him even though he would technically be my number two if I became Alpha as it was in his bloodline to be my lieutenant. "Back the fuck off Scott" I hissed through my teeth clenching my jaw tight. He glared at me for a couple of seconds assessing my dominance, seeing if he could take me. If he tried I would put him down, he knew that which was why he looked down at the floor pretty quick and stepped back respectfully. I took a deep breath and slapped his shoulder letting him know everything was ok, I didn't hold grudges. "I was kidding man seriously, you like the friend then go for it" I said honestly.

I had no interest in fighting over a girl, if he wanted this one there would be plenty more at the party for me to fuck. This party would be teeming with humans and shifters alike, personally I liked to fuck shifters. They were more flexible, had more stamina and out of respect of me being Alpha's son they were more than happy to try anything I wanted, hoping I would mate them and make them the Alpha female. That wasn't gonna happen though, I didn't want a mate, why tie myself down to just one girl? The Alpha bloodline ended with me, I wasn't ever having kids. I couldn't get anyone pregnant without mating, I was infertile until I chose someone and connected their body to mine. So I had no doubt in my mind whatsoever that there would be no more Phillips Alpha's.

People started arriving and a bunch of female shifters paraded themselves in front of me hoping tonight was their lucky night. One girl in a slutty blue dress wrapped her hand around my wrist, "Wanna dance with me Jayden?" she purred as she swayed seductively. Fuck this was a good party already!

"Sure baby why not" I said winking at my boys and following her swaying ass to the dance floor.

After a couple of hours I spotted part of my pack brothers all standing around chatting so I made my way over to them. "Hey guys" I said throwing my arm around Rick's shoulder.

"Hey Jay" he said grinning.

"Good party huh?" I asked looking around at the packed house, the music was banging and everyone was dancing, drinking and laughing.

"Awesome man" Seth said grinning.

"Got your eye on anyone?" Seth asked looking around and stopping at a group of humans in the corner.

I grinned "Nah man, I'll take anything, you know me" I said shrugging.

"Not going for the hottie with Mel Porter?" he asked a little shocked. I grinned this must be the girl Scott likes.

"No man, Scott's called dibs, where is she anyway?" I asked looking around for this girl that had my best friend so worked up, he had been crazy about this girl for years, I remember him talking about her.

"I don't know, but trust me you'll know her if you see her, she is smokin hot! Definitely the hottest fucking girl in here" Seth said, the other boys nodded their agreement.

I frowned, she can't be hotter than the shifter girls, they were all beautiful, it was part of our race to be perfect looking which is why so many of us ended up as models or actors. "Scott didn't say she was a shifter" I said scanning the room for her again.

Seth shook his head "She's not, she's human, smokin though" he said blowing out a sharp breath and running his hand through his hair. I shrugged, whatever I said to Scott he could have her anyway.

"I'll see you guys" I said slapping Rick on the shoulder as I made my way to the kitchen to see Scott and Paul doing shots. "Hey, I'll have one of those" I said grabbing another cup and holding it out to Paul who was pouring them another. "Everyone's going on about this mystery girl of yours" I said laughing as we counted to three and downed the shots, Paul immediately poured another three.

"Yeah I know, she's got a boyfriend though so" he said shrugging.

I laughed "Come on, that shouldn't stop you, you're Scott Porter!" I said punching his arm maybe a little harder than I thought as he winced and rubbed his shoulder. Shit I wasn't used to this extra coming of age strength yet, I guess it would take a few days.

"I know, I keep trying but nothing" he said sadly, I smiled reassuringly.

"You'll get her, but it's not like she's the one man, she's human, you know she's not for you anyway" I said shrugging. It was no big deal, shifters could have sex with humans and could maybe have relationships with them but they never lasted. A shifter could only mate with another shifter so we could have our fun with humans but it would never go any further than that.

I had heard about one shifter who apparently fell in love with a human but they only lasted a couple of years, love for a shifter faded, it was the mating that created the unbreakable bond that kept them together and in love. This was another reason I didn't ever want to mate, once mated you would never want anyone else. A male shifter would do anything for his mate, anything, she was literally the centre of his world and if anything ever happened to her he would be alone until the day he died.

This was what happened to my father, when his mate died, my Mother, he sort of lost his grip on everything, like she was the only thing tying him down. He left me, unable to love now that his mate was dead, I understood how he felt and never blamed him for it but I just don't get how people could want to put themselves through that. What the hell could be worth risking everything for? I would never take a mate because I would never want to end up like my father, a lonely, bitter and twisted old man with no love or compassion for anyone, even his own son.

After a couple more shots we went to dance, "You fucked anyone yet Jay?" Paul said laughing.

I shook my head and smiled "Not yet, it's only ten" I said shrugging, I didn't want to choose too early, I'd get stuck with whatever girl I chose for the night probably and I wanted to have some fun tonight. Two girls came over dancing with us eyeing me and Scott with flirty expressions. Scott got a good amount of females too because he would be my number two, shifter girls wanted to be mated to powerful males. I smiled nodded over my shoulder "I'm gonna go pee" I shouted over the banging music, they nodded and started dancing with the girls as I weaved my way through the drunken people heading to the bathroom.

I tried the one downstairs but it was locked so I headed upstairs to my en-suite, desperately needing to pee now after downing all this liquid. I crossed my room and went to the bathroom sighing with relief as I emptied my full bladder. As I was washing my hands I heard someone rattle the door handle, I smiled, someone else who couldn't wait for downstairs. I could smell something that I smelt yesterday at Scott's, it was glorious and it made my stomach clench up tight. I had no idea what the smell was but it was intoxicating and I hadn't been able to stop thinking about that scent all night last night.

I opened the door and my heart stopped. The most beautiful girl I had ever seen in my life was standing in front of me. She had glossy chocolate brown hair to just above her shoulders, her skin was pale and was flawless, she was wearing a black silk dress that clung to her perfect body showing off all of her glorious curves underneath. Her legs were long and toned, I opened my mouth to speak but nothing came out so I closed it again. She was so perfect, I had never seen anything more beautiful and I knew I never would.

I felt my wolf jump and I clenched my fists willing my feet not to close the small distance between us. I dragged my eyes back to her face to see her beautiful hazel brown eyes were wide and a little bewildered as she stared at me as I was doing to her. I couldn't move, I needed her, I felt the hairs on the back of my neck rise as my canines extended. Holy shit what the hell?

I gritted my teeth and tried again to speak, come on Jayden you can do this! "You need the bathroom?" I asked my voice husky and thick with lust. She gulped and her eyes dropped to the floor, I wanted so much to lift her chin and look into her eyes again but instead I stepped to the side and held the door open for her. She looked at the door and shook her head slightly looking confused before heading in and locking the door behind her.

What the fuck was that? I went over to the mirror and opened my mouth looking at my canines that were just going back to their correct human teeth. What the hell happened then? I rubbed my hand up my arm and looked back at the door, I wanted to see her again. I wanted to touch her and run my fingers through her silky brown hair, as I thought about it my canines extended again.

I slapped my forehead confused as hell, suddenly I heard her speak and my heart took off in overdrive "You ok?" she asked. Her voice was so beautiful, it was like an angel singing and I would do anything to hear her speak again. I looked up to see her standing there looking a little uncomfortable with her arms crossed over her beautiful body hugging herself tightly.

I nodded and willed my teeth to return to normal, I ran my tongue over them and they retracted allowing me to turn to her again. "I'm fine, you enjoying the party?" I asked wanting to hear her speak again, she smiled and I felt like my world started to spin too fast, happiness bubbled inside me and I wanted to see that smile again.

"Yeah, it's good, you?" she asked looking me over biting her lip slightly.

I took a deep breath, taking in another lungful of that intoxicating scent, I took a step forward and sniffed again, shit it was her! She was the smell from Scott's! Her beautiful eyes looked a little startled as they came back to mine, my wolf jumped forward wanting me to take her, wanting me to claim her. I couldn't help but close the distance between us, her breath seemed to catch in her throat as I reached my hand up and brushed a stray lock of her hair back into place. Her hair felt like silk between my fingers and my whole body was screaming for me to touch her skin.

Our bodies were about a foot apart and I was just considering if I could close the distance when she did. She pressed herself to me, her perfect body touching every inch of mine, I gritted my teeth as my wolf growled in my chest. He wanted her now, I was fighting it as best I could but her scent was driving me wild. I was stiff as a board, it was almost painful how hard I was, I bent my head and touched my lips to hers. My whole body tingled with pleasure as her warm soft lips pressed against mine lightly.

She made a small moan in the back of her throat and I couldn't hold it any longer. I wrapped my arms around her tight and pulled her closer to my chest as I moved walked her backwards to the bed. Shit I had to have her now! Her hands went up around my neck pulling me closer, as we got to the bed she laid down, I hovered above her and pulled her up the bed more before laying on top of her gently keeping all of my weight off of this perfect angel not wanting to hurt her. I would never hurt her.

Her hands went down to the back of my t-shirt pulling it up over my head throwing it on the floor, her eyes and hands trailing over my chest making me shiver. I licked along her bottom lip wanting to deepen the kiss, she opened her mouth eagerly and I slipped my tongue into her mouth. She tasted even better than she smelled and I couldn't think about anything else, she took over everything, her scent, her taste, they were driving me out of my mind.

I pulled my head back to look at her. She was so beautiful, like a perfect angel, my wolf jumped forward again, so close to the surface now, I was fighting a loosing battle, he wanted her, he wouldn't stop until she was his. I was sweating and panting for breath, fighting with all of my might to get the hell off of her before it was too late, but I couldn't move, I couldn't force even one inch of space between us. I was gonna take her and there was nothing either of us could do about it. She looked at me, her hazel eyes showing concern, she raised her hand and touched my sweating forehead.

"Are you ok?" she asked in her angels voice, that tipped me over the edge.

My canines extended again, further than I had ever felt them, "I.......can't control....can't" I choked out. She frowned confused and I lost the battle, I felt him take over as I lunged for her throat and bit her deeply marking her as my own.

CHAPTER 4

As soon as my teeth sank into her skin my whole body throbbed with love and passion for her. She was my world, she was my everything, my whole life before her had been a lie, everything that I had found beautiful, everything that I had found interesting or that made me happy were nothing, nothing could compare to this girl. I pulled my mouth away from her neck tasting her sweet blood on my lips, my teeth retracted and I looked into her eyes.

She was shaking, her whole body trembling as she looked at me shocked, "Shh, It's ok, I'm sorry I hurt you, but I'll never hurt you again, I promise, never" I cooed smoothing her hair from her face. She nodded and I bent my head to kiss her again, the kiss was a hundred times better, her taste was a hundred times sweeter and her scent a hundred times more intoxicating. She gripped her hands into my hair pulling me closer as I ran my hands down her perfect body, my angel, my world.

I kissed down her neck, when I got to my mark on her neck I licked the blood away to heal it and close the teeth marks I had put there. She moaned and I smiled as I kissed it making her moan and wriggle underneath me. A mark was sensitive, almost like another g-spot when it was touched by your mate. Her fingers dug into my back as I kissed it again and ran my nose up her shoulder breathing in her beautiful scent that was now mixed with mine. I brushed my nose over her mark, "Oh God" she moaned grinding her hips against me making me moan.

I kissed further down her body, trailing little kisses right down to her feet, I unbuckled her shoes pulling them off kicking mine off at the same time. I ran my hands up her smooth toned thighs slipping them under her dress, I gripped the edge of the silky material as I pushed it higher exposing a sexy black thong that set my world on fire. I pushed it higher and pulled it completely off over her head leaving her in a sexy little lace bra and matching thong, God I got even harder, how the hell is that even possible?

She gasped and blushed covering herself up with her arms as I looked her over. I frowned and moved her arms, I wanted to see every part of her, "Could we turn the light off?" she asked uncomfortably. What the hell would she want that for?

"Why?" I asked confused as I laid back down on my side next to her just memorising every beautiful inch of her body.

She grimaced "I don't want you to have to look at me" she said wincing slightly, I looked at her, I was even more confused now.

"You don't want me to have to look at you? I don't understand, why wouldn't I want to look at you?" I asked pulling her face to look at me, she was bright red and looked even more beautiful. The pink on her cheeks made her hair seem to take on a slight red tinge.

"Don't, I know what I look like, we should just turn the light off" she said sitting up and moving to get up from the bed. My wolf lunged forward refusing to allow her to leave but I pushed him back, he wouldn't hurt my angel, I grabbed her hand stopping her from getting off of my bed and moved to sit up too.

"You are the most beautiful thing I will ever see in my life, you're perfect, and seey as hell, I want the light on so I can see every inch of your perfect body" I said honestly.

I could see her eyes filling with tears as she shook her head, "No I'm not, you don't have to say that to get me to sleep with you" she said a tear falling down her face.

I wrapped my arms around her and pulled her small frame into my lap as I wiped the tear from her face. "I swear on my life, you take my breath away, you're incredible, you're so beautiful" I said as I kissed her passionately. She wrapped her arms around my neck pulling me closer kissing me hard, I laid her back down and ran my hands down her body my hands lingering on her flat toned stomach, her curvy hips, I gripped her pert little ass and I moaned, God she was just incredible.

I would die if I didn't take her soon, I kissed back down her body unclasping her bra and pulling it off trailing my finger-tips across my mark making her buck her hips into me as she moaned loudly. If I could only hear one sound for the rest of my life, that would be it, that moan of pleasure, it was the sexiest thing I had ever heard in my life. I looked down at her pert, perfect breasts before looking back to her face, she was watching me nervously. "So beautiful" I murmured as I kissed down to them, massaging them gently before taking her nipple into my mouth sucking on it gently and rolling my tongue around it and pulling back to blow on it making it stand out even further.

She gripped my hand and pulled me higher, as my face was level with hers she kissed me, running her hands down my back scratching gently, when she got to the waistband of my jeans she followed the material round to the front her fingertips slipping inside touching tickling my skin making me shiver with desire.

I continued to kiss her and massage her breasts, kissing across her cheek and biting on her ear lobe gently making her gasp. She unbuttoned my jeans and slid them down over my hips her hand trailing round to my ass, when they were down as far as she could reach she raised her legs, catching her feet in them and pushing them the rest of the way down. I smiled, that was sexy as hell, she smiled back and I felt that happy feeling return, I would do anything to make this angel of mine smile. I would make her happy, give her anything that she wanted.

I kicked my jeans off of my feet and moved back down her body wanting to kiss every inch of this girl that was now mine. As she moved I noticed she had a large bruise on her side, I lifted her arm to look at it, it looked a couple of days old. "How did you get this?" I asked trailing my fingers over it tenderly, wishing I could make it disappear.

"Um, I fell" she said. Wow ok I need to watch out for her even more that I thought if she's a little clumsy, I even had to protect her from herself!

I bent my head and kissed the bruise gently before making my way further down, kissing over her flat stomach dipping my tongue into her belly button. Her hand was tangled in my hair, her breathing was coming out faster now as I moved further down to her centre. I slipped my fingers into the sides of her thong and pulled it down slowly trailing my hand down her legs. God she was so soft and delicate, it was like touching the petals of a delicate flower. I was scared to touch her in case she disappeared. What if this is a dream? What if I wake up and she's just a dream? How the hell would I cope with the loss? I don't think I would.

I smiled and kissed my way back up her body. I stopped to look at my mark, it was incredible, it looked a little sore and red, but it was fascinating looking at my teeth marks on her perfect creamy skin. She rubbed her hands down my chest gripping hold of my boxers pulling them down, she looked down and I saw a shiver run through her as she looked at me. Her hazel eyes met mine and they were filed with lust and passion, I smiled at her and got a heart stopping smile in return.

My wolf was growling inside me now that we were both naked, he wouldn't wait anymore. I moved back on top of her nudging her legs open further. She wrapped one of her long legs around my waist as I bent my head to kiss her, I could feel myself lined up with her entrance and I pushed forward ever so slightly making her gasp and whimper. Damn it, I'm going to hurt her, she's too tight.

I stopped immediately and looked at her, "You ok?" I asked concerned, she bit her lip and nodded looking a little scared. Oh God I did hurt her! I pulled back and rolled to my side pulling her to my chest so we were facing each other.

"What's wrong? Why did you stop?" she asked breathlessly looking hurt and upset.

I ran my fingers through her hair, "I don't want to hurt you" I admitted, she frowned and looked at me confused.

"I don't want you to stop" she said rolling me onto my back and moving to straddle me. My wolf growled, he wanted to be in control, he didn't like being dominated, but I could let her dominate me, she was my angel, she could do whatever the hell she wanted.

She kissed me as she moved to hover above me. I gripped her hips stopping her from taking me into her. "No don't, it'll hurt you, I can feel it" I said scared as hell, she was gonna tear or something, I wasn't gonna fit.

She shook her head, "Please" she begged. My wolf roared that she wanted something as I fought against him not to let her have it, "Please" she begged again breaking my heart. I had to give her what she wanted but how could I watch her hurt herself? She pulled her head back to look at me, "Do you really think I'm beautiful?" she asked quietly, she looked so nervous and insecure. What the hell has happened to this girl for her to think that she's anything less than perfection? I looked deep into her hazel eyes, eyes that I hoped she would pass onto our children.

"I don't think you're beautiful, I know you're beautiful, the most special and precious thing I have ever seen, you're just perfect" I said honestly.

A tear fell down her face and I kissed it away, "Thank you" she said gratefully.

"Anytime" I said as I bent my head to kiss my mark. She wriggled and moaned as I ran my tongue over it.

I was memorising every expression, every line of her face, every fleck of darker brown that was in her hazel eyes. I memorised the beautiful scent of her breath as it blew across my face, the way her chest was rising as she took a breath. I wanted to be able to picture this moment with crystal clarity. "Please" she breathed, I closed my eyes, I could take it slow, maybe if I was really careful I wouldn't hurt her, "Please" she begged. I couldn't refuse her, my now mated body needed to give her anything she asked for, I opened my eyes to look at her. There was no indecision there, only lust and passion and need, I nodded and kissed her rolling her onto her back praying I could do this without hurting her.

When we finally broke apart we were both breathless and sweaty, I was careful and she was fine, well better than fine actually she definitely enjoyed herself. She closed her eyes, "God I'm tired" she mumbled, I smiled and wrapped my arms around her perfect body, pulling her to me.

"You can sleep now shortie" I said smiling and loving the feel of her in my arms.

"I'm not short" she mumbled sleepily against my chest making me laugh.

Within a minute she was asleep so I pulled back to look at her. She was so beautiful, and she was mine, I smiled happily, watching the rise and fall of her chest, her breathing being the most important thing in the world to me. Wow I was mated! And I didn't even know my mates name for Christ sake.

That was just crazy though, what the hell was that? I couldn't not mate her, it was like she was supposed to be mine, from the first second I saw her I needed her. Is that how it usually happened? I thought you talked about becoming mates then did it, I didn't know it was just pure need like that. I kissed her forehead and closed my eyes drifting off into a peaceful sleep next to the most perfect girl in the world. My girl, my mate.

Chapter 5

Brook's POV

I woke up feeling safe and warm and so damn comfortable, where the hell was I? I raised my head from the comfy spot I had found to see I was laying on a boy's chest. My eyes went wide as I remembered what had happened, wait what the hell did happen? I came up to use the bathroom and the most beautiful boy in the world was already in there. The second my eyes met his I felt funny, my heart had started beating way too fast, my fingertips starting to tingle. I had wanted him so bad, so bad it was almost painful, the need for him had almost killed me.

I bit my lip and raised my head to look at him, he was so incredible. His brown hair was messy and sticking up everywhere. He was asleep and looked so peaceful, he was pure perfection, he was actually beauty personified and I could feel my body throbbing in need for him again. My hand moved to brush his hair from his forehead but I caught myself before I touched him. I didn't want to wake him, I dragged my eyes down his naked body across his chest and sculpted abs, his body was tanned, toned and perfect.

I bit my lip and pushed back off of the bed slowly trying not to wake him, god I was naked! I grimaced thinking about that fact that he had seen my body, but he didn't seem to flinch away from me earlier and he said he thought I was beautiful. I climbed slowly out of the bed and grabbed my bra and thong pulling them on, not taking my eyes from his face. Oh god please don't wake up!

I pulled my dress over my head and grabbed my shoes from the floor, I tiptoed over to the door and held my breath as I opened it and crept out closing it behind me. I could hear the music banging downstairs, I leant against the wall trying to calm myself. How the hell could I have done that? If Trey found out he would literally kill me then he would kill my Mom. I gulped and smoothed my hair and dress before heading back downstairs. I didn't want to do this, I wanted to go back into the bedroom and have him wrap his arms around me again, but I had to leave. I couldn't let Trey hurt my Mom.

I weaved my way through the throng of people looking for Mel, I spotted her chatting and laughing over the other side with her brother and a group of boys. As I walked up she grabbed me into a hug, "Where the hell have you been? I've been looking for you for like two hours!" she cried hugging me fiercely. I opened my mouth to speak but she but me off, looking at me confused, "You smell different" she said shaking her head confused. I smiled she was always crazy.

"I smell different? Are you drunk?" I asked laughing as I took her cup and downed the contents.

Scott was looking at me a little weird too, "You do smell different, where have you been?" he asked looking at my hand that I held my shoes in.

I blushed and dropped my eyes to the floor, "Nowhere, I was dancing, look Mel can we go?" I asked embarrassed as to why everyone was staring at me again.

She frowned "Go? It's only just after twelve" she said pouting.

I looked at her pleadingly, "Please? I need to go, please" I said.

She sighed and nodded "Yeah ok, but you'll tell me what this is about right?" she asked curiously. I nodded and looked around at the boys who were all staring at me looking me over but all looked slightly bewildered for some reason. "I'll come too" Scott said wrapping his arm around my shoulders, his hand brushed my neck and I shuddered, it felt so wrong, I shrugged his arm off quickly feeling a little sick.

He looked at me strangely but didn't say anything as we walked to his car, I slipped into the back and gulped knowing the interrogation was about to start. "So why did we have to leave? What happened?" Mel asked taking my hand as she slipped into the back next to me. I glanced at Scott who was driving, not paying attention, or pretending not to be paying attention anyway. I took a deep breath and looked at my best friend tin the world.

"I cheated on Trey" I said wincing at how bad that sounded, she gasped and gripped my hand tighter.

"You're shitting me! With who?" she cried looking slightly excited, I smiled and shook my head.

"I don't even know his name, I didn't ask! Can you believe that? Damn it I'm such a slut!" I said shaking my head disapprovingly.

She laughed "You don't know his name? Oh my god Brook!" she said laughing her ass off.

I giggled "It's not really funny, if Trey finds out he'll go crazy" I said my laughter stopping immediately thinking off all the pain he would cause to me, or worse, to my Mom or even the beautiful boy I had just had the most amazing sex ever with.

"He won't find out, how can he? He's in Denver and he wouldn't know anyone here anyway" she said reassuringly, I nodded she was right. There shouldn't be anything tying me to this at all. "So what did he look like?" she asked excitedly.

I sighed and closed my eyes picturing his perfect face, "He's got brown hair, kinda messy, and dark green eyes, my god he is so hot it's unreal, and his voice, shit his voice is the sexiest thing I have ever heard in my life" I said a slight shiver running through me.

She frowned "What was he wearing?" she asked curiously.

"Um, jeans and a t-shirt, a white t-shirt" I said nodding, she shrugged "I didn't see him" she said.

"Was he good?" she whispered, I giggled and nodded biting my lip trying not to think about just how good he was.

"Oh god Mel, it was unbelievable, seriously fucking mind blowing" I admitted.

She looked at me jealously and smiled "I told you that dress was made for you" she said raising an eyebrow.

"I still don't like the dress" I said pulling it down slightly trying to cover my legs more.

She laughed "But it got you mind blowing sex, you so owe me" she said laughing her ass off again.

I nodded "Yeah ok, I'll give you that one" I said grinning wickedly at her.

"So I can't believe you didn't even ask his name! What the hell happened?" she asked as we pulled up outside her house. I climbed out and waited for her to walk around to my side.

"God I have no idea, I went to use the bathroom and he was in there, when he opened the door it was like bam and that was it, he must have felt it too because he looked like he was having trouble speaking" I said smiling remembering how he opened his mouth and closed it struggling to get his words out.

She smiled "That's so romantic, are you seeing him again?" she asked happily as she skipped over to the freezer pulling out a carton of ice cream and two spoons.

I shook my head "No, I'm with Trey" I said sternly as I dug into the chocolate ice cream hungrily.

"He was ok with that?" she asked curiously.

I shrugged "I have no idea, I didn't tell him I had a boyfriend, we fell asleep after, when I woke up he was still asleep so I snuck out and came to find you" I admitted a little sheepishly.

She burst out laughing again and shook her head "Wow you are a slut!" she teased making me laugh, I nodded eating another spoonful of icecream.

"I know, I just pray that Trey doesn't find out" I said feeling slightly sick at the thought. Scott was watching me curiously from the doorframe looking like he was trying to work out a complicated puzzle.

"Let's go watch a movie finish this ice cream off" Mel suggested nodding towards the lounge.

"Ok, I'm just gonna go change first, I don't feel comfortable in this" I said waving my hand over my scantly clad body, she nodded and headed off to the lounge to choose the movie. I went upstairs pulling the dress off and grabbed a loose fitting t-shirt and sweats and pulling them on instead. As I walked past the mirror I noticed my hair was all messed up and tangled so I grabbed a brush and brushed out the snarls pulling my hair back into a loose pony tail.

I frowned as I saw a red mark on my neck and bent closer to look at it pulling the edge of my top down so I could see. Just at the base of my neck where it meets my shoulder there was a big red bite mark. I gasped as I tilted my neck to look at it better, it looked deep but it didn't hurt, I could clearly see four perfectly round puncture holes, two on each side surrounded by normal looking teeth marks forming two crescents. It was healing and looked like it had happened a couple of weeks ago not something that happened tonight.

I poked at it and rubbed it but it didn't fade or change, I closed my eyes thinking back to him biting me. I remembered him looking like he was in pain then he said something about not being in control and then his eyes changed from green to a almost black colour and he bent forward and bit me, no his eyes didn't change colour that's just stupid! Must have been a trick of the light or probably a trick of the alcohol more like it. It didn't hurt when he bit me, it actually felt nice, if he had bit me hard enough to leave a mark like this it would have really hurt me, wouldn't it? Maybe I had a reaction to it or something?

I rubbed it again but it wouldn't go, the teeth marks actually felt a little raised, it was definitely a reaction, I hope he didn't give me anything. I thought back to the $ex, shit we didn't use a cond0m or anything either! I grimaced, I was on the pill so I knew I wouldn't get pregnant but what if he had some sort of STI? Oh great Brook, just fucking great!

I heard shouting from downstairs, I let my hair back down not wanting to have to explain the bite to Mel tonight and made my way downstairs. "Scott, I don't know what happened! Honestly I needed to, I couldn't help it!" a sexy voice shouted angrily, I gasped, it was him. The boy I slept with, he was here! I sat on the bottom step not wanting to go and face him, maybe he was just here to see Scott, he couldn't even know I was here, no he definitely didn't know who I was, there was no way he could.

I wrapped my arms around myself praying he would just leave, this was just a one night stand, I had a boyfriend. A boyfriend who would kill me, my Mom and him if he ever found out. I felt sick, the thought of Trey hurting him was worse than the thought of him hurting my Mom, my heart was crashing in my chest. Oh god, Trey's gonna find out! How the hell could I have been so stupid?

Jayden's POV

I woke up and instantly noticed she wasn't in my arms, I raised my head looking for her, maybe she'd rolled away or something. But the bed was empty. I sat up quick and looked around my room, her clothes and shoes were gone too. I jumped out of the bed pulling on my jeans and t-shirt slipping on my trainers and ran to the en-suite but I knew she wasn't there I couldn't smell her anymore, she had left the room.

I ran down the stairs, and scanned the room quickly, where the hell is she? I pushed past people into the kitchen but she wasn't there either, my wolf was growling, he wanted her near him, he didn't like the fact that she had snuck away. I turned and went to the bathroom, someone was in there and I relaxed, calm down Jayden she's in the bathroom! I waited a couple of minutes and the girl in the blue dress that I had danced with earlier came staggering out. "Shit!" I cried angrily, did she leave the house?

Paul was walking past me so I grabbed his arm, "Paul, you seen a really sexy girl with brown hair? She's wearing a black dress" I asked desperately.

He shrugged "Don't think so man, why what's up?" he asked looking at me curiously.

"I mated" I said scanning the room again

He gasped and grabbed me "You fucking mated? What the hell Jayden? Who?" he cried shocked.

I shook my head "I don't know where she went, we fell asleep, I just woke up and she was gone" I said pushing past him needing to find her. I didn't even know her name for Christ sake!

I could feel him following me close on my heels as I walked around the room, I spotted a brown head and my wolf rejoiced as I ran over pushing past people and took her hand. She turned and smiled seductively, my heart sank, it wasn't her. "Hi Jayden" the girl purred.

I let go of her hand "Sorry, I thought you were someone else" I said turning away quickly.

I looked back over my shoulder to see Paul had grabbed Seth and Rick and a couple of other boys from my pack who were all trailing along behind me wanting to meet my mate. She would be Alpha female when I made the challenge so they would need to show their respect to her. I walked over to them, "I can't find her, have you seen her?" I asked desperately, oh god what if she was in trouble or something? I felt my wolf ready to come out at the thought of her being in trouble and I forced him back down, I couldn't shift in front of all of these people, some of them were humans.

"We don't even know who she is man, what's her name? We could ask around" Seth suggested.

I shook my head "I don't know her name, she's beautiful, about five six or seven, brown hair, just above her shoulders, brown eyes, smokin body, she's wearing a little black silk dress, black shoes" I said looking at them pleadingly.

Seth frowned "The only girl I've seen like that dude was Mel Porter's friend, she left with Mel and Scott a little while ago" Seth said shrugging.

I breathed a sigh of relief, that was her, I smelt her last night at Scott's, oh shit that means I've mated the girl he wanted to sleep with! He was gonna be pissed. I took off at a run to my car and jumped in heading over to Scott's as quick as I could. Why the hell did she leave me? How could she leave me? I was her mate, she should have wanted to stay in the bed with me and not leave without saying goodbye. After five minutes of frantic driving I skidded to a halt outside their house. I could smell her as soon as I stepped out of the car and my wolf rejoiced inside that I was so close to her. She was safe, Scott had looked after her for me.

I ran to the door knocking quickly, God please be awake! I looked at my watch it was just after one in the morning. The door opened and a surprised looking Scott opened the door, "Hey Jay, what are you doing here?" he asked smiling as he stepped to the side to let me in. Shit this is gonna be hard!

"Um Scott man I need to talk to you" I said uncomfortably, it wasn't my fault, I know I said he could have her but I just couldn't help myself. He tensed immediately and looked behind me for trouble, I shook my head and closed the door.

"Scott man, something's happened, I mated" I said swallowing my guilt, I can't believe I've done this to him! Shit what if he had actually wanted to mate her instead of just sleeping with her? My wolf growled at the thought if him wanting her so I closed my eyes calming myself.

He gasped "Shit Jayden! You mated? I thought you said you didn't ever want a mate" he said watching me looking shocked, proud and a little jealous too.

Most shifters wanted to be mated, it was an unbreakable bond between two shifters that was stronger than anything, most of us wanted that strength and closeness, but I had always shyed away from it. God I was so stupid, the feeling was incredible, to love someone more than anything else in the world, to be willing to give your life for them in an instant, it was overwhelming, the joy of having a mate, I can't believe I didn't want this.

I nodded "I know, I didn't want one, it just kind of happened, I couldn't control myself, as soon as I saw her I had to have her, I just couldn't stop" I said frowning at the feeling of losing control. I would never loose control with her again, ever.

He pulled me into a hug and slapped my back happily, "I'm so pleased for you! Who is she? What's she like?" he asked excitedly. I smiled sadly, ok shit here it goes.

I opened my mouth to say when Mel walked into the hallway, "Hey Jayden, how's it going? Great party" she said grinning. I smiled, it was a fucking awesome party, best party ever.

I nodded "Yeah it was" I said.

Scott turned to her excited "Jayden's mated!" he said happily.

She clapped her hands excited and jumped a little on the spot, "Oh god that's incredible! Congratulations!" she said happily.

I nodded to the lounge "Can we go in there?" I asked uncomfortably rather than standing in the hallway, Scott nodded and we went in, he sat down on the sofa and I sat on the armchair. "Scott man, I'm really sorry, I didn't know who she was, honestly I just couldn't stop, I tried to not mark her but my wolf, he wanted her" I said grimacing waiting for him to explode at me.

He looked at me confused, "What?" he asked giving me his 'what the fuck' face, ok did she not tell them she had mated? I heard her moving around upstairs and I wanted to go to her and wrap her in my arms.

"Mel's friend, I don't even know her name" I said frowning.

Scott laughed, "That's funny dude, seriously who did you mate with?" he asked laughing his ass off.

Why the hell is that funny? "What's her name?" I asked curiously, I just couldn't remember it, I know he'd told me before but I just never paid that much attention to it, she was just Mel's friend then.

"Who Brooklyn?" he asked still chuckling, fucking hell that was a beautiful name, Brooklyn Phillips, I smiled, that would sound awesome, maybe we could get married soon, I loved the thought of her being Mrs Phillips.

"Is she upstairs?" I asked standing to go to her, Scott looked at he confused until understanding shot across his face. His eyes darkened and he jumped up in front of me, I clenched my fists controlling my wolf, I didn't want to hurt my best friend, but I WOULD NOT allow him to challenge me.

"You didn't!" he shouted angrily.

Mel gasped "You can't mate her! She's human" she said horrified.

My eyes snapped to hers, human? She can't be a human! I had definitely mated her, she was mine, she was supposed to be mine, that's why I couldn't help but claim her. "She can't be human, I marked her" I said sternly.

Mel shook her head "No! She's human, she is, Scott she's human, he can't have" she cried looking at him confused.

Scott stepped forward to me "You better fucking not have Jayden, you know I like her" he growled.

I stepped forward looking straight into his angry black eyes, "Don't you fucking dare challenge me Scott, sit the fuck down now" I ordered. He took a deep breath and stepped back and sat down, his posture still alert, his eyes still black, his wolf still wanting to kill me but he was showing me respect by backing off. "I didn't mean to, I couldn't stop, the first time I saw her my teeth extended, my wolf, he wanted her, she's mine" I said sternly.

"But you can't mate her she's human" Mel said again sounding like she was trying not to cry.

I shook my head, "She can't be human, I need to speak to her, she's probably from another pack and hasn't told you" I said confidently. Shifters couldn't mark humans so there had to be something else, some other explanation.

Scott was glaring at me, "She was supposed to be with me, you know I liked her, if she's a shifter I would have mated her" he growled angrily.

I stepped forward towards him, he wanted to mark my mate? My wolf wanted to show him I was in charge, he wanted to beat him senseless for even thinking of my angel in that way. "It's done, she's mine now" I growled warningly.

He shook his head, "How could you do this to me?" he shouted looking at me angrily. Shit I didn't do this to hurt him!

"Scott, I don't know what happened! Honestly I needed to, I couldn't help it!" I shouted angrily trying to make him understand.

She was coming downstairs now, I could hear her, I looked at the hallway waiting for her to come around the corner. She didn't, she'd stopped on the stairs, I stepped around the chair to go to her and Scott grabbed my arm. How dare he touch me! I snapped my eyes round to his, so angry my hands were shaking, my wolf trying to force me to shift and rip his head off. He must have seen this in my eyes as he let go immediately and dropped his hand to his side, his eyes turning back to their usual blue. I took a deep breath willing mine to do the same before I walked to the bottom of the stairs.

CHAPTER 6

B rook's POV

I sat there uncomfortable on the stairs pulling my t-shirt down over my knees, oh God just go! Why wasn't he leaving? They had stopped shouting at each other now so he should be leaving any minute. I closed my eyes and put my chin on my knees waiting for the sound of the front door.

"Hi", I snapped my eyes open and looked up to see him standing at the bottom of the stairs looking like a damn Greek god or something. His green eyes boring into mine making me feel weightless, shit what the hell do I say?

"Um hi" I said uncomfortably as I stood up, he smiled making my heart try to break it's way out of my chest.

"I didn't get your name, I'm Jayden, or Jay whatever you want" he said grinning as he looked me over.

"Um, Brooklyn, or Brook for short" I said swallowing loudly, he nodded and stepped up a step so our faces were level. I could feel the heat rising in me, god I wanted him to touch me so bad, my whole body was aching for him again.

"Why did you leave?" he asked quietly as his eyes tried to drag the answer straight from mine, I blushed at the close proximity and stepped back another step to put some distance between our bodies.

He frowned and looked a little hurt, "I just thought, you know, I'd leave before it got awkward, kinda like it is now Jayden" I said uncomfortable. His eyes flashed with excitement as I said his name, I would imagine mine did too, his name rolled off my tongue like chocolate making me shiver slightly.

"It's not awkward, we need to talk though I guess, get to know each other" he said smiling happily.

I shook my head, that couldn't happen, I couldn't get to know him, I could barely be around him, my body was screaming at me to grab him and hold him and I couldn't do that I had a boyfriend. "No, I'm sorry if I gave you the wrong impression, well I guess I definitely gave you the wrong impression, I mean shit we had sex, but I can't do this, I have a boyfriend" I said blushing like crazy as I rambled on and on making myself sound like a complete idiot.

He frowned angrily, "No, you're mine" he said as he stepped up to the step I had just vacated. His? What the hell is he talking about? Wow he's some kind of super possessive guy, jeez I only slept with him once! His face was so close to mine, I could smell his sweet breath blowing across my face making me want him so bad it hurt.

"No I'm not, look this was a mistake" I said stepping to the side and moving quickly down the stairs to find Mel, hopefully the possessive hot guy would leave then.

"Mistake? We're mated, that's it, you can't have a boyfriend, you're mine" he said sounding angry, mated? What's that? Mated like a dog?

"Mated? What the hell? I'm not some kind of dog, I don't mate for goodness sake, shit are you crazy? That's just great, all those people at the party and I have to sleep with a crazy guy" I said laughing even though this really wasn't funny.

He looked at me a little shocked, "We're mated" he said again, I looked at Mel and Scott for help, they were just watching speechless.

"Look, Jayden is it? You're a really good looking guy and wow you were good in bed, but seriously, you need to get some help" I said shaking my head. He moved so quick I didn't even see him move, he wrapped me in his arms, tingles were spreading through my body, my core was throbbing with need and I was more turned on than I had even been in my life.

His nose skimmed across my jaw making me whimper with desire, "We're mated, I can smell me on you, you have my mark, you're definitely mine, I can tell" he whispered in my ear making me shiver. "You know you're mine, I can smell how aroused you are, you want me right now just as much as I want you" he whispered. I bit my lip to stifle my moan of desire, he was right I did want him, I couldn't speak. What the hell was there to say? I could barely even think about anything other than his glorious body pressed against mine.

"Maybe you should go Jay" Scott said from behind him, oh god thank you! He shook his head pressing me closer to him possessively, he kissed my neck and I unconsciously tipped my head back wanting him to kiss lower where he bit me earlier. He smiled against my neck and pulled my t-shirt aside and ran his tongue across the bite mark. A shot of pleasure shot straight to my core and I moaned bringing my hands up to grip the back of his head holding it there as my body set on fire with passion.

He pulled back to look at me and I whimpered, I didn't want him to stop, I didn't want him to ever stop. He chuckled "See" he said happily, I still didn't understand, what does that prove other than the fact that he was a fucking sex god and his mouth could set me on fire?

I shook my head "I have a boyfriend, this was just a one night stand, I'm sorry" I said honestly. I was sorry, I wanted this, I wanted him for some reason even though I didn't even know him. I didn't want to be with Trey anymore, I hadn't wanted to be with him for almost three years, after the second time he hit me, when I was fourteen I wanted to leave him then but it was too late he wouldn't let me go.

"We're mated!" he shouted angrily making me flinch back from him, he immediately calmed down looking at me apologetically, "Don't be scared, I wouldn't hurt you, ever" he said stepping back to me brushing his hand across my cheek gently.

I looked at Mel for help, she looked from me to Jayden, "She's not what you think she is! Look at her she has no idea what your talking about Jay" she said sternly.

He looked at me closely, trying to drag the answers from my eyes again and suddenly he stepped back looking at me shocked. "Shit!" he gasped running a hand through his messy hair, I smiled ok now he's getting the idea that he's a crazy dude!

"Finally" I mumbled I said stepping to Scott's side, Jayden's eyes flashed and went darker just like when he bit me, they were almost black and looked scary as hell. He stepped up to me and took my hand pulling me away from Scott, ok wow what the hell is going on? I wrenched my hand out of his. "What the fuck is this about? And what the hell is going on with your eyes? Shit your eyes have changed colour! I thought I imagined it before" I cried angily. I wasn't scared, I felt no fear whatsoever, I believed him when he said he would never hurt me.

He took a deep breath and his eyes changed back to the beautiful shade of green and I felt my heart throb. "Come for a walk with me, I'll explain" he asked, almost pleadingly, holding out his hand for me to take. I watched his face turn from hope to disappointment when I didn't take his hand. I felt sick, he looked so sad, I couldn't make him sad! I put my hand in his and he grinned happily. "Thanks shortie" he said smirking at me.

I laughed "I'm not short!" I said shaking my head.

"You're shorter than me" he said teasingly. I laughed, of course I was shorter than him, he was probably about six foot two of total perfection.

"I expect most people are shorter than you Jayden, you're built like a freaking god" I said shaking my head in amusement, he laughed a beautiful laugh and pulled me towards the front door.

"We'll be back in a bit" he called over my shoulder. I glanced back at Mel, she looked strangely excited but shocked and scared at the same time, Scott looked sad and murderously angry, ok what the hell is this about?

He walked me out of the house and towards the woods still holding my hand, as we got to the edge of the tree line I stopped. I didn't want to go in there, Mel had told me stories about things that lived in the woods when I was a kid and it had scared the crap out of me. He stopped and looked at me before nodding into the tree's, wondering why I had stopped. "I can't go in there, I don't like it" I said feeling slightly sick.

He stepped closer to me and cupped my face in his hands, his face less than an inch from mine, "You have nothing to be scared of shortie, I'll never let anything hurt you I swear" he said tenderly. I could hear the truth in his voice and thinking about his eyes earlier I knew he was scary himself.

"There's animals in there, Mel told me when I was a kid" I said frowning looking into the tree's scanning for some type of killer animal.

He chuckled "Brook, it's fine I promise, you trust me?" he asked raising his eyebrows at me, I nodded, I did trust him, he was crazy and possessive but I trusted him, definitely, even though I had nothing to base that trust on at all. He smiled and stepped towards the tree's again giving me a little tug, I took a deep breath and stepped into the tree's with him. He smiled happily as he led us forwards going deeper and deeper into the woods, it was so dark, how the hell could he see where he was going?

"Jayden, that's enough please" I begged looking back the way we had come longingly.

He stopped and pulled me over to a tree that had fallen over, he brushed the moss off of it and motioned for me to sit down. He crouched down in front of me, "Do you have any idea what I am?" he asked curiously, what he is? What does that mean?

"Sagittarius?" I offered shrugging making him laugh, he shook his head.

"Ok you have no idea, this is fucking crazy, I don't know how this happened, it shouldn't have happened" he said frowning confused.

When he didn't continue I cupped his cheek, "Jayden, please tell me what the hell this is about, it's cold" I said hugging myself against the cold night, he stood and immediately pulled off his t-shirt standing there with a bare chest making me so hot I could catch fire, well that definitely warmed me up!

He bent down wrapping the shirt around my shoulders. "Sorry that's all I've got, I could give you my jeans too but I've not got any boxers on" he said looking at me playfully. I laughed and shook my head pulling his t-shirt around my shoulders tighter, he knelt down in front of me rubbing his hands up my arms trying to warm me.

"So, I'm not like you, please don't freak out, ok?" he asked making me instantly weary, when people say 'don't freak out' that usually pretty much guarantee's a freak out. I nodded biting my tongue trying to keep myself focused. "I'm a shifter, the animals Mel warned you about in the woods when you were a kid, that's me" he said cocking his head to the side watching me intently. I smiled, ok great, possessive, crazy and now delusional, just great and I'm in the middle of the dark woods with him and actually have no idea which direction we even came in from!

He smiled "You ok with that?" he asked curiously.

I nodded playing along "Sure, what kind of animal are you?" I asked trying to hide my amusement, he seemed to relax and breathed a sigh of relief.

"I'm a wolf, my father's Alpha of the pack, I'll be Alpha one day" he said still trying to warm me up.

I nodded "Ok great, now I know, can we go back to the house? Son of Alpha, it's cold" I said trying not to show my sarcasm too much.

He laughed "You don't believe me, ok I thought that was too easy" he said standing up and unbuttoning his jeans. My smile faded as I watched him pull them off standing there naked in front of me making my body yearn for his. "Don't run Brook, my instincts are to chase you" he said warningly, chase me? I gulped and he suddenly exploded into a huge brown wolf.

I screamed and jumped up clamping my hand over my mouth to stifle the piercing scream that was coming out of me. I felt sick, my whole body was shaking with fear, I closed my eyes and prayed for this to be over quickly. Oh shit please don't maul me, kill me before you eat me, please! I was jostled and I screamed again struggling against something hard. I opened my eyes to see Jayden there with his arms tight around me, "Shh, it's ok, I won't hurt you I swear, it's ok shortie, shh" he cooed stroking my hair.

Holy fuck did he really just turn into a wolf? Am I still asleep? Is this a dream? Am I that creative that I would dream up this beautiful boy then have him explode into a wolf in the middle of the dark woods? I don't think I am.

He pulled back to look at me, "It's ok Brook, it's ok" he said pressing his forehead to mine, I could barely breathe. "Calm down please" he begged holding me tight, I pushed him away and looked at his face, was this some sort of joke? How the hell could he fake something like that?

"How did you do that?" I asked barely recognising my own voice.

He shrugged "I was born like this, my whole family are shifters" he said casually as if we were discussing the weather. I nodded and sat back down on the tree my legs feeling a little weak, he pulled his jeans back on watching me curiously.

He bent back down in front of me, "There are lots of us, the Porters, they're shifters too" he said.

"What? No way! I've known Mel and Scott for years, seriously no, she isn't a....a... whatever you said" I said sternly.

He smiled "A shifter" he said casually.

"Shit! Will you stop saying that!" I cried, god that word was fucking crazy! Maybe I was crazy, maybe that's what this was, it wasn't a dream, this is some sort of psychotic episode or something, I'm really in some padded cell, in a white jacket, dribbling.

"Ok, I need to tell you about mating" he said quietly, looking a little unsure, my hand shot up to my neck, he said I had his mark, that I was his. I traced the teeth marks on my neck and he looked at me apologetically, "Did that hurt?" he asked grimacing.

I shook my head "No not really, it felt a little weird, but it was nice actually" I admitted, he smiled and reached out a hand to touch it. As soon as his fingertip touched it, my core throbbed and I moaned breathily as my body pulsed with excitement.

He smiled his sexy little smile and pulled his hand away, "That is the sexiest thing I have ever seen, my mark on your skin, it's driving me crazy" he said looking at it lustfully.

I gulped and dropped my eyes to the floor, "Ok tell me about mating" I said wanting to make him stop looking at me like that.

"Ok, well shifters they can date and stuff like humans can, but when they find the shifter they want to be with, the male will mark the female creating a bond between them, claiming her as his, other shifters won't go near a female once she's been mated" he said running his hands up my arms again trying to warm me as I started to shiver again, but to be honest it wasn't the cold that was making me shiver, it was the casual use of the words 'shifter' and 'humans'.

"So you claimed me?" I asked shocked, he nodded looking at me apologetically, "But why? Why would you do that? You don't even know me, look at me, why would you want to claim me?" I asked confused looking down at my fat ugly body. He gasped and moved my legs apart moving his body in between them and pressing his chest to mine.

"Why the hell wouldn't I want to claim you? You are the most beautiful thing I have ever seen, every single guy in that party was talking about you tonight" he said wrapping his arms around me.

I laughed and shook my head, wow ok, add blind to the list too! "What the hell has happened to you? Why do you think you're so hideous? Honestly Brook, you are stunningly beautiful, if I could only see one thing for the rest of my life it would be you, without question" he said looking deep into my eyes. Oh my god he is so damn sweet!

"Ok we'll agree to disagree, but anyway why did you claim me? You don't know me" I said watching his face turn angry.

"God stop that! You don't see yourself the way other people see you!" he said fiercely.

I sighed "Please answer the question Jayden" I said, he sighed and pressed his face into my neck breathing deeply.

"I don't know, when I saw you, my body wanted you, my wolf wanted you, I knew you were supposed to be mine, I couldn't help it, I tried not to but I lost control and claimed you" he said shaking his head as if this was some sort of weakness he had.

"That's when you said you couldn't control it, that's when you bit me, your eyes changed colour to black just before you did it, but when you pulled back they were green again, I thought I imagined it" I said shaking my head.

He nodded "That was my wolf, he took over, he claimed you" he said.

I pulled back "So your wolf claimed me? That means YOU don't want me?" I asked frowning.

He gasped and shook his head fiercely "Of course I want you! My wolf is part of me, but it's the dominant part that comes out when something needs to happen, it's not some other person that's inside me, I AM my wolf, that was just how I explained it, I should have said I claimed you, but it was my wolf instincts that made me sink my teeth into your skin" he explained. "I don't know how this happened, you're human, I shouldn't have been able to claim you" he said looking at confused again.

"Shifter's don't claim humans?" I asked frowning confused.

He shook his head "Never" he said positively. Ok this is just getting weirder and weirder!

"Never?" I asked watching his face.

He shook his head again, "Never, I didn't even think it was possible, your body's different to mine, your gene's are different, I shouldn't be able to claim you, I can only claim another shifter, you sure your not?" he asked looking at me hopefully.

I laughed "I think I'd remember something like that Jayden" I said sarcastically making him laugh.

"Hey, I had to check!" he said innocently.

"Ok so what do we do about this then? How do we get un-mated?" I asked.

He looked at me horrified, "What? You can't get un-mated, you're mine now, I'm yours, I'll never want anyone else, if you were a shifter you'd feel the same about me, but obviously you don't, which I guess is a big problem for me" he said looking at me sadly.

I wrapped my arms around him and pulled him close to me, "I'm sorry, I have a boyfriend" I said quietly, wishing I didn't.

"You know, you haven't once told me that you're in love with him, you've just said you had a boyfriend, not that you loved him or that you didn't actually want me" he said pulling back looking at me hopefully. Oh god I didn't love Trey but that had nothing to do with it, I needed to protect my Mom and now I needed to protect Jayden, Trey would go crazy if he found out any of this.

But could I tell Jayden I didn't want him? I only met him a couple of hours ago but I could feel the bond that he was talking about, I trusted him, I wanted him. But I couldn't have him, I needed to get this sorted and go back home and wait for Trey to come back, hopefully he wouldn't notice the huge bite mark I have on my neck. Wow ok that's gonna be hard, but I guess he doesn't actually like to look at me too closely because of how I look so maybe I could get away with it if it faded soon.

"I'm in love with him Jayden" I lied watching his face fall, he looked so sad my heart started to break. Oh god I can't do this!

His eyes flashed to black again and he shook his head fiercely, "You can't you're mine, we're mated, you need to be with me" he growled.

"I'm sorry, I didn't choose this, you forced this on me, I can't be with a shifter Jayden, I love my boyfriend, we've been together a long time" I said.

He closed his eyes taking a couple of deep breaths, when he opened them they were the beautiful green again, "How long?" he asked taking my hand.

I smiled sadly "Four years" I said trying not to grimace.

He nodded "That's a long time, so I guess I don't know anything about you" he said faking a smile.

"I guess not" I said squeezing his hand gently.

"Well how old are you?" he asked curiously.

"I just turned seventeen three weeks ago, you?" I said looking at his beautiful face feeling myself being drawn to him.

"I turned twenty today" he said.

I gasped, "It's your birthday? Wait! Was that your party we were at?" I asked shocked, he nodded smiling. "Oh, sorry I didn't realise, well happy birthday" I said frowning, ok wow I so screwed up his birthday!

"Yeah it is" he said rubbing small circles in the back of my hand. I shivered again, "You think maybe I could come back to Scott's and we could talk some more?" he asked hopefully.

"Do you think that's a good idea? I mean shouldn't you just go home and mate someone else or something?" I asked, surely getting to know me would just make this worse. I know it would make it harder for me, being around him was hard work, all the time I needed to watch myself so I didn't jump him. But then again, it was probably different for him, he's so damn hot and I'm, well I'm not.

He shook his head "I need to be in your life Brook, if you don't want to be with me I still need to be around you" he said shaking his head looking pained.

"Well how the hell is that gonna work?" I asked rolling my eyes.

He smiled sadly, "I don't know, but we can try right? I can be your friend, I just need to make you happy, so I'll be whatever you need me to be" he said looking at me pleadingly. Oh god he was so sweet! Damn stupid Trey!

"Jayden, why torture yourself like that? Just go sleep with a bunch of girls and mate someone else" I suggested.

He looked at me horrified and shook his head, "Maybe later on I will, but for now I just want to get to know you, please" he asked looking at me pleadingly. My god I can't say no to that face! I nodded slightly and his face exploded into happiness as he jumped up holding out a hand for me again.

CHAPTER 7

I let him pull me to my feet and took his t-shirt from around my shoulders holding it out to him. He smiled and took it wrapping it back around my shoulders again, "You need it more than me, my body runs hotter than yours" he said taking my hand and putting it on his chest. God he was so warm! I was standing so close my whole body was tingling for him. "Come on then shortie, let's get you in the warm" he said wrapping his arm around my waist where it seemed to fit perfectly and helping me walk along in the dark, lifting me gently when there was something in my way or when I stumbled on something I couldn't see.

"Can you see where your going?" I asked curiously squinting through the blackness in front of me.

He chuckled "Yeah, I can see fine" he said guiding me around a big rock that I only saw when I was practically on top of it. Finally we made it out of the woods and I breathed a sigh of relief.

"I hate the woods" I said shuddering.

He laughed "The woods aren't too bad, it's only because you can't see where your going" he said giving me a little squeeze.

He let me go as we walked up to the house, I gave him back his t-shirt and took my last look at his glorious body as he pulled it on. As soon as I was through the door Mel almost jumped on me. "What the hell hap...oh hey Jay" she said stopping as she spotted him over my shoulder.

He smiled "Hey Mel, do you think maybe I could stay for a while so Brook and I can talk for a bit?" he asked curiously. Mel looked over her shoulder and I saw Scott sitting on the sofa, he nodded and Mel turned back to Jayden.

"Sure, ok" she said a little uncomfortably, "So I'm gonna go to bed I guess, give you two some time to talk then" Mel said smirking at me, ok she obviously thought we were together and would be doing more than talking!

"Thanks, I'll be up in a bit" I said hugging her, she skipped off up the stairs.

"Ok well, could you re-lock the door once Jayden leaves?" Scott asked looking at me.

I nodded, "You ok?" I asked, he looked so sad about something.

He smiled "Yeah I'm fine Brooklyn, see you in the morning ok" he said hugging me and nodding at Jayden before skulking off towards the stairs. Ok what the hell is that about?

"He doesn't look too pleased with me" I said grimacing.

Jayden chuckled "It's not you he's pissed with, it's me, he liked you, I think he wanted to date you, if he knew you could be mated I think he would have mated you" he said shaking his head looking uncomfortable. I looked at him with wide eyes, Scott really did like me? This was just too crazy!

"Don't be stupid, god what is it with you and Mel? Scott's not interested in me, I've known him since I was three years old! He used to push me over and throw water balloons at me, he even stole my first bra and hung it from that tree out the front so everyone could see it!" I said frowning.

Jayden burst out laughing, "Well if that doesn't tell you he likes you nothing will" he said laughing his ass off. Ok what the hell?

"What will?" I asked curiously, what the hell was I missing from him being a pain in my ass when I was younger?

"It's standard behaviour for telling a girl how you feel, one, touch her as much as you can, so pushing you over would be where that fitted in, two, make her clothes see though so you can cop a look, hence the water balloons, but I got nothing for him stealing your bra, that's going a little too far, maybe bordering on stalkerish" he said teasingly.

I laughed and rolled my eyes, he was a really funny guy, "Right ok, well want a coffee or something?" I asked heading to the kitchen and flicking on the kettle. He came and sat on the worktop next to me smiling at me happily as I made coffee, "How do you take it?" I asked grabbing the sugar and putting two in mine with extra milk.

He smiled "Not like yours, wow I'm surprised you have any teeth left!" he said looking at me with fake horror.

I rolled my eyes and flashed him my teeth, "All mine, I like sugar, I shouldn't have it though" I said grimacing.

"Why? Your not diabetic or anything are you?" he asked looking a little concerned.

I smiled "No nothing like that, sugar's not good for you that's all" I said not wanting to get into the whole, 'your beautiful' thing if I told him I shouldn't be eating the calories.

"Well I just take milk in mine, just a little" he said nodding at the cup, "What's your boyfriends name?" he asked faking a smile as he asked but I could see that this was hurting him.

"Trey" I said almost apologetically, he seemed like a really nice guy, and I was hurting him, god I felt like shit!

"Is he in your school?" he asked taking the two cups and leading us to the lounge plopping down on the sofa.

I sat next to him, "Um no Trey's older than me" I said not really wanting to talk about this.

He looked at me interested "Yeah how old is he? Where did you two meet?" he asked, I grimaced.

"Well, Trey's twenty four and we met when I was out shopping with some friends" I said, his mouth dropped open and he looked at me shocked.

"He's seven years older than you? Wow that's a big age gap, you've been with him for four years which means you met him when you were thirteen and he was twenty right?" he asked turning his nose up slightly. I nodded "What the hell kind of twenty year old would approach a thirteen year old when she was old shopping with her friends? That's like me hitting on a thirteen year old" he said looking a little disgusted.

I smiled and rolled my eyes, "Ok like I haven't had heard that before!" I said chuckling.

He laughed "Yeah I guess you got that lecture from your Mom and Dad huh?" he said grinning a little smugly.

I nodded "Yeah, from my Mom, I never knew my Dad" I said shrugging.

He watched me looking interested "No? You mind if I ask what happened?" he asked curiously.

"No I don't mind, it was a long time ago, my Mom slept with someone on a one night stand and got pregnant, when she told him he gave her money and told her to get rid of me, she didn't, he left town, that's that" I said shrugging, ok why the hell did I just tell him all that?

He frowned, "Your Mom raised you on her own then or do you have a step dad or something?" he asked taking my hand and playing with my fingers.

I shook my head, "Just me and my Mom, she's awesome, she put herself through college while I was at school, worked in the evening's to pay the rent and still managed to be the best Mom in the world, she's a doctor now" I said proudly.

He looked at me smiling happily, "She sounds great" he said honestly.

I nodded "What about you?" I asked.

He shrugged looking a little sad as he weaved his fingers through mine. "My Mom died when I was five, my father left just after, I was raised by my Aunt, she was my legal guardian, but she died last year" he said sadly. I gasped, god he sounds like he had a really hard life!

"Oh god Jayden, I'm sorry" I said squeezing his fingers tightly.

He smiled "It's ok, my Aunt was great, a little crazy, but great, she would have really liked you" he said smiling happily.

"She must have been nice to take on a five year old" I said honestly, he nodded smiling fondly. I guess I need to talk about the whole shifter thing now, we seem to have avoided it pretty well up until now. "So your father's Alpha of the shifters?" I asked grabbing my coffee and wrapping my hands around it trying to warm myself up.

He nodded looking a little annoyed, I got a sense that he didn't like his father at all. "Yeah, he's pack Alpha" he said frowning.

"How many shifters are in your pack then?" I asked curiously as I pulled my knees up to my chin.

"Well there's probably about fifty or sixty families across the towns" he said shrugging.

"Shit! Seriously? Sixty families? And your father is in charge of all of them?" I asked a little shocked.

He nodded "Yeah, the Alpha passes down through bloodlines, there's been a Phillips Alpha for the last two hundred years" he said casually.

I smiled "So that's your last name? Jayden Phillips, got any middle names?" I asked curiously.

He grinned "Yeah, Richard" he said rolling his eyes, "You don't like your middle name?" I asked smiling.

He shook his head "Nah, it's my fathers name, bit boring" he said grinning.

I laughed "Boring? My middle names Logan, that's a boy's name!" I said laughing.

He grinned "It's nice, what's your surname?" he asked happily.

"Mill's" I said yawning.

He smiled sadly, "Want me to go so you can sleep?" he offered looking like he really didn't want to leave, I shook my head, I didn't want him to go either, not yet. He grinned "So what do you like to do in your spare time? You have any hobbies or anything?" he asked looking really interested.

I smiled "I love to read, I want to be a book editor when I leave college, I like to swim, I like dancing, I love watching scary movies as long as I'm not in the house on my own after and I love to eat strawberry cheesecake" I said trailing off a list of my favourite things.

He smiled "What about things you hate?" he asked curiously.

I grimaced "I hate it when people crack their knuckles, Trey does that all the time, drives me nuts, um, I hate spiders, I hate tequila and I hate getting bit by random boys at birthday parties" I said teasingly making him laugh his ass off. God he was so hot when he laughed! I rested my head against the back of the sofa, "Tell me yours" I said closing my eyes listening to his silky sexy voice.

"I love playing football, eating, I eat a lot it's part of the shifter thing, I love old classic cars, I like to fix them in my spare time, I'm studying law, my Mom always wanted me to be a lawyer so I decided I'd do that for her" he said casually.

I snapped my eyes open to look at him, "You don't want to be a lawyer but your doing it anyway?" I asked shocked.

He shook his head frowning "No way, it's so boring, but it's what my Mom wanted for me so" he said trailing off. Oh god he is so adorable! He's studying Law because of his Mom but actually hated it?

"That's incredible Jayden, seriously, you must have really loved your Mom, It's sweet" I said honestly.

He grinned "Yeah or I'm a sucker for a sob story either way" he said laughing. I smiled, "I'm taking a weekend course in car's though, I should just about be a qualified Mechanic at the same time as I qualify as a Lawyer" he said laughing.

"Wow a car fixing Lawyer, you don't see many of those these days" I said laughing, he grinned and rolled his eyes at me.

God I was getting cold again! I could feel the heat seeping out of his body so I scooted closer to him, "I'm cold" I said quietly, he smiled and closed the distance between us wrapping his arm around me tightly. I rested my head on his shoulder and yawned again, "So what about your hates?" I asked closing my eyes again.

"Well I don't really hate anything, I dislike rats but I don't hate them, I don't like flying too much but I can cope with it, I don't like" he said but I didn't hear anymore, he was just too comfortable and warm and safe.

CHAPTER 8

Jayden's POV

I woke up with a really stiff neck, I moved my head up from the funny angle where I had fallen asleep sitting up on the couch and looked down at the angel in my arms. She was still sound asleep, curled into me happily, I smiled at how beautiful she was, she looked so peaceful and perfect. I glanced at my watch, it was just before six around about the time I usually woke up, it didn't matter what time I went to bed I only really slept for five hours at the most and was always awake by six am. It was a male shifter thing, like an internal body clock I guess, we all needed less sleep than humans, female shifters could sleep for longer. I guess it was something to do with the male being the provider, so I guess the wolf would go out looking for food for his mate, something like that anyway I don't know.

I brushed her hair away from her face, god how the hell am I gonna pull this off just being friends with her? My whole body was screaming for her, but if it was either put myself through agony of watching her with someone else everyday just so I could be close to her or cut her out of my life completely. There was only really one option, and although it would hurt like hell and be the hardest thing I will ever have to do, the other option would kill me, I know it would.

I had to be around her, I told her last night I would find someone else later on but that just wasn't gonna happen. I wouldn't even be able to look at another girl now, she was my everything, it was either her or no one, that's what a mating was, a pairing for life. It's typical of me though to choose someone who I can't be with. I decide never to get mated then end up mating with a girl I shouldn't even be able to mate with in the first place, the bond turns out to be one sided so she doesn't feel anything for me, and on top of that she has a serious boyfriend! Fuck my life!

I heard someone coming down the stairs, I glanced over my shoulder to see Scott look over. I smiled sadly and moved so I could grip her tighter, I moved my body off of the couch and eased her down onto her back as I slipped my arm out from under her. I stood up and looked at her, hating the fact that I had to leave but I had left a raging party at my house last night, I dread to think of what the place will look like today! My wolf growled, he didn't want to leave her, especially with Scott now that I knew he wanted her. I bent down and kissed her forehead, ignoring the blast of desire that pulsed over me making me want to rip her clothes off and take her right on the couch.

I stood up and walked into the kitchen to talk to Scott. "Hey" I said a little sheepishly, he smiled but it didn't quite reach his eyes, I wasn't forgiven.

"Hey" he said putting some toast in the toaster.

"Scott man, I'm sorry, I swear I couldn't help it, I didn't know who she was, I literally lost control and mated her" I said shaking my head still not able to comprehend the need for her.

"It's ok, I just don't understand how you say it happened, how could you just need her like that? It's not an urge to mark someone, it a decision, you must have decided to mark her" he said shrugging obviously still really pissed off.

I shook my head "Scott, I walked out of the bathroom and my canines extended, I almost mated her instantly but I managed to hold off long enough to let her past me into the bathroom then when she came out it was twice as bad, the hairs on the back of my neck were standing up, my teeth were out longer than they had ever been before, it was her voice that tipped me over the edge, I was fighting it, I wasn't doing well, but then she spoke and I snapped, that was it I swear" I said honestly.

He looked at me a little shocked, "I've never heard of that" he said shaking his head.

"I've never heard of a shifter mating a human before either" I said confused. Maybe I should go speak to my father about this see what he says. "Listen I need to go back to mine, I left the party going on last night, I'll be back later once I've cleared up, if she wakes up before I'm back can you give her my number and ask her to call me?" I asked feeling like a piece of shit that I had him doing my dirty work for me when he was totally pissed with me right now.

He nodded "Sure, make sure you're there with her when she dump's that asshole she's seeing, just watch him ok, Mel said he's a real piece of shit, she said he can be an ass to her but she wouldn't elaborate" he said. My wolf jumped wanting to rip his head off just in case he would ever hurt her or anything, I pushed him back. She's not dumping him anyway so he would have no need to get angry with her.

"She's not dumping him, she doesn't want to be with me" I said casually trying to pretend like she wasn't ripping my heart out.

He gasped "What? How?" he asked shocked, I smiled sadly.

"I guess the mating didn't work with her because she's human, it only works for shifters by the look of it, so she wants to stay with her boyfriend and I'll have to be content with being her friend" I said trying not to show the pain of the words.

Scott slapped my shoulder as a supportive gesture, "Shit Jayden that sucks! You really mated with her, like a proper mating? And it has no effect on her?" he asked shaking his head in disbelief.

"Mine's a proper mating, I'd do anything for her, I'll even watch her make a life with her boyfriend if that's what she wants, not much else I can do" I said honestly. "I better go, keep an eye on her for me, I'll be back, and Scott I'm really sorry man" I said apologetically.

He smiled sympathetically, obviously deciding that a lifetime of unrequited love is enough punishment for stealing a girl he wanted to fuck. "It's ok Jay, I'm sorry man, shit I bet you wish you'd not mated her now huh?" he asked grimacing slightly.

I laughed "I'm glad I mated her Scott, I get to make her happy, that's enough for me" I said honestly.

He snorted "Wow dude, you got it bad, this suck's ass" he said.

I smiled "She's worth it man, I'll see ya" I said as I walked out heading to my car.

I drove the five minutes to my house, fighting the urge the whole time to go back and lay with her, maybe she was cold without me there, she didn't have a blanket. I sighed and pulled into my drive, there was still car's parked around so I knew there was still people inside. I groaned as I made my way up the drive picking up empty beer cars and paper cups as I went, I dumped them all on the porch as I went in.

The door was wide open and the house was a fucking mess. There were drinks bottles and cups and can's everywhere, people were asleep on the floor in various states of undress. I went to the kitchen and turned on the faucet flushing the vomit from the sink before it made me gag. The kitchen was a mess, the punch bowl smashed leaving a puddle of sticky liquid and fruit all over the side and floor. There was even more empty alcohol containers in here, cigarette butts everywhere and a nice little burn on my carpet where by the looks of it the carpet had caught fire. I laughed, well it could have been worse I guess, the damn fire could have spread burning down the house along with everyone at the party and all my stuff, so whatever else there is wrong, it could have been a lot worse.

I went upstairs to see people asleep in the hallway, every bedroom was full of couples, in some cases three people. None of my stuff seemed to be missing or broken though which was a bonus. I went back downstairs grabbing a frying pan and wooden spoon. Banging on it as loudly as I could a couple of times "Every one up! Get the hell out of my house or help clean it, the choice is yours" I shouted. I banged it again and heard people groaned and gasping, there was movement everywhere as people got up and got dressed leaving the house quickly, not one of those assholes stayed behind to help! Typical!

I got to work, I was pretty fast being a shifter so it actually didn't take that long. When I was finished I grabbed a glass of orange juice and sat on the sofa closing my eyes, the first thing that popped into my head was Brook. God was she ok? I glanced at my watch, it was after ten now, I wonder if she's awake. She hadn't called me, I asked Scott to ask her to call me, but I guess that doesn't mean that she would do it just because I asked her to.

I grabbed some food from the fridge making a sandwich and grabbing a bag of crisps and an apple. I shoved the food down my neck as fast as I could then went back to my car to go back to see Brook. I pulled in to their drive a few minutes later and practically skipped to their door I was so excited. I let myself in as usual, being quiet in case she was still asleep, I went straight to the couch but she was already up.

I spotted Scott and Mel in the kitchen, "Hey morning, where's Brook?" I asked grinning, the whole house smelled like her and it was making me so aroused I could climax just from the thought of her alone.

Scott looked at me apologetically, "She went home" he said quietly.

"What? When?" I cried angrily.

"About an hour ago, she got a text from Trey and packed up her stuff and left, he's home a day early apparently, wanted to see her" Mel said grimacing slightly.

I felt so jealous and angry I wanted to smash something, my wolf wanted to come out and rip the place to shreds at the thought of what he could be doing to her now, his hands on her body, my mate's body. I growled and slammed my hand down on the worktop, "What's her address?" I shouted, Mel looked at Scott a little scared and he stood up quickly.

"Jayden, calm down dude, you said yourself she wasn't your mate, she didn't want you, if you go there now you'll more than likely shift and rip his throat out" Scott said trying to calm me down. He was right, I clenched my fists willing myself to calm, I agreed to be her friend, nothing more, she wanted her boyfriend, the sick fuck who dated her when she was thirteen, fucking paedophile!

I gripped my hands in my hair, "Ok, I'm ok, I need her address, I won't do anything, I just need to check she's ok" I said calmly, I must have passed their inspection, either that or my Alpha blood claim was strong today because Mel grabbed a piece of paper and immediately started writing her address and phone number. I took it, this was about thirty minutes from here, nice neighbourhood. "Thanks" I said nodding as I left the house at a sprint jumping over the hood of my car instead of running round and wrenched the door open.

I sped to her house as fast as I could without killing anyone and pulled up outside the address Mel had written. I didn't want to be too obvious so I pulled up a couple of houses away, there was a huge expensive looking truck in the drive that didn't look like it would be the type of car Brook or her Doctor mother would choose. Shit he's probably there with her now! I can't just walk up to her house she'll think I'm some crazy fucking stalker! I took a few calming breaths and grabbed my phone, I could just call her and see if I can come over or something, give her the choice instead of just turning up unannounced.

I dialled the phone number Mel had given me and closed my eyes, I felt sick, this was harder than I thought. How the hell was I gonna cope with this? Knowing that he's in there with her, touching her, his hands on her body. I could feel the growl trying to rip it's way out of my throat as the phone continued to ring, why the hell isn't she answering?

CHAPTER 9

Brook's POV

I woke up and rolled over jerking back as I felt myself almost fall off of the sofa, I snapped my eyes open to see Mel's living room. Oh shit I fell asleep on Jayden! I sat up quickly looking around for him but he wasn't there, I couldn't help but feel disappointed. But another part of me was glad he was gone, my body re-acted to his presence and drove me crazy, but my head was still telling me I needed to stay the hell away from him. The more time I spent around him the more I was gonna start to like him, I could feel it seeping in, and in a few weeks I would be crazy about him I could tell.

I got up being quiet hoping he had actually left after I had fallen asleep rather than be sitting in the kitchen or something, this was already too weird for me. I mean shit a shifter? How the hell has all of this happened? Did I believe in any of this? I mean I plainly saw him explode into a wolf, there was no way he could fake any of this, was there?

I tiptoed to the kitchen praying he wasn't there, and if he was maybe I could sneak to the stairs and find Mel and get her to tell him to leave. I glanced round the corner to see Scott sitting there on his own and I breathed a sigh of relief that I wouldn't have to deal with him today. "Morning" I said quietly as I walked in, he smiled at me a little sadly.

"Hey Brooklyn, you sleep ok?" he asked, I nodded, actually I slept really well even though I was on the sofa.

I trudged over and sat at the stool next to him, "Scott, where's Jayden?" I asked looking around uncomfortably.

"He left, he needed to go and sort out his house after the party, he wanted me to give you his number and ask you to call him" he said pulling out his phone.

I shook my head, "I don't want his number Scott, I can't do this" I said putting my forehead on the counter trying desperately not to cry.

He rubbed my back tenderly, "Brook, everything's gonna be ok, don't cry, come on" he said softly. How the hell is everything gonna be ok? I have a boyfriend who I don't love, who is literally gonna kill me if he ever finds out, and a damn wolf boy who thinks I'm the only girl in the world for him!

I felt the tears start to fall so I sat up and wrapped my arms around Scott hugging him tightly as I cried on his shoulder. "Shh, It's ok Brook, you don't have to be with Jay if you don't want to, he told me this morning you two are gonna try to be friends" he said softly as he stroked my hair. I nodded squeezing my eyes shut, I needed to stop crying! I hated crying in front of people.

"I know, I just don't know how this happened, I mean is this real Scott? Jayden said that you and Mel are......" I said trailing off not really wanting to say the word.

He cupped my face in his hands and smiled reassuringly, "Mel and I are shifters too, but we're still the same people who you grew up with I promise" he said kissing my forehead and pulling me back into another hug. "Are you really human Brook?" Scott asked pulling back and looking at me intently, he looked confused as hell.

I sniffed and wiped my face, "Yeah" I whispered not trusting my voice to speak properly.

He sighed and shook his head, "You know, if I knew you could be mated I would have asked you out a long time ago" he said turning away and getting up from the stool taking his plate to the sink. I gasped, shit, he really did like me! How the hell could I have not seen this? Why the hell would someone like Scott even be interested in me in the first place? I mean I know I grew up with him of sorts and he is adorable, he could probably see past looks seen as he knew me so well.

I smiled thinking about how sweet he was, and I always had a huge crush on him! Looking at him now though I could see he was good looking but I just didn't feel that attraction anymore, there was no draw for me there, if he was to strip his shirt off I wouldn't be staring lustfully after him like I would have done a couple of days ago.

"You know Scott, if you'd have asked me out I would have said yes if I wasn't with Trey, I always liked you" I admitted chuckling.

He laughed humourlessly and turned back to me rolling his eyes, "A day too late Brooklyn, but thanks for letting me know" he said shaking his head at me.

"Why the hell would you want to be mated to me anyway Scott? You could have any girl you wanted, I mean look at you, you are so damn hot, I swear I always fancied you" I said laughing and blushing that I had just told him that.

"Why would I want you? Your smart, kind, funny, adorable, thoughtful, generous, and a thousand other things I could put in a list, but none of this matters now, your mated with Jay" he said shrugging. Aww he is so sweet! I smiled at him.

"Can people get un-mated? Jayden said no" I said frowning slightly, I couldn't go through life mated to a damn wolf while dating someone else.

Scott laughed and shook his head "It doesn't work that way Brook, when he marked you he created a bond between the two of you, your linked now, he's yours, he'll always be yours and there's nothing you can do about it" he said looking at me sadly.

Holy shit, there really was nothing I could do about it! "But I don't want him" I said crying again, he wrapped me in his arms.

"That's sad Brook, and it's gonna be really hard for Jay, but he needs to be friends with you, a shifter has to be near his mate, I've never heard of a mate pair just being friends before but I'm pretty sure Jay can make this work, he's a really great guy" he said stroking my face and wiping my tears away.

God I felt like shit! Poor Jayden! Scott just held me tightly until I stopped crying. "How did this happen then? Jayden said shifter's couldn't mate humans, just other shifters" I said my voice croaky where I had been crying.

He shrugged, "I have no idea, he shouldn't have been able to claim you, he said he had to, that he lost control, but it doesn't work like that, it's a decision, like a marriage proposal of sorts I guess" he said sounding confused.

I smiled sadly, "I saw him Scott, he was sweating and shaking, he looked like he was struggling not to, he definitely lost control, I saw his eyes change" I said frowning.

Scott just looked even more confused, "Well it's done now anyway, however it happened, you really not leaving Trey?" he asked starting to make me some toast and coffee, I shook my head trying desperately not to wince at the sound of his name.

"No, I'm with Trey and that's it, I guess Jayden and I can try to be friends if he wants to, but I really think he's better off away from me, I mean why the hell would he want to torture himself?" I asked shrugging.

Scott smiled "I can't explain it to you, and to be honest I've never felt a mating bond so I can't be sure, but from what people tell me about it, as soon as he marked you, you should have felt it, like a rush of love and passion for him, you'd do anything for them and your one purpose in life is to make them happy and keep them safe" he said looking at me in awe, maybe he wanted to be mated.

"I didn't feel that, I just, I don't know, he drives me crazy, literally, him being near me gets me so excited I could cry, but I didn't feel love, I'm not in love with him" I said honestly.

Scott laughed "Yeah the physical stuff comes with it too, that'll always be there, if you were a shifter you wouldn't be attracted to anyone else now, like you said you fancied me, you still look at me like that now your mated?" he asked curiously.

I narrowed my eyes and looked him over playfully, "Honestly, no, you just don't do it for me anymore" I said laughing.

He pushed me playfully setting my food in front of me, "Well I'm not dressed to impress today! Maybe I should go change see what you think then" he said faking hurt, I slapped his arm and rolled my eyes. "I think the mating has worked to a certain extent then, obviously the physical side is there, can I see your mark?" he asked nodding at my neck. I grimaced and pulled my t-shirt to the side watching his face as he tried not to react to it.

I rubbed it, it was still slightly raised, "Will it fade? It feels raised, will it leave a scar?" I asked turning my nose up slightly.

He reached out a hand and touched it, the second his finger tip touched it I started to feel sick, it felt wrong, I flinched away from his hand and he smiled, "You don't like me touching it" he said laughing.

I shook my head grimacing, "It makes me feel sick, is that normal too?" I asked.

He nodded "Yeah, it's part of the bond thing, it'll be sensitive for Jay and everyone else it'll feel a little weird, it won't fade though Brook, it'll go like a scar, it won't always be red like now" he said almost apologetically.

"How the hell am I gonna explain a damn bite mark on my neck to Trey and my Mom?" I asked panicking again slightly.

He took hold of my hand, "I don't know, you could say you got attacked at the party or something, you could tell your Mom I did it if it helps" he said shrugging.

I laughed "My Mom would kick your ass Scott and you know it" I said chuckling, he nodded grimacing,

"I know" he said faking horror making me laugh harder.

He really is adorable and I was really sad that I didn't mate with him, when I was a kid I always dreamed one day he would want me, he was always my fantasy husband when we played weddings and house, but then I got stuck with Trey and all my dreams disappeared. If only he had asked me out before I met Trey, and mated with me before I met Jayden, he would have made me really happy. I ate in silence after that, he just kept his hand on the small of my back rubbing gently until Mel came down about half an hour later.

She was so damn excited to talk to me as she skipped over looking around "Where's Jay?" she asked confused.

"He went to sort out his house early this morning" Scott said kissing the top of both of our heads as he went to walk off. "I'll let you two talk then, if you need to talk about anything Brook then I'm here ok" he said winking at me as he walked out.

"Show me" Mel chirped as soon as he left the room, I looked at her and gave her my best 'what the fuck' face, she rolled her eyes and pulled my t-shirt off of my shoulder looking at my mark. "Wow this is hot! It's an Alpha mark, did you see how the teeth next to the canines are slightly bigger than the other teeth, that's an Alpha trait, you're so lucky Jay is hot! And he's really nice, such a player though but you won't ever have to worry about that" she said happily.

Ok why the hell is she so excited? "Mel babe, I'm not with Jayden, I'm with Trey" I said.

She gasped looking at me horrified, "But you can't! You're mated! You are mated right?" she asked suddenly looking at me unsure.

I nodded "Apparently" I said watching her face change back to happy again.

"I can't believe you mated an Alpha! Well he's not Alpha yet but he will be" she said bouncing in her seat and looking at me a little jealously.

"Mel calm down! I'm with Trey, Jayden and I are gonna be friends, I'm not like you" I said quietly watching the smile fade from her face.

"You really are human, you're not from another pack?" she asked quietly.

I shook my head "I didn't even know what the hell a shifter was Mel and to be honest I'm pretty pissed with you that you didn't tell me" I said honestly.

She looked at me apologetically, "I couldn't tell you, we're not allowed to tell people otherwise I would have done, you're my best friend" she said pleadingly.

I rolled my eyes "I get it, don't worry" I said nodding, I understood and to be honest I would have thought she was tricking me anyway. "I'm gonna grab a shower ok?" I said as I stood up.

"Sure, are you seeing Jay today?" she asked curiously.

I shook my head "I don't think so Mel, he wants to be friends but I don't know if I can, I'm with Trey and I don't think he'd like it, he gets jealous you know that" I said honestly.

She nodded "If Jay finds out Trey hit you that time, he'll flip out" she said grimacing.

I gasped "Don't tell him! Don't say anything to Scott either, you promised me" I said feeling sick, god if Jayden went mad and started a fight or something, then Trey would end up finding out

I slept with him he would kill my Mom, then me and probably Jayden too!

She shook her head, "I won't don't worry, Jay would literally go crazy, he's a badass anyway, but now he's mated he would kill for you in a heartbeat" she said with wide eyes. I frowned, I couldn't bear the thought of him in a fight or anything, I mean what if he got hurt or something?

"I'm going for a shower then" I said leaving before she asked me anything else, I couldn't talk about this anymore, I just needed to go home and pretend that none of this happened.

After a shower I felt much better, I packed up my stuff once I was dressed, I was planning on staying here tonight but I didn't want to see Jayden again today so I was gonna leave in a couple of hours, Mel was gonna stay at mine instead. I grabbed my stuff and plopped it by the front door, it was only half nine and she wanted to shopping, again! I plopped down on the sofa next to Scott, "Ok?" he asked curiously, I nodded and plastered on a fake smile so they couldn't see how hard this was for me.

"I'm great, Mel wants to go shopping again, woo hoo!" I said sarcastically rolling my eyes.

He laughed "I honestly have never met another girl that didn't like shopping, something else that would have been on the list" he said winking at me. I sighed and leant against him, leaning forward when he wanted to move his arm and put it around me, he just sat there with his arm around me while we watched TV.

My phone buzzed and I grabbed it opening a new message from Trey, my heart was beating out of my chest as if he would somehow be able to tell I had cheated by me reading a text.

'Hey baby, I'm back early, I'll be over in half an hour' he wrote.

I jumped out of the seat "Shit!" I cried before I could stop myself, Scott jumped up and pulled me behind him protectively looking towards the door. I couldn't help but laugh, bless him what the hell was he expecting? I grabbed his hand laughing my ass off at him, he looked at me shocked.

"What? What's wrong?" he asked his body relaxing slightly.

"Trey's home that's all" I said still giggling, he blew out a big breath and ran his hand through his hair.

"You scared the shit out of me!" he said shaking his head laughing now too.

I went to the kitchen to see Mel, "Mel babe I gotta go, Trey's home a day early, he wants to see me, he just text me and said he'll be round in half an hour, I'm sorry hon, I'll make it up to you I promise, come stay tomorrow instead" I said apologetically.

She smiled "It's ok, I got bucket loads of homework to do tonight anyway so I wouldn't have been much fun, I'll see you tomorrow at school, be cool, there's no way he'd know ok?" she said hugging me tightly. I nodded but I felt so scared, if he found out this was gonna hurt, bad! I grabbed my bags from the front door and headed out to my car feeling the dread settle in.

CHAPTER 10

I pulled up outside my house, his car wasn't in the drive so I breathed a sigh of relief as I ran to the house quickly wanting to hide the dress that I wore to the party in case Trey saw it, he would fucking kill me if he knew I went out looking like that! I screwed the dress up and threw it to the back of my wardrobe putting all of my shoes on top of it. I should have just chucked the damn thing out of the window on the way home!

I went back downstairs, my Mom wasn't home, god I wished she was here, I was so scared. There was no way he could know, no possibility at all, I kept repeating this to myself as I made a coffee with shaky hands. After about twenty minutes I heard his car pull up and I squeezed my eyes shut, oh god please help me get through this! He let himself in as usual and I held my breath, please be in a good mood!

He smiled and I let the breath out, "Hey baby" he said happily as he came into the kitchen.

"Hey boyfriend" I said smiling and trying not to flinch as he wrapped his arms around me and crashed his lips to mine. He kissed me hungrily running his hands down my body to grip my ass. When he pulled away we were both a little breathless. "I missed you" I said trying to keep him sweet. He grinned happily, wow he is in a really good mood today, the deal he went for must have gone well!

"Well I missed you too baby" he said pulling me towards the lounge, he plopped down on the sofa and pulled me into his lap stroking my back slowly as he looked at me lovingly. I actually liked this Trey, he could be really sweet when he wanted to, when we first started going out he was thoughtful and kind and I fell hard for him, but after about a year he started getting angry with me and possessive and finally he started hitting me.

"So why are you back early Trey? Your business go ok?" I asked curiously as I wrapped my arms around his neck tightly.

He laughed and ran a hand through his hair, "Yep, the deal was awesome baby, it got wrapped up pretty quick so I came home to see my girl" he said kissing me again. I kissed him back but I felt a little sick, like I really shouldn't be doing this. I hadn't felt attracted to Trey for a long time but this was something else, I felt guilty, I felt like I was cheating and I hated it.

He pulled out of the kiss and slipped his hand into his jacket pocket bringing out a small rectangular leather box and offered it to me. Oh god he bought me something! I smiled sweetly as I took it, "What's this for hon?" I asked curiously.

He laughed "I saw it and I thought you'd like it" he said pulling me closer to his chest watching me excitedly. I opened the box wondering what the hell it would be, to see a diamond bracelet nestled against the cream silk. I gasped, it was so beautiful, this must have cost him a fortune!

"Shit Trey, this is beautiful" I said honestly.

He chuckled "Thought you'd like it" he said taking the box out of my hands and pulling the bracelet out of the box, holding it out to put it on me. I held my hand out watching as he snapped the beautiful thing to my wrist.

"God Trey thank you so much, I love it, thank you" I said running my finger over the diamonds.

He lifted my chin and pressed his lips to mine again, shit ok now I need to pay for it I guess! He moaned in the back of his throat and laid me down on the couch climbing on top of me his hands roaming over my body lustfully. Suddenly he pulled away a little confused, "Did you change your perfume or something?" he asked curiously. My perfume?

"No, why?" I asked confused.

He bent his head and inhaled, "You smell a little different" he said frowning.

I laughed "I slept at Mel's last night hon, I used her shampoo and body wash" I said shaking my head.

His eyes hardened slightly, "You slept out while I wasn't here?" he asked looking slightly pissed off.

I nodded "Only at Mel's, we watched a movie and painted our toenails" I said starting to get scared. Any little thing like this could set him off, he was still frowning, shit come on Brook think of something! "We waxed our legs too if you're interested in checking them out" I said trying to sound sexy, his face softened and a small smile tugged at his lips.

"Yeah? Now that I'm interested in" he said waggling his eyebrows at me as he kissed me again. Wow that was close!

I closed my eyes and tried to pretend that I loved him and as he pulled at my clothes, all I could think of was Jayden and what he would say if he could see me right now. My phone started to ring from the table but Trey didn't even break stride as he used my body, at least he was being gentle today, he had obviously missed me. Just as I thought he didn't take my top off, he never did anymore, but did push it right up so he could see me anyway so I might as well have taken it off. Thank God he didn't see the bite mark on my neck with my top bunched up there.

I wrapped my legs around his waist as he continued to thrust into me, kissing all over my face. He was nearly done, I could tell by his face, I pulled his face to mine and kissed him hard, digging my fingers into his back just how he liked, and that made him finish. He grunted and collapsed on top of me almost crushing me, I trailed my fingers down his back as I pretended to be catching my breath and calming down.

He pulled back to smile at me after a minute or so, "I really missed you Brook, how about you come and stay with me tonight?" he asked as he kissed across my cheek. I groaned internally, I hated staying at Trey's, he always wanted to stay up late and I had school tomorrow! Plus I hated the guys he hung around with, they were complete assholes and treated me like shit, expecting me to clean up after them and stuff.

"Um I can't, I have a lot of homework to do tonight hon, I didn't know you'd be home today so I didn't do any yesterday as I was planning on doing it tonight" I said biting my lip, if he insists and worse comes to worse I'll just have to ask for an extension.

He rolled his eyes and nodded, ok wow if he's letting it go he really is in a good mood today! "You think I can stay here then?" he asked hopefully.

I laughed, "I'll ask, but you know my Mom won't let you" I said shrugging.

He groaned and laid his head on my shoulder, "She has to let me surely, she knows we have sex! I don't see what the problem is" he said grumpily.

I smiled "She just doesn't like to know it goes on under her roof that's all" I said chuckling. My Mom knew we had sex as she had got me on the pill when I was thirteen, she let me stay at Trey's occasionally, but she still wouldn't let him sleep here.

He pressed his face into my neck inhaling, "I don't like this body wash baby, it smell's wrong on you" he said turning his nose up slightly, I gripped my hands on the back of his head and smiled.

"Ok, I'll be sure not to buy that one then" I said laughing. He chuckled and pulled himself off of me pulling me up to sitting, I instantly pulled my top down to cover myself embarrassed. My phone was still going crazy on the table and he grabbed rejecting the call without even looking at it.

"Let's go eat, I'm hungry" he said standing up and pulling on his clothes quickly, I nodded grabbing my jeans and panties pulling them while he was getting dressed so he wouldn't be watching me.

We made our way to the kitchen and I grabbed stuff to make a sandwich with, he sat on the counter watching me not even offering to help as usual. The doorbell rang, I kissed his lips as I walked past to get it, he slapped my ass chuckling to himself. I wrenched the door open and my heart stopped as I saw Jayden standing there looking like a fucking Greek god on my doorstep, my body went crazy with need for him, he smiled and I felt my heart skip a beat. Oh Jesus he is so damn hot! I wanted to jump on him and have him rub his hands down my body. I couldn't take my eyes from his, he was the only thing I could think about. "Who is it baby?" Trey called, I instantly snapped out of my own little world, oh shit! Trey!

CHAPTER 11

Jayden's POV

I rang again but she still wasn't answering her damn phone! My wolf was going crazy, he wanted out, right now. He wanted to go in there and rip this Trey's head off for touching my girl, I waited another five minutes before calling her again, the call went to voice mail for the hundredth time. Right I can't stand this anymore I need to see her!

I got out of the car and made my way to her house, taking deep breaths willing myself to be calm, obviously she wouldn't want him to know we had slept together so I'd have to be cool. But I just needed to see she was ok and ask her to call me later, I couldn't go a whole day without speaking to her. I rang the doorbell and heard her footsteps, a guy laughed and I clenched my fists tight digging my nails into my palms concentrating on the small sting to keep myself from bursting through the door and killing him.

She answered the door looking so beautiful it was unreal, her beautiful hazel eyes met mine and I couldn't help but smile at her. Her face went from shock to happiness as she smiled back at me and I felt my stomach clench up tight that she was pleased to see me. Neither of us spoke, I just looked over her beautiful face, happiness bubbling up inside me that she looked almost as pleased to see me as I did her.

"Who is it baby?" her guy called from inside, her smile faded immediately a look of horror crossed her face.

"Um no one Trey" she called as she stepped out of the door and closed it behind her. "Shit, what the hell are you doing here? You need to go Jayden!" she whisper yelled at me, ok yeah great she thinks I'm a fucking stalker!

"I'm sorry, I needed to see you, I thought you'd call me, you didn't even leave me your number, I had to get your address from Mel" I said trying not to show her how much she was hurting me.

She glanced back at the door, "Go please!" she begged looking like she was scared or something. My wolf jumped needing to touch her and I stepped forward putting my hand on her cheek, she pressed her face into my hand and closed her eyes, I could feel my body yearning for hers. "Please Jayden, go" she begged again.

"Ok, I'm sorry, will you please call me later, just so I know your ok? You should have about ten missed calls on your phone with my number on" I asked quietly, chuckling at how obsessive that actually made me sound. Damn it, oh well I can't take it back now! The door opened and I stepped back quickly dropping my hand as a he walked out of the house. Damn I wanted to kill him so bad, I'd never wanted to kill anyone before but this guy had my girl! He was about my height but was built a little bigger than me, with short brown hair and angry looking brown eyes.

Ok think Jay, don't get her in trouble she won't forgive you! "Hey, you don't know an Emma Thompson do you? I was just telling, err sorry I don't know your name" I said turning to Brook.

She swallowed looking at me shocked and confused, "Brook" she said quietly.

I smiled "Right, I was just telling Brook, I'm supposed to pick this girl up for a date today but I can't find her house and I've lost the damn address she gave me!" I said looking up and down the street.

The guy laughed and wrapped his arm around Brook pulling her to his side, "No idea, we're busy though so run along and tell your life story to someone else" he said looking me over slowly. Holy fucking shit my wolf was so close, I couldn't look away from him, my wolf refused to back down, he glared at me for a few seconds before turning to Brook "Go finish making lunch baby" he said kissing the side of her head. She nodded and turned to walk off instantly, I dug my heels down as my wolf was trying to make me follow her, she turned at the door and mouthed 'I'm sorry' looking at me apologetically before disappearing through the door.

As soon as the door shut he stepped up to me, "You hitting on my girl you little shit?" he asked angrily. I couldn't help but laugh, his girl yeah fucking right!

"I was just looking for Emma, I thought she might know her, she's about the same age" I said trying to keep the aggression out of my voice. If he started a fight I would have to finish it and I didn't really want to have to do that, for one thing Brook wanted to be with this asshole for some reason.

"I fucking hope so, leave now" he said stepping forward again, fuck it I hated to be disrespected! Part of my Alpha bloodline made me react to any challenge and he was definitely pushing my buttons!

"Don't fucking talk to me like that" I spat angrily, he frowned and we glared at each other for a couple of seconds my body was alert waiting for him to hit me.

Brook opened the door again "Trey" she said quietly.

His eyes snapped to her for a split second "I'm now coming" he said angrily, she didn't leave, she stood there waiting for him so he backed off and went to her side wrapping his arm possessively around her and pulling her inside.

I stood there glaring at the door for a few seconds before I turned on my heel and went back to my car so fucking angry I wanted to smash something. He was a fucking asshole! He didn't even deserve her anyway! What the hell did she see in that guy? Because I couldn't see a single thing good about him, I mean girls probably thought he was probably good looking but I didn't think she was one to go for looks, she didn't strike me as that kind of person. But then again I only really had one conversation with her, how the hell would I know what she was like and what attracted her to him? I climbed in the car and I slammed the door with so much force that the window shattered spraying glass into my lap on onto the street. "Fuck it!" I shouted gripping my hands into my hair, this is bad, this is really bad, I can't do this!

Brook's POV

As soon as I shut the door I pressed my ear against it listening to them talking, I wouldn't let Trey hurt Jayden, I couldn't! "I fucking hope so, leave now" Trey said making me flinch, oh god Jayden please go before he hurts you! I knew that tone in his voice too well, he was seriously close to loosing it!

"Don't fucking talk to me like that" Jayden said sounding so angry that I cringed, shit this was it, Trey was gonna kill him! I wrenched the door open quickly.

They were standing about a foot away from each other glaring angrily, Trey looked like he wanted to kill him, in all honesty he was probably was thinking of HOW he wanted to kill him, by the looks on his face it would be the slowest most painful way he could think of. Jayden actually looked just as angry, shit he's gonna get himself hurt! "Trey" I said quietly trying to break the tension, his eyes snapped to mine they were hard and angry, I tried desperately not to flinch.

"I'm now coming" he said angrily, his tone was warning, he had told me to go inside and I came back out, he wasn't happy with me at all! His eyes flicked to the door telling me to go back inside but I just stood there waiting for him, he backed away from Jayden and wrapped his arm around me tightly clamping me to his side and led me inside. I couldn't look at Jayden again, I didn't want to see the look of hurt in his eyes that I was in here with Trey instead of out there with him.

As soon as the door shut Trey's arm went from around my waist to my upper arm as he dragged me into the kitchen. "Who the fuck was that?" he asked shaking me roughly, his top lip was twitching like it always did when he was trying to control his temper.

"I don't know, he just knocked he was looking for some girl called Emma" I lied wincing as his grip tightened on my arm.

"I don't believe you" he said pulling me to him.

"It's true! I promise, I don't know who he is! Trey please your hurting me" I begged tears filling my eyes.

"I'll do more than fucking hurt you if I find out your lying to me" he spat as his other hand grabbed the back of my hair jerking my head back. I bit my lip hard enough to draw blood and whimpered, "Did you arrange for him to come here because you thought I'd be out of town still? Did my coming back early ruin your little sex session?" he asked sneering at me.

I gasped as he pulled my head further back, "Oh god please Trey! I swear" I cried grabbing his hand in both of mine trying to lessen the pressure on my hair.

He shoved me roughly into the kitchen counter making pain shoot through my hip as I banged it hard, my leg gave way and I sank to the floor. "Please Trey, please, I love you, please" I begged sobbing in a pile on the floor, tingles were shooting down my right leg where I had hit it so hard and my scalp was burning. Oh shit this is bad, if he finds out who Jayden is he will literally kill me. I put my arms around my head protectively as I sobbed uncontrollably, pain shooting round my whole bottom half.

He gasped, "Shh, It's ok baby, I love you too" he said as he bent down and picked me up, carrying me into the living room, I was still sobbing. He sat down on the sofa and settled me on his lap wrapping his arms around me tight and started rocking me gently, "I'm sorry baby, you just make me so fucking angry,

I'm sorry, shh it's ok" he said smoothing my hair from my face and wiping my tears.

He lifted my chin to make me look at him, "I'm sorry, forgive me?" he asked tenderly, I nodded quickly wanting this to be over so I could go and put some ice or something on my leg. "That's my girl" he said kissing me softly.

"My hip and legs hurts" I whispered.

He hissed through his teeth and rubbed it gently, "Come on baby I'll run you a bath" he said picking me up again gently, I wrapped my arms around his neck tightly trying to keep my leg as still as possible as pain shot right down to my toes making me whimper.

He sat me on my bed and went to my en-suite running the water while I grimaced in pain, I rolled into a ball. It could have been worse, he could have hurt Jayden. After a couple of minutes he came back smiling apologetically, "I'm so sorry baby" he murmured as he unbuttoned my jeans starting to pull them down.

I screamed as his hands brushed across my hip, "Stop stop!" I cried breathless, he winced and took his hands away quickly. "I can do it" I said gritting my teeth and easing them down to my knee's, he pulled them the rest of the way off. I looked down to see a huge red and purple mark on my hip spreading down the top of my thigh, oh shit that looks bad!

He trailed his fingers over it tenderly, "Shit, this looks bad Brook, you need to see someone?" he asked looking at me pleadingly. I shook my head, I couldn't face the questions, I couldn't keep up with the lies that I had to tell all the time.

"Can you just get me a cold flannel maybe?" I asked biting my lip, he nodded and kissed my forehead before running to the en-suite and coming back with the flannel. He held it on gently just looking at me apologetically, he was always like this, he felt really guilty about it after if he hurt me badly, a few bruises here and there were nothing to him but if he made me cry like that he knew that he'd gone too far. He was always super sweet looking after me and stuff for a couple of days afterwards though.

I laid back on the bed and just let him hold the cold flannel in place as I closed my eyes trying to think of anything but the burning pain in my leg. I felt the bed dip next to me and he wrapped his arm around me pressing into my side, I turned my face and pressed it into his chest praying for the day he would finally kill me and this would all be over, I didn't want a lifetime of this, I couldn't take it. "I love you Brook, I love you so much, I'm sorry" he whispered turning the flannel to the cold side.

I nodded "I know Trey, I love you too" I said knowing he needed reassurance, he always needed reassurance that I wouldn't leave him. I think deep down he was quite insecure.

"Want to get in the bath?" he asked stroking my hair.

I shook my head "I don't want to move" I admitted, he closed his eyes.

"I'm sorry, I just thought, shit, forget it, I'm sorry" he said kissing my face softly.

After about half an hour the pain had faded slightly to be replaced by a dull ache, he helped me off the bed, I went over to the wardrobe and grabbed a pair of baggy sweats so they wouldn't rub or squeeze my bruise that I had coming. He even finished making lunch bringing it up to me in my room, we sat on the bed watching TV for a while until I heard my Mom come home.

He held my hand tightly as we went downstairs, my Mom was cooking dinner, "Hey Brook, hey Trey" she chirped happily.

"Hey Mom" I said faking a happy smile, she hugged me tight and then set back to making dinner.

"Ask her if I can stay" Trey whispered in my ear rubbing his hand up and down on my back trying to be loving.

"Mom do you think Trey could stay over tonight?" I asked immediately.

She gasped and looked at me a little disapprovingly, "I'm sorry guys, you know I don't like it" she said shaking her head. I breathed a sigh of relief.

"Beth, you know I love your daughter, we've been together forever now, we're always very responsible, this isn't some fling, I know I'm a lot older than her, but I love her more than anything, if you say you don't want us to have sex in the house then that's fine, but I just want to hold her I swear, I've missed her so much this weekend" he said kissing the top of my head softly.

She sighed and closed her eyes, "I guess you two have been together a long time, I should maybe just get over it huh?" she said chuckling slightly. I felt my heart sink, oh god please don't let him start staying here, they were my nights off!

"Yeah? Does that mean I can stay?" Trey asked excitedly.

She sighed and nodded "Yeah ok, but I don't want to hear anything! I'm serious, we'll see how it goes tonight, like a trial ok?" she asked winking at me, she obviously thought this was what I wanted seen as I asked for it.

"That's great Mom, thanks" I muttered plastering on a fake smile. Shit I couldn't call Jayden now! He asked me to call him but Trey was gonna be here, damn it!

Trey and my Mom started having a conversation about his trip so I kissed his cheek, "I'm just gonna go to the bathroom" I said as I slipped out almost un-noticed trying desperately not to limp in case my Mom saw. I grabbed my phone and found the eight missed calls all from a while ago, I pressed call and went to sit on the toilet.

"Brook?" he answered almost immediately, I sighed, god he had such a sexy voice!

"Hi, I'm sorry about earlier" I said quietly.

"No it was my fault, I shouldn't have come over like that, I'm really sorry" he said sadly.

"Don't worry about it, but you can't do that again ok? You can't just come over when Trey's here, he can sometimes get a bit jealous" I said closing my eyes and putting my forehead against the wall.

"I won't I just freaked out a bit, I need to get used to it, it's hard Brook, I can't explain it to you, he didn't say anything did he?" he said quietly.

"No he was fine" I lied closing my eyes. "Look I know it's gonna be hard, but you need to understand that I didn't choose this Jayden, you forced this on me, I can't just change my whole entire life because of what happened at the party" I said trying to explain how I felt without hurting him too much. To be honest if I wasn't with Trey this would be easy, I would be there like a shot, I didn't have the instant devotion that Scott was talking about but there was definitely something there, I couldn't deny it.

"I'm sorry, can I come over and we can talk or something?" he asked sounding a little hopeful.

"Not tonight, Trey's here still" I said grimacing slightly as I moved making my leg start to ache again.

"Oh, well how about tomorrow daytime?" he asked.

"I have school Jayden, we don't all have college holidays you know" I said teasingly making him laugh.

"Lunchtime? Or after school?" he asked, I sighed, god I wanted to see him too, I couldn't keep putting this off.

"Err lunchtime I guess" I said quietly.

"Yeah? Awesome! What time? Shall I pick you up from school?" he asked excitedly.

I nodded "Yeah, ok about one?" I offered biting my lip.

"Definitely, I'll see you then, can I call you in the morning?" he asked sounding a lot happier now.

"No! No, I'll just see you at one at the school ok?" I said quickly, "Look I gotta go, bye Jayden" I said snapping the phone shut. I'd been in here too long already. I made my way downstairs they were still talking in the kitchen, they didn't even notice I was gone.

I went to the medicine cupboard and grabbed some painkillers for my aching body Trey wrapped his arms around me from behind and kissed my neck. Oh god he was so close to Jayden's mark! I pulled away quickly before he could touch it, "Can you get me some water Trey? I want to take these" I said holding out the pills, he nodded looking at me apologetically and went to get the drink.

After dinner Trey went to watch TV with my Mom while I sat up the kitchen table doing my English essay for tomorrow. I strung it out as long as I could, I didn't want to have to get up, it took me a long time to get comfortable I didn't want to have to start all over again. At nine I went into the living room, "Hey Trey, I'm pretty tired, want to go to bed?" I asked hopefully. At least I could pretend to be asleep and just lay still.

"Sure baby, you sure this is ok Beth?" he asked smiling happily.

She nodded and rolled her eyes "Yeah ok I guess" she said smiling.

I kissed her head "Night Mom, see you in the morning" I said grabbing Trey's hand and pulling him towards the stairs.

"Night Beth and thanks" he called as he followed me grinning like a mad man.

"Night guys, just keep it down ok?" she called making Trey chuckle behind me.

When we got to my room he was beaming, "So this is a first huh? Me getting to sleep here" he said as he pulled me into a hug.

"Um Trey, I'm pretty tired hon, I don't think I can do anything, my leg's hurting really bad" I admitted. He nodded and bent to pull my sweats off for me being careful of my hip, he stripped out of his clothes so he was just in his boxers. He pulled me towards the bed, I unclasped my bra pulling it off so I was in a t-shirt and panties.

He pulled the covers back and nodded for me to get in first before following me in and pulling me close to his side. "I love you Brook" he said as he kissed me gently, god I wish he was like this all the time.

"You too Trey" I lied quickly.

"Want me to kiss it better?" he asked suggestively, I smiled and rolled my eyes.

"Honestly? No thanks, I think it'll hurt" I said.

He laughed "I'll be careful" he said running his hand down my body slowly. I stiffened, oh shit if he starts he won't want to stop, I don't want to sleep with him again!

"Trey, come on hon, it'll hurt me, please? Besides you promised my Mom you just wanted to hold me, she won't let you stay again if she hears anything" I said teasingly.

He sighed and flopped down on the bed next to me, "Yeah, you're right, night baby" he said as he brushed his lips against mine gently.

I closed my eyes and willed myself to fall asleep but I just couldn't stop thinking about Jayden, Trey was wrapped around me breathing in my ear and I couldn't stop wishing he was Jay. Why the hell was I so damn excited about seeing him tomorrow? Shit this was not gonna end well!

CHAPTER 12

I woke to the feeling of being tickled gently, I frowned confused before remembering Trey slept over last night. I moved to roll over and pain shot down my leg making me gasp and clamp my teeth together tightly. Trey stopped rubbing his hands on my side, "Ok?" he asked quietly, I nodded and slowly opened my eyes to look at him. He was half propped up on his elbow watching me.

"How long have you been awake?" I asked rolling more carefully onto my side to face him.

He bent forward and kissed my lips gently, "About half an hour" he said shrugging.

"So you've just been watching me sleep for half an hour? Pervert" I joked making him laugh.

He rolled his eyes "You ok today?" he asked his eyes trailing down to my hip.

I nodded "Yeah, it just aches a little, it's fine" I said pressing my face into his chest. "What's the time Trey?" I mumbled against his skin.

"Almost seven" he said kissing the top of my head.

"I think I'm gonna go grab a shower" I said needing to get out the bed before he started wanting sex, I really don't think that would help the whole sore leg situation.

He grinned "I'll come with you, wash your back" he said happily as he climbed out of the other side. Shit if he sees me naked he'll see Jayden's mark!

"Um Trey" I started not knowing how the hell to say I didn't want him anywhere near me.

He sighed and wrapped his arms around me, "You think it'll hurt you, so you'd rather I didn't" he said matter of factly, I bit my lip and nodded, that wasn't exactly the reason but hey if it worked! He kissed me gently before pulling back to look in my eyes, "You know I love you right?" he asked tenderly. I knew he loved me, he had problems but I didn't doubt that he loved me, he just had a funny way of showing it sometimes.

"I know you do, I love you too" I said forcing a smile.

He grinned and kissed my forehead "Good, I'll go make breakfast, you want a fruit salad or something? You're still on a diet right?" he asked raising his eyebrows. I nodded dropping my eyes to the floor, "Good girl" he said kissing my lips again gently before heading out of the room.

I stripped out of my clothes and jumped in the shower, being careful not to look in the mirror, I hated to look at myself naked, I hadn't seen myself fully naked for about a year and half. I disgusted myself, it was bad enough I had to see myself in clothes, I didn't want to look at my actual body. I stood under the shower and cried, my tears mixing in with the spray, I had to turn my body as the slight pressure from the water was making my leg ache more, I'd have to fake a letter to get out of gym today.

My mind went to Jayden and how adorable he was, what the hell did he come here for yesterday? How the hell can I explain to him he can't just turn up like that? The more I thought about him the more excited I got, I was actually really looking forward to seeing him today. I could picture his green eyes and the exact shade of his brown hair, how handsome he was, how his voice sounded. Just the thought of him was turning me on, I traced my hand over his mark on my neck, it was still raised, I fingered the little marks of each of his teeth and couldn't help but smile a little.

After awhile I got out and went to my bedroom praying that Trey wasn't in there, if he saw me in just a towel I had no doubt he would want sex. He didn't like to look at my body, but he had no problems using it whenever the hell he wanted to. Maybe he had really changed this time, he promised my Mom that he just wanted to hold me and he did. Maybe this would be the last time he would hit me, maybe he knew he went too far, I couldn't help but hope. But a small part of me knew that I had got my hopes on this exact thing dashed on too many occasions to believe that he would change, he'd never change. One day he would kill me, and then I'd all be over and I wouldn't have to worry about my Mom anymore because he would have no reason to hurt her.

I got dressed quickly in jeans and a loose fitting black round neck t-shirt, I looked in the mirror to check that Jayden's mark was hidden before heading downstairs. Trey was sitting up the table with my Mom eating bacon sandwiches, in the spot where I usually sat there was a bowl of chopped up apple and banana. My stomach was hurting at the smell of the bacon, I was so hungry it was painful.

I sat down and picked up my fork, "Morning" I said smiling at my Mom, she smiled and nodded at the bowl, "Trey said you didn't want a sandwich, you're gonna be hungry if you don't eat properly" she scalded.

I smiled "I'm having breakfast with Mel" I said shrugging, her face brightened.

"Oh! I didn't realise, hey is Scott home from college yet?" she asked cheerfully. My Mom loved Mel and Scott like crazy, she was good friends with the Porters and our Mom's used to share our childcare when we were younger so they could both go back to work on different days without having to worry about us kids, so she knew them really well.

"Yeah he came home Friday" I said smiling, Trey's face snapped round to mine and I felt my stomach drop, oh shit, I already told him I stayed at Mel's!

"Scott's Mel's brother right? The blonde one?" he asked frowning at me angrily, ok I needed to stay near my Mom then he wouldn't be able to hurt me.

"Yeah" I said shifting in my seat uncomfortably as he continued to glare at me.

"How's he getting on in college? Did you speak to him?" my Mom asked.

I shook my head, "No I didn't see him, he stayed at one of his friends" I lied taking another bite of my banana and trying to ignore the look of pure rage that was stretched across Trey's face.

"Oh that's a shame, he's such a nice boy, maybe we'll invite the Porters round, I haven't seen Rachel or Paul in ages" she said grabbing her plate and walking off towards the sink.

"Yeah good idea Mom" I said keeping my eyes on her, if she left the room I would too, there was no way I was staying in here with Trey while he was looking at me like that.

"I'll drive you to school today and pick you up, then maybe we could go out tonight" Trey said his face still hard. I tried to swallow the mouthful of banana but the damn thing didn't want to go down so I just nodded instead.

"Right guys I'm off to work, I swapped a shift with Mary so I'm in today but off tomorrow" my Mom chirped as she kissed the top of my head.

"Ok bye" I said watching her longing to go with her, I didn't want to be on my own with Trey.

As soon as the front door closed he slammed his fist down on the table making me jump. "You stayed with this Scott guy?" he demanded angrily.

I shook my head fiercely, "No! I stayed with Mel in her room, Scott stayed out, I think Mel said he was at a party" I said nervously. He held out his hand for me, I placed my hand in his willing him to believe me, as soon as my hand was in his he squeezed it hard making a sharp pain shoot up my wrist, "Ow Trey I promise!" I lied squeezing my eyes shut tight.

"If I find out you're lying to me" he said warningly.

I jumped out of the chair and moved round the table to him, he didn't loosen his grip on my hand the whole time. I sat on his lap and wrapped my other arm around his neck putting my forehead to his. "I swear Trey" I whispered, he sighed and closed his eyes as he let go of my hand.

He cupped my face, "Ok baby I believe you" he said kissing my nose, I breathed a sigh of relief and nodded kissing him hard trying to make him forget he was angry with me.

Half an hour later he dropped me at school, "I'll pick you up after baby ok?" he said kissing my lips gently. I nodded and smiled happy that I was finally getting away from him, at least for a few hours anyway! I found Mel leaning against the side of her car waiting for me.

"Hey! How'd it go?" she asked watching Trey drive away.

"Ok, he didn't know anything" I said shrugging.

She grinned, "There then, nothing to worry about! So Scott tells me your meeting Jay for lunch" she said looping her arm through mine as we started walking towards the school. I grinned, god I was so fucking excited about it!

"Yeah" I said trying to squash the ridiculous happiness I felt just thinking about seeing him.

She sighed "Well I can't stand here gossiping all morning, I need to go speak to my English teacher, so I'll spend all afternoon gossiping instead!" she said teasingly.

I laughed "Alright, see you later" I called as she turned to skip off.

The morning passed unbelievably slow, every second seemed like an hour as I was watching the clock waiting for lunch. Finally the bell rang and I started to get nervous, I mean what if we had nothing to talk about and it was just embarrassing? Or even worse what if I couldn't keep my hands off of him? Oh god please don't let me cheat on Trey again! I threw all of my stuff in my bag and made my way to the front door, oh shit what if he doesn't even come? I'll look like a real idiot standing here if he doesn't turn up!

I walked nervously out of the door and spotted him immediately, he was leaning against an old red sports car, he looked kind of nervous too. When he spotted me his face lit up into a beautiful smile making my heart beat a little faster. As I walked down to him his eyes didn't leave mine once.

"Hi" I said my voice sounding a little higher where I was excited.

"Hi" he said grinning and pushing my hair behind my ear his fingers lingering on my cheekbone for a split second, making my body yearn for his. "Ready to go?" he asked opening the passenger door.

I nodded "Sure, where do you want to go?" I asked climbing in and watching him run round to his side, his beautiful smile stretched across his face.

He grinned at me as he pulled away, "I don't know, wherever you want" he said casually, ok he's easy going! "I know this little Italian that's quite nice, you like Italian?" he asked glancing at me.

I grinned "Yeah I love Italian food" I said happily.

"Great, we'll go there then, you have to be back at two right?" he asked curiously.

"Yeah I got double science this afternoon so if you don't want to come back that's fine with me, I'm supposed to be dissecting a frog" I said grimacing at the thought.

He laughed and turned his nose up, "I remember doing that, gross" he said shaking his head.

"So what have you been doing with yourself this morning?" I asked curiously, turning in my seat so I could look at him while I spoke to him.

He grinned but didn't look at me, "Not much actually, I've been sitting around waiting to come and meet you" he said, my heart started to speed up, he was so damn sweet. And my God he was so hot! He was wearing light blue ripped jeans and a nice fitted pale yellow t-shirt. I couldn't keep my eyes off of his body. I actually thought I was doing well to keep my hands off of his body though, as I wanted so badly to kiss him, well actually that's a lie, I wanted to rip the damn sexy clothes off of his body and run my tongue over every square inch of him! "What about you? What lesson's have you had today?" he asked as he pulled into a little car park, he stopped the car and turned in his seat too, a smile stretched across his beautiful face.

"Um French, History and English, I had gym too but I got out of that" I said happily.

He frowned, "How did you get out of that?" he asked curiously. Oh shit! Way to go Brook!

"Um I hurt my leg, fell over yesterday" I said shrugging and opening my door needing to get away from his intense gaze.

He jumped out and came round to my side shutting my door for me, "Your leg ok? How did you manage to fall over?" he asked looking at me concerned.

I sighed dramatically, "Carrying too much stuff, tripped and fell, the end, shall we go eat?" I asked nodding to the restaurant.

"Sure" he said taking my hand, I pulled my hand away quickly looking around, shit what if someone who knows me sees and tells Trey? "Sorry" he muttered dropping his gaze to the floor, shit this is hard for me I dread to think what it's like for him!

"It's ok, I just can't have Trey find out I'm here with you, he wouldn't like it" I said shrugging, wow that's the understatement of the century! He nodded and opened the door for me letting me go in first.

The restaurant was really cute, small and intimate, we were sat in the back and were the only people in there. He sat opposite me and just watched me until I started to get uncomfortable, like he seemed content to just look at me not speaking or something. "Jayden, stop staring at me, seriously" I said laughing.

He laughed "Sorry, right yeah, not doing a very good job of showing you I'm not some obsessive stalker am I?" he joked happily.

"No your not" I said still giggling.

"So how about I tell you two things about myself and you do the same?" he offered.

Ok this sounded fun, "Sure, good juicy stuff though something other people don't know" I said leaning forward excitedly.

He grinned leaning in too, "Ok well, you already know I don't want to be a lawyer no one else knows that, um, when I was three I stole a packet of sweets from the local shop and ate them under my bed, I was so scared that my Dad was gonna find out that I flushed the packet down the toilet but the damn thing wouldn't go so I had to put my hand down and get it out" he said grinning.

"Eww!" I said laughing. "Did you get caught?" I asked shaking my head chuckling.

"No I snuck out when my parents were asleep and buried it in the garden" he said shrugging. I laughed harder, he really was funny.

The waitress came over to take our orders and was totally eye shagging Jayden but he didn't even notice. "Um can I get the tomato pasta but without the cheese?" I asked quickly scanning the menu for the thing with the least calories.

Jayden frowned "You don't like cheese?" he asked cocking his head to the side.

"Yeah I love it, but it's fattening" I said then bit my lip, why the hell did I say that?

"You are kidding me" he said shaking his head disapprovingly, he turned to the waitress and she grinned at him seductively, "I'll have the lasagne, and can we get some extra fries? And make sure you put the cheese on her pasta" he said shaking his head amused.

She nodded "Sure thing, anything else I can get for you?" she asked smiling flirtily, I laughed, ok wow does she not see me sitting here?

"You want anything else shortie?" he asked looking at me again making her scowl, I don't think that offer was directed at me!

"Um no thanks" I said handing her back my menu a little uncomfortable under her glare. She took it and stalked off making me chuckle again, jeez could she be more obvious?

Jayden looked at me curiously, "What's funny?" he asked confused.

I nodded towards the waitress, "You've got a fan, jeez if looks could kill I'd be dead already, you are so in there if you're interested" I said laughing, he didn't laugh, he frowned at me looking a little pissed off.

"I'm not interested" he said looking at me like I should have already known that.

"It was a joke Jayden, jeez, will you lighten up?" I said rolling my eyes at him, he sighed.

"Right yeah ok, so tell me your two" he said his face brightening again.

I shook my head "No way! I already knew the lawyer one so you need to give me another" I said sternly, he rolled his eyes.

"Ok how about, it took me five attempts to pass my driving test?" he said fighting a smile.

I laughed "Five times? Seriously?" I asked unsure as to whether he was just saying that to get out of telling me something more embarrassing about himself.

He nodded looking a little sheepish, "Yeah, I can't park for shit!" he said shrugging, "I told everyone I passed first time and quickly took my test again, and again until I passed" he said chuckling. I laughed and shook my head, ok bless him! "Now tell me yours" he said as the food came over. I watched the waitress try unsuccessfully to get his attention from me and shoot me another couple of death glares before walking off.

"Ok let me think" I said racking my brains trying to think of something no one else knew about me. I dug into my pasta, "Oh God this is good" I said shovelling more in, I was so hungry, I hadn't had anything other than half of the bowl of apple and banana this morning.

He smiled watching me eat, "Want some fries?" he offered pushing the plate towards me, I smiled and munched on a couple while I was thinking.

"Right I got one, when I was twelve I wore a white swim suit on holiday" I said shrugging.

He frowned "A white swim suit? What's so bad about that?" he asked confused.

I laughed "White doesn't hold up so well when it gets wet, so the damn thing went see through at the beach, not the thing a young developing girl needs" I said laughing, he burst out laughing.

"Right now I get it, hey you still got it?" he asked raising one eyebrow looking sexy as hell.

I shook my head smiling "No, but even if I did it wouldn't fit me now anyway" I said rolling my eyes. His eyes drifted down slowly, oh shit he's checking me out! "Jayden, my eyes are up here" I said laughing and waving my hand at my face.

"Just imagining it" he said smirking at me.

"Yeah because that would be such a good image" I said frowning and pushing the pasta around on my plate not wanting to eat anymore.

He reached across the table and took my hand "It's the best image I could ever think of, actually scratch that, take the swimsuit off, that would be better" he said winking at me flirtily.

"God, are you a pervert Jay?" I asked rolling my eyes but fighting a smile.

He smiled "Of sorts I guess, I never used to be, but I just can't get you out of my head" he said shaking his head as if this was some sort of weakness he had. I didn't know what to say, I wanted to hold him and tell him that everything was gonna be ok, but I couldn't do that, because it wasn't nothing about this was ok.

"Want to know my other one?" I asked pulling my hand from his and eating again just for something to do, god this tasted good! He nodded still looking a little embarrassed, "That night at your party was the first time I've ever been with anyone other than Trey" I said watching his face fall at the mention of Trey.

He put on a fake smile "I honestly can't say the same, I'm sorry" he said apologetically.

I laughed "Yeah I kinda guessed that from your mad skills in the bedroom" I said then blushed like crazy as he started to laugh. "Mel said you were a player" I said shrugging and looking at him as I stole a few more of his fries.

He smiled sadly, "I was I guess, not anymore though" he said casually.

"Jay, Scott said that you won't even fancy girls anymore, is that true?" I asked feeling like shit. He smiled and nodded but he didn't actually look too bothered, I closed my eyes, fuck this is bad, "Will it always be like that for you?" I asked not opening my eyes, I couldn't see how much I had screwed up his life.

"Yep, I'll only ever want you" he said as if this was no big deal that he may not ever get to have sex again.

I felt tears welling up in my eyes, "I'm so sorry Jayden" I said honestly, he put a finger under my chin lifting my face up, I opened my eyes and the tear fell down my face, he wiped it away tenderly.

"Shortie, it's fine, I promise, it's not a problem" he said stroking my cheek tenderly sending ripples of desire through my body. God did he know what he was doing to me? A pained expression crossed his face and he pulled his hand away quickly looking like he was trying not to breathe.

"Tell me another one" he said changing the subject, I tried to think of anything other than his body and how kissable his lips looked.

"I can't sleep with my closet door open" I said glad for the change of subject.

He frowned looking amused "And why's that?" he asked curiously.

"Monsters" I said shrugging making him laugh again.

"Monsters? What kind?" he asked eating his food but his eyes not leaving my face.

"Werewolves" I joked.

"Ha ha, your funny" he said sarcastically.

"Nah, I used to think there was a one armed man who lived in my closet who could only get out at night if the door was left open, he'd come out and strangle me with my clothes, it just kinda stuck so I still make sure the door is shut tight before I go to sleep" I said grimacing slightly.

He was laughing so hard he had tears in his eyes, "How the hell did you make something like that up?" he choked out.

I shook my head "I didn't make it up, someone told me and scared the crap out of me when I was like five or six" I said.

"Yeah and who was that?" he asked still amused.

"Scott" I said shrugging, he burst out laughing again, "It's not funny! For over ten years I've had this fear, damn asshole!" I said frowning.

When he stopped laughing he looked at his watch, "It's quarter to two, you really want to skip this afternoon? We could go catch a movie or something, I'll drive you home after" he suggested hopefully. Oh god I would love that, this hour seemed to have gone so fast, it just wasn't enough, I didn't want to leave yet, but I had to. Trey was picking me up today so I needed to be at school.

"Um I can't sorry, Trey's picking me up today" I said grimacing slightly as he closed his eyes and gulped nodding slightly. "I'm sorry" I said quietly.

He nodded "It's ok, can I maybe take you out tomorrow?" he asked sadly.

"Jay seriously is this really a good idea? Is it not better to just try out of sight out of mind?" I asked curiously.

He gasped "No! I need to see you, I don't think you realise what this feels like for me, it's hard as hell to sit here and be your friend but it would kill me to not see you" he said looking at me pleadingly.

I sighed "Ok, well I could see you for lunch again I guess if you want" I said trying not to show him how excited it was at the thought of seeing him again tomorrow.

He grinned "Yeah, great, same time then" he said standing up and pulling out his wallet throwing money on the table. "Come on then shortie, let's get you to school so you can dissect that frog" he said teasingly.

"Oh shit I forgot about that" I said grimacing and feeling slightly sick, maybe I should have gone for something a little lighter in case I throw up! He chuckled and waited for me to get up and move to his side before we walked out, "So when do you go back to college?" I asked as we got to his car.

"Two weeks" he said looking a little sad about it.

He opened my door for me again "Wow Jay, you really are a gentleman" I joked, he did a little bow making me giggle as he shut the door. We chatted a bit on the way back to the car, it was nice, he was really easy to talk to and was a really great guy, I could see why Scott liked him.

As we pulled up at the school he looked at me sadly, "Ok, so I'll see you here at one tomorrow" he said looking right into my eyes making me feel a little tingly.

"Yeah ok great" I said biting my lip.

"You think maybe I could call you later?" he asked.

"I don't think so, Trey's taking me out tonight so I don't know what time I'll be home" I admitted. Hopefully Trey wouldn't want to stay at mine again tonight! I heard him curse under his breath and he gripped the steering wheel tightly his knuckles going white. "I could call you if you want, if I can" I said quickly seeing the tension across his face.

His eyes snapped to mine, "I'd love that" he said nodding eagerly.

"I'll ring if I can, if I can't ring I'll text you ok?" I suggested.

He was grinning happily again now, "Great" he said looking like a kid on Christmas morning and I couldn't help but smile back.

"Ok well I'd better go, tomorrow I'll buy ok" I said opening my door quickly before I had to kiss him, he was too close and I was starting to want him again. What the hell is wrong with me? Is this part of the mating like Scott said? Every time I looked at him I wanted to jump his bones! It was almost embarrassing and I was glad he had no idea otherwise I would literally die of embarrassment.

He grabbed my hand as I went to get out of the car, "Thank you for coming today shortie" he said as he kissed the back of my hand tenderly. I gulped and nodded unable to speak, I climbed out of the car and almost ran to the school before I wouldn't be able to leave him. Crap this was bad! The more time I spent with him the more I liked him, god why is my life always so damn hard? Nothing's ever straightforward!

CHAPTER 13

The rest of the week flew by, everyday Jayden would come and meet me for lunch. He was so sweet and funny that he made my heart ache for him and I couldn't help wishing things were different and I could be with him and make him happy. He took me to different places each day for lunch, everyday we would play the 'tell each other two things nobody else knows' game, which was actually really fun. I felt like I knew him really well and he was just so damn easy to be around!

I called him when I could, I didn't let him call me though in case he called when Trey was around. Jayden was awesome, so sweet and kind and tender, he hadn't once moved to kiss me or anything which I was totally grateful for, because if he kissed me I knew I wouldn't be able to stop ravaging his body until both of us were physically exhausted.

Even Trey was actually being sweet still. He hadn't hit me or anything since he hurt my hip which was great, he seemed to have calmed down a lot which made life a lot easier now that I wasn't walking on egg shells all of the time, maybe he really had changed this time. Mom had changed her house rules now, so she let him stay over again which he loved as it meant he got to have me anytime he wanted which seemed to put him in a really good mood. I couldn't help but start to hate Trey now, I haven't liked him for a long time but now that all I could think about is Jayden and how good it would be with him, I resented Trey more and more.

Today was Saturday and I was staying at Mel's tonight, Trey had given me his 'permission' and said it was ok for me to stay there as he was working tonight, he had a deal he needed to finalise or something. I didn't ask for details, I didn't want to know what really went on with him, I knew his business wasn't legal and that it involved drugs but anything more than that would get me in trouble too if he ever got arrested so I never asked anything.

I headed to Mel's just before lunch as we were going to a BBQ at one of Scott's friends, as I pulled up I saw Jay's car in the drive and happiness rushed through me. I grabbed my overnight bag and headed to the house trying to calm my excitement. I didn't bother knocking, I practically lived here when I was a kid so it's kind of like a second home for me.

I dumped my stuff down by the door, "Mel?" I called as I walked up the hall to the kitchen.

"Yeah in here" she called back.

I smiled as I walked round the corner, the first person my eyes spotted were Jayden, I couldn't look away from him, he was so damn hot. "Hey" I said grinning.

"Hi shortie" he said his face matching mine as he came to stand next to me. Neither of us spoke, we didn't really need to, I was too busy taking in every single perfect inch of his face, enjoying the heat seeping from his body into mine where he was standing so close.

Someone cleared their throat loudly and I heard people laughing, I reluctantly dragged my eyes from his and looked at my best friend. She was laughing hysterically, then I noticed there were four other guys in the kitchen all laughing looking at me too. "What? What's funny?" I asked confused.

Mel shook her head, "I was talking to you" she said still giggling, she was taking to me? I didn't hear anything.

"You were? Sorry, what did you say hon?" I asked blushing slightly, I must have been too busy staring at Jayden imagining all of the things I wanted to do to him.

"I said we're going to a pool party at Seth's" she said happily, oh shit, a pool party? I can't get half naked in front of a load of people!

"Um Mel I don't, err" I said uncomfortable,

She shook her head "I've got a spare bikini you can borrow don't worry, I know you don't have one with you" she said dismissively.

I burst out laughing, did she seriously expect me to wear a bikini in front of people? And one of hers? She was like a twig! "Yeah because I'll fit into one of yours" I said laughing harder.

She smiled and nodded at my chest "I know, you may have to tape them bad boys in or something, that killer cleavage will be on show quite a bit, but you don't mind that do you Jay?" she said teasingly. I gasped and dropped my eyes to the floor as everyone's gaze fell to my chest.

"I don't mind that at all" Jayden said flirtily from next to me making me roll my eyes, I couldn't help but smile.

Mel grabbed my hand and dragged me up to her room, "Mel I don't want to go to a pool party" I whined, Mel didn't understand my issues with my body. When I first tried to talk to her about it she just dismissed my worries as stupid, I didn't try to talk to her about it again, she didn't understand. Silly girl thought I was beautiful because she was looking at the real me, she was biased because she was my best friend, bless her.

She pushed me onto her bed and went to the drawer, she turned back to me with a bikini in each hand, "Black or blue?" she asked holding her hands out to me. Oh god they were so damn small!

"Mel, I can't wear that! For one thing it won't fit me, and for another I don't want everyone to see me in a bikini!" I said willing myself not to cry.

"Black it is then" she said ignoring me as she tossed it into my lap.

"Mel, come on please" I said horrified.

She sighed "If it's that bad then wear a t-shirt over the top, some people will wear t-shirts over" she said shrugging, ok I guess I could do that, I could just say I didn't want to get sun burnt or something.

I sighed and stood up, "Fine! But you owe me for this, there better be alcohol" I said shaking my head as I crossed the room to her bathroom to change.

I pulled on the ridiculously small bikini, I mean it fitted me because it stretched but Mel didn't have much of a chest so my breasts were very obvious with the little triangles that just about covered me. I groaned but refused to look in the mirror as I pulled my clothes back on over the top.

Mel was sitting on the bed waiting for me, "Where is it? Have you got it on?" she asked suspiciously.

I grimaced "Mel, It's fucking tiny, seriously it's embarrassing, you sure other people will be wearing t-shirts too?" I asked, I didn't want to stick out like a sore thumb and embarrass myself in front of everyone!

"Yes! Now come on then. Let's go, I'm starving" she said handing me a towel and dragging me back downstairs.

We took two cars, I went in with Jayden, Mel, Scott and some other boy called Paul and the others went in another car. We pulled outside a really nice looking house, "Wow" I said looking it over as Mel dragged me out and round the back.

"Swim or eat first?" she asked as we plopped out towels down on a lounger.

"Drink first" I said nervously.

The pool was nice, quite big, there was a lot of people already here, people stopped to look at us as we walked in. Everyone seemed to be looking at me, a lot of the girls were glaring at me for some reason. What the hell is that about? Jayden stepped closer to me and shot them all a look that should be able to kill them on the spot making them all drop their eyes to the floor, "Why are they looking at me like that? What have I done?" I whispered to him stepping a little closer to him feeling so damn uncomfortable.

He sighed "You're my mate shortie, girl shifters want to be mated to an Alpha so you've blown their chances" he said casually.

"Oh god" I groaned, great they all hate me already!

He laughed "Don't look so uncomfortable! They'll get used to it, the way we mated was so sudden, people are curious about you that's all, not everyone here is a shifter though so don't say anything to anyone in case they're not ok" he said bending slightly so our faces were on the same level.

I nodded and smiled, "Ok, I'm going to get a drink then I guess" I mumbled heading off after Mel in the direction of the house. Jayden followed close behind me glaring at girls as they looked at me a little disapprovingly. After three vodka shots I felt a little better so we went to sit down, a couple of girls were wearing t-shirts so I didn't seem to be standing out when I left mine on too.

Even though it was a pool party no one seemed to be swimming, everyone was sitting around talking, some people were dancing, there was a huge BBQ going with all sorts of food that had been burnt beyond recognition where the guy cooking it was slightly too drunk to care. I was sitting chatting to Mel and Jayden, I was already on about my sixth drink so I was definitely feeling a little tipsy. Scott was standing by the edge of the pool talking to one of his friends, "Excuse me a minute" I said to Mel and Jay as I stood up and walked over to Scott.

As I got close to him I saw his face change, "No" he said warningly shaking his head.

"Oh yeah" I said as I closed the distance and pushed him hard into the pool. He grabbed my hand and dragged me in too making me squeal, both of us came up laughing.

"Dammit Brook, how the hell am I supposed to pull looking all wet and soggy?" he whined as I splashed him in the face.

"You'll just have to try harder" I said shrugging and laughing as he reached to grab me.

I swam away as fast as I could and climbed out ignoring that way the wet t-shirt was stuck to my body as I ran and hid behind Jayden. Scott was walking over to me smirking "You know your gonna pay for that Brooklyn" he said teasingly. I gripped Jay's waist pressing into him from behind laughing, I could hear him laughing. Scott darted to one side so I ran off in the other direction, he caught me easily and tackled us both back into the pool making water shoot up my nose. Scott and I had a slight water fight for a bit, it was fun, he was always like this, I would kill to have a brother like him.

I saw Jayden move from the corner of my eye and I stopped to watch him as he stripped out of his t-shirt exposing his sexy muscled chest and abs. "Oh shit" I gasped as I saw him in just his shorts, the desire for his body was overwhelming, I was so turned on I could actually have climaxed. He was just perfect, the only time I had seen him with no clothes was at his party and my mouth was actually watering at the sight of him now.

He walked over to the edge of the pool and I could barely breathe, "Shit Scott I need to get out of the pool, right now" I said trying unsuccessfully to look away from Jay's awesome body. If he came anywhere near me there was no way I wasn't fucking his brains out and I couldn't do that.

Scott looked at me strangely, "Why?" he asked splashing me again, I didn't care because at that moment Jayden dived into the water. He swam underwater and came up just in front of me, his brown hair slicked back and shining in the sun. His green eyes were sparkling with happiness and love. I closed the distance between us unable to stop myself and wrapped my arms around his neck crashing my lips to his taking him completely by surprise.

He moaned a little and wrapped his arms around me pulling me tight against his chest, I wrapped my legs around his waist squeezing my whole body as close to him as I could as I kissed him hard. He moved forward a little and pushed me against the side of the pool tracing his tongue along my bottom lip. I opened for him eagerly, oh god he was such a good kisser!

His arms tightened around me and I swear I heard a low growl resonate from his chest, it was sexy as hell. Where I was wrapped around him I could feel how hard he was already and I wanted him so bad I could burst. He pulled away to kiss down my neck tracing his tongue over his mark making pleasure shoot round my body, I bucked my hips slightly grinding against his erection making him gasp slightly.

I forgot where we were, I forgot everything, I forgot about Trey and the reason's why I shouldn't be doing this. I couldn't think of anything other than Jayden and how much I needed him and how he was setting my whole body on fire. Suddenly he pulled out of the kiss making me whimper, I pulled his face back to mine needing more but he pulled away again.

"Trey's on the phone" he whispered sadly his arms loosening around me slightly, he looked devastated. What the hell is he talking about? Trey was on the phone? Oh shit! I looked over to see Mel talking on my phone waving frantically for me. I looked back at Jay, he honestly looked heartbroken.

"I'm sorry" I said honestly, he nodded and let me go as I reluctantly unwrapped my body from his, damn stupid Trey! I hated him so much! I swam to the stairs and pulled myself out, I didn't look back at Jayden again, I couldn't see that heartbroken face again. I didn't ever want to hurt him, but I had no choice, I needed to keep him and my Mom safe from Trey and this was the only way I could do that.

I ran to Mel and took the phone grabbing a towel and wrapping it around myself, "Hey hon" I said quickly.

"Where the fuck are you?" he growled angrily, my whole body stiffened.

"I'm at Mel's" I said closing my eyes.

"Don't fucking lie to me Brook, she just told me you were at some asshole's pool party" he said his voice shaking slightly where he was so angry.

"Um yeah, it's one of Scott's friends" I said knowing I needed to tell the truth.

"Scott, Mel's brother? That fucking prick that wants to screw you?" he spat angrily, shit even he knew Scott liked me and he's only met him once!

"Trey hon" I started but he cut me off.

"Give me the address, I'm coming to get you" he shouted, I flinched slightly. Fuck me if he's this angry something's gonna get broken this time, I felt sick, I could barely breathe.

"I don't know the address, I'll come home, I'll get Mel to give me a lift back to hers and pick up my car and then I'll drive to yours" I said trying to calm him down.

"Give me the fucking address now" he roared making me jump.

I turned to Mel quickly, "What's the address here?" I asked desperately.

"1021 Riverside" she said looking at me apologetically.

I repeated the address to Trey, "I'll be there within half an hour, be ready when I get there, if I have to come in and get you I swear to god Brook I'm going fucking to kill someone" he shouted making me cringe again.

I nodded "Ok, I'll be out front" I said snapping my phone shut and throwing it in my bag so I could dry off quickly.

"You leaving?" Mel asked shocked.

I nodded "Yeah, Trey needs me" I said towelling off my hair, I noticed my hands were shaking.

"Is everything ok?" I heard Jay ask from behind me, I couldn't look at him, knowing that after what just happened I was leaving to be with my boyfriend.

"Everything's fine, Trey needs help with something" I said pulling on my jeans over the top of my wet bikini bottoms. The t-shirt I had on was still plastered to me, it wasn't going to get dry even though I continued to wipe the towel over it.

"Here shortie" Jay said handing me his t-shirt, god he is so damn sweet! But I couldn't wear that, Trey would want to know who's it was and it would just end up causing me more trouble.

"Um no thanks, it's fine it'll dry don't worry" I said quickly still not able to look at him. Trey ruined a perfect fucking moment, that was everything I had been thinking about for the last week and Trey has to choose that exact moment to ring, fucking asshole!

I slipped my shoes on, "I can't stay at yours Mel, I'll call you tomorrow" I said hugging her quickly. I turned to walk off but Jayden caught my hand making me stop sending another wave of desire through my body. God every time his skin touched mine I wanted him more and more!

"Will you call me later?" he asked pleadingly. I closed my eyes, shit this was getting so hard, it wasn't just the lust that I felt for him now, there was definitely something there, and I didn't want to leave his side, I wanted to stay here with him so bad.

I nodded "If I can" I said as I pulled my hand from his and practically ran to the front of the house, I sat on the curb and put my head in my hands unable to stop the tears from flowing down my face. I don't know what I was crying for the most, the pain I was soon to feel or that heartbreaking sadness that was stretched across Jayden's face.

Jayden's POV

I watched her walk away taking my heart with her, she was killing me, this whole situation was killing me. And that kiss! Fucking hell that was so damn hot, I would give anything to hold her again, I didn't care if I never had sex again in my life, but I needed to feel her delicate skin on mine, hold her hand and kiss her goodnight.

She had practically ran away from me to go to that asshole, I moved to go and wait out the front with her but Mel caught my arm making me stop. "Don't get her in trouble with Trey, just stay away" she said pleadingly, she looked a little scared. Why the hell were the two of them so jumpy for? Brook looked like she was almost shaking when she was talking to him on the phone.

I took a deep breath and sat down on the sun lounger, "What did he say he needed her for?" I asked Mel knowing that she spoke to him too.

She shrugged "I don't know Jay he didn't say" she said plopping down next to me.

"What did he say then?" I asked curiously.

"He asked to speak to her, I said she was swimming, he said he didn't know we had a pool, so I told him we were at a pool party, then he just demanded I call her and get her to speak to him, sounded pretty pissed actually" she said, she bit her lip as she looked at me like she shouldn't have said anything.

"He sounded pissed, what do you mean? Do you think he would have shouted at her?" I asked jumping up as anger took over.

She grabbed my hand "Jay chill, she won't thank you for getting involved, she wants to be with Trey" she said ripping my heart open further. I knew she did, it just hurt even more when someone actually said it out loud, I sat back down and nodded still unable to get rid of my anger completely. If I find out he shouted at her I swear I'll rip him limb from limb.

Scott put another burger in my hand, "Chill, eat, she'll call you later, you need to start relaxing Jay" he said patting my shoulder sympathetically. I sighed and nodded, I know I needed to relax, she wasn't mine, as much as I wanted her to be, it was her choice. I sat back eating my burger trying to think of anything other than her, "So that kiss was fucking hot Jay, seriously, if her phone hadn't rang I think you would have banged her in front of everyone" Scott said laughing.

I smiled, actually I probably would have done, my wolf had almost taken over, the only reason I stopped is because I could hear Mel shouting for Brook that Trey was on the phone, it was like I snapped out of some sort of passion fuelled trance or something. I shook my head "No man I had it under control" I lied, he smirked at me knowingly making me chuckle.

"She was the same though, it was so funny one minute we were mucking around then she just stopped, looked like she even stopped breathing, when I looked round you were taking your top off, she goes 'Shit Scott I need to get out of the pool right now' and she couldn't take her eyes off of you, she wanted you bad" Scott said laughing. I grinned, I knew how much she wanted me, her hormones were going crazy, I smelt them as soon as my head broke the surface of the water. I closed my eyes willing myself not to remember I didn't need another hard on, she did that to me enough already, I didn't need one when she wasn't even near me!

I couldn't stop thinking about her, what if this Trey guy was angry with her for coming out to a party or something? After an hour I asked Mel to call her, she sighed unhappily but rang her anyway, I think just to stop me whining, but Brook didn't answer her phone. After another half an hour she tried again but still no answer, "I can't do this anymore, I need to go and see if she's ok" I said standing up quickly.

"Jay you can't! You said you've already knocked once and he saw you, you can't pass yourself off as a stranger this time" Mel said disapprovingly.

"You said he sounded pissed, I can't get it out of my head, I need to hear she's ok, if she won't answer her phone then I'll have to think of something else, maybe get one of the neighbours to knock or something" I said not knowing what the hell I was talking about.

"Want me to come? I could knock" Scott suggested.

I shook my head "No it's fine, keep calling her Mel, and if you get through to her call me" I said. I grabbed my t-shirt and keys and ran for my car. Something was wrong I just knew it, she always answered the phone to Mel, always.

CHAPTER 14

I sped to her house and parked a couple of houses away, his car was in the driveway so I knew they were here. I called Mel quickly, "Have you spoken to her?" I asked desperately.

She sighed "No Jay, still no answer, honestly I think you should just leave it, she won't thank you if you start causing trouble between her and her boyfriend" she said pleadingly. I squeezed my eyes shut at the word boyfriend, maybe she wasn't answering the phone because they were having $ex! I groaned as pain ripped through my heart, I knew she had $ex with him, I could smell him on her occasionally when we met for lunch, but I tried my hardest not to ever think about it, it was just too painful.

"Thanks, I'll let you know how I get on ok" I said snapping the phone shut unable to hear anymore of her protests.

I opened my phone again and called Brook, after about ten rings I was just about to give up and go and knock when Trey answered. I gripped the edge of the seat hard enough to tear the leather refusing to shift as jealousy ripped through my body. "Yeah?" he said lazily.

"Hi can I speak to Brook please?" I asked trying not to sound too aggressive.

He sniffed loudly, "Who the f*ck's this?" he asked angrily, my wolf fought to get free, he wouldn't be disrespected.

"A friend of hers from school" I answered squeezing my eyes shut tight. Come on Jayden keep it together, you need to get used to this asshole if you want to be in her life!

"Baby, someone on the phone for you" he called away from the phone.

"Who is it hon?" she asked, I heard her gasp.

"Some guy from your school, hurry the f*ck up and get rid, tell him not to call you again" he growled angrily.

"Ok" she said quietly. There was a rustling with the phone, "Hello?" she said curiously, obviously my number not appearing on her caller id, she had memorised it so she wouldn't have too many calls and texts from me on her phone, she said that he used her phone a lot.

"Brook, it's Jayden, you ok?" I asked gripping the seat harder and tearing the leather even more.

"Um yeah, I'm fine thanks, listen I can't speak to you now" she said clearly uncomfortable.

"Hurry the f*ck up!" I heard him shout angrily. If he shouts at her again I swear I'm going in there and ripping his head off!

"Brook, is everything ok? I could come over" I suggested looking longingly at her house, please say yes, please!

"No! No, I'll see you in school ok?" she said quickly.

"Tell him not to f*cking call you again Brook, NOW!" he ordered sounding really pissed. I heard her make a little yelping noise and I burst out of the car nearly taking the door off.

"I have to go, don't call me again ok?" she said breathlessly, she hung up and I ran towards her door.

As I ran up the drive I heard a bang, she whimpered again, if he's hurting her I'm gonna f*cking kill him! I tried the door to see it was unlocked so I let myself in, ok wow if I'm wrong about this, I am gonna in so much trouble with her!

"Why the f*ck is a guy calling you?" he asked angrily.

"He's just a guy from school, that's all, he needed help with something! A project, we're doing a project together" she said breathlessly. My hands were shaking my wolf wanting out so bad I could barely hold him back.

I listened, they were upstairs at the front of the house, "A project? Why can't you do it with a girl? You sleeping with him? Huh? You f*cking him you little tramp?" he shouted.

I took the steps three at a time, "No!" she cried. I heard another bang and she cried out in pain.

"He wouldn't f*cking want you anyway, who the f*ck would want you? Look at you! Get up! You're f*cking lucky I still want you, if I didn't love you I wouldn't even be able to stand looking at your fat ass" he said.

I burst into the room, she was pinned against the wall, he had his hand round her throat, her cheek was bright red, her lip was split, she was crying and clutching at his wrist desperately. I grabbed his shoulder and jerked him backwards away from her as I punched him hard in the face, his head snapped back his eyes rolling back into his head. I punched him again snapping his nose, he was a little limp so I threw him away from me, he slammed against the other wall hard leaving a huge dent in it as he slumped to the floor like a rag doll. I was so f*cking angry I wanted to kill him, sh*t, could I stop myself from killing him? I stepped towards him my hands shaking, my wolf wanting revenge on him for hurting my mate, I couldn't think of anything else but how I was gonna kill him, how much of his blood I would spill before I finally let him die.

I heard Brook move behind me, she gasped for breath, the sound seemed to snap me out of my rage, I took a deep breath and turned back to her, she was rubbing her neck as she looked at me shocked. "Shit! Are you ok?" I asked moving quickly back to her side and putting my arm around her waist, she winced as my arm went around her, obviously he'd hurt her ribs or back. I gritted my teeth as the rage started to take over again, I raised my hand and stroked her bruised cheek with my fingertips. She nodded and gripped my arm, her eyes were wide and scared.

"What are you doing here?" she asked her voice breaking slightly as she continued to cry.

She clung to me tightly, "I thought you were in trouble" I said frowning and looking back at the piece of shit who was slumped on the other side on the room.

His arm twitched and then he started to push himself up off of the floor, what the hell? He should be in a coma right now how hard he hit that wall! When he was standing he wiped the blood from his face with the back of his hand and took a step forward glaring at me looking murderously angry. The rage was building inside me and I knew I was gonna kill him, if he wanted to live he needed to get the hell away from me right now. I felt a growl trying to rip it's way out of my throat, my wolf trying to force me to shift. Brook whimpered so I shoved her behind me quickly, there was no way he was getting anywhere near her, she cringed into my back.

His hands started to shake as he sneered at me. I saw his eyes turn black, HOLY SHIT! He's a shifter! I stepped back forcing Brook against the wall behind me pinning her there, I needed her out of the way if he was gonna shift. I can't believe she's dating a shifter!

"You're gonna die now boy, then your f*cking mother Brook, but not before I r*pe the sh*t out of her, and your coming home with me" he said angrily.

She screamed behind me, "NO! Trey please! Please! Nothing happened, I swear, please don't hurt my Mom please" she screamed, she was banging her fists against my back squirming trying to get out of the little cage I had created with my body, trapping her against the wall. "Move Jayden! Move!" she screamed hysterically.

"You come anywhere near her or her Mom and I'll kill you and your whole pack" I growled.

He looked at me a little shocked, "You're a shifter?" he asked smiling with a wicked glint in his black eyes, I nodded waiting for him to move. "You know who I am?" he asked smiling cockily.

I shook my head "Should I?" I asked looking him over, he was quite big but I was confident I could take him, I was from Alpha bloodline and I had my mate to fight for which would give me extra will to kill him.

He laughed "I'm Trey Newton, from The Trident pack, Alpha of The Tridents actually" he said smiling. My blood froze in my veins, he was an Alpha! The Tridents was a really bad pack, they were basically all the badass' that didn't want to belong to my father's pack and any rogues that decided to join them instead of us.

"Jayden Philips of Willow creak" I said not taking my eyes off of him once.

"Philips? As in Alpha Philips? Any relation?" he asked raising one eyebrow.

"He's my father" I said staring at him, fighting my wolf that wanted to kill him.

"Father really? I met him once, he's an ass so I decided to go to the Tridents instead" he said sneering at me, obviously trying to provoke me into a fight so I would leave Brook unprotected, but that just wasn't happening.

"He is an ass, your right" I said honestly.

He smiled "Well maybe you should leave that shitty pack and join up with the big boys" he said waving a hand at himself.

"Big boys, right, I don't think so, but thanks for the offer" I said turning my nose up, his eyes narrowed at the disrespect and I could see he was fighting with his wolf now too.

Both of us were ignoring the still struggling and screaming Brook behind me, suddenly he laughed "So it appears that my girlfriend wants out from behind you, you'd better let her go" he said warningly.

"No, you'd better f*cking leave here right now and never come back or I swear to you I will rip your heart out and give it to her as a present" I growled angrily.

He stiffened at the threat, "I am Alpha! You will show me respect" he demanded sinking into a slight crouch, I matched his posture readying for his attack.

"You're not my Alpha, get the f*ck out of here, if you hurt her or her Mother, you'll be begging for death long before I give it to you" I said angrily, my hands were shaking needing to shift, I clenched them tight trying to stay in control.

"Brook get here now" he demanded.

She started up again, "Jayden please move! He'll hurt my Mom please!" she begged sobbing as I refused to let her go.

"He won't get anywhere near her shortie, I promise you" I said, her hands gripped the back of my t-shirt as she pressed her body against mine tightly.

"Yes I will Brook, you know me baby, I'll have all my boys r*pe her two at a time, then I'll slice her from groin to neck and let her bleed to death" Trey said smiling wickedly.

She screamed and started beating against me again. "Please Trey, please! I'll do anything, please, anything you want I swear please!" she begged her voice breaking. Her breathing hitching as she continued to sob, she was breaking my heart, I hated to hear her so upset, I wanted to comfort her. But I needed to make her safe first.

"What the hell would I want from you that I haven't already had?" he asked laughing.

"Please Trey, I love you" she cried desperately, I felt sick, her words were killing me, his face softened slightly, I could see he loved her.

"Come here to me and I won't hurt your mother" he said pointing to the floor in front of him.

"I can't, please, he won't let me go!" she cried, "Please Jayden" she whispered.

I shook my head "What do you want with her anyway? You can't mate her" I said watching his face closely, his jaw snapped tight.

"None of your f*cking business" he said scowling, I'd obviously hit a sore spot there, had he tried?

"Have you tried to mate her?" I asked curiously.

"I can't! She's a f*cking human in case you didn't notice" he growled angrily.

I nodded "Yeah I noticed, I just wondered what would happen if you tried" I said shrugging.

He laughed "Well I can help you there, nothing happens, she bleeds" he said chuckling, my wolf lurched at the thought of his teeth on her neck but I forced him away. He had tried to mate her and it didn't work? What the hell does that mean?

"Nothing happens? Really? Show him your neck shortie" I said sternly, she whimpered.

He frowned confused, "What about it?" he asked, "Show him shortie, it's ok, I promise, you trust me right?" I said moving my hand from the wall to touch her leg but still pinning her behind me.

"Yes" she whispered.

I moved slightly to one side so he could see her, she moved behind me, obviously moving her shirt to the side. I knew the exact moment he saw my mark on her neck. His face went red, his hands shook and a split second later he exploded into his wolf leaping towards us. I grabbed her arm pulling down towards the floor making her drop, I spun slightly and just as the wolf's teeth were snapping at my face I gripped hold of him around the throat and threw him as hard as I could away from us, readying myself to shift. "Stay down Brook" I said sternly, I saw her nod slightly as she cowered on the floor.

He skidded along the floor and slammed into the wall as I shifted and lunged for his throat. He twisted at the last second so my teeth sank into his shoulder making him yelp and jerk away from me. I lunged for him again forcing him back away from Brook, I couldn't have this happen too close to her she could get hurt by accident. He dodged again his teeth snapping at my face missing me by mere millimetres, I raised up onto my back legs slightly to come at him from a different angle and sank my teeth into the back of his neck twisting trying to snap it, but I didn't have a good enough grip.

He threw me off and ran at me the force of his body hitting mine slamming me into the wall knocking my breath out of me. He immediately turned towards Brook, my blood boiled in my veins, I pushed myself up and jumped over the top of him landing in front of her putting my body between him and her. He wouldn't get anywhere near her, no f*cking way. I could hear her sobbing behind me, he was sizing me up thinking of how to attack me, I wouldn't wait for him to attack, I couldn't have him any closer to her than he already is.

I lunged forwards again at the same time he did, I bent low putting my head in his chest and pushed forward as hard as I could throwing him backwards making him loose his balance. When he was on the floor I buried my teeth as hard as I could into his shoulder feeling the bones beneath my teeth. He yelped and I lifted him and whipped my head to the side throwing him towards the wall. I must have thrown harder than I thought, I still wasn't used to all this extra coming of age strength yet.

His body flew through the air and smashed straight through her bedroom window, I heard him yelp before he disappeared. I shifted back and ran to Brook's side, I grabbed her hand and yanked her to her feet pulling her quickly to the window not wanting to leave her for a second in case he came back up the stairs behind me. I leant out of the window in time to see him laying on his side, he shifted back pushing himself to his feet. Blood all over his back, neck and face.

He looked up at the window murderously angry, his face the picture of rage as he sneered at me, "You're dead Philips, your all dead and it won't be painless either, I'll kill her mother first, and then I'll make you watch as I kill Brook slowly, making her scream for you" he said spitting blood onto the floor.

Rage took over again, he needed to die. I threw one leg over the windowsill about to jump and finish this but Brook grabbed my hand "NO! Jayden please don't, please don't leave me" she begged crying hysterically. Trey just sneered at me and turned walking towards his truck, obviously not man enough come back up and take me on his own. My wolf was trying to force me after him, I wanted so badly to jump out of the window and tear him limb from limb, but I couldn't leave Brook alone, not while she was clinging to me like that. She wanted me to stay so I had to stay, it was part of my mating to give her whatever she asked for. I watched him get in and pull away before I turned to her and wrapped her in my arms.

She was sobbing, her legs gave out so I picked her up bridal style and carried her to the bed sitting her on my lap as I rocked her gently. She wrapped her arms around my neck and sobbed onto my shoulder, "Oh God! Are you ok? Did he hurt you?" she asked desperately pulling back and looking all over my face and neck concerned.

"I'm fine shortie" I said honestly, he didn't get anywhere near me.

She started sobbing again and hugged me tight, "This is all my fault, I should never have gone to the stupid party, I should have just left my phone turned off, I should have told you we couldn't be friends, now he's gonna kill my Mom!" she said gripping her hand into my hair.

I rubbed down her back as I continued to rock her as her sob's slowly calmed down. "It's ok shortie, I promise, I'll sort everything" I said soothingly. Suddenly she pulled back to look at me, she looked really angry, her eyes were red and puffy, her cheek had a blue and red tinge to it where he had hit her, her lip was slightly swollen but had stopped bleeding now.

"Why the hell did you do that? Why didn't you let me go? Then he wouldn't be after my Mom, he wouldn't want to hurt you!" she cried slapping her hands on my chest.

I caught her wrists making her stop in case she hurt herself hitting me, "I couldn't let him hurt you" I said simply.

She shook her head "I'd cope with it, I always cope with it, it doesn't matter, but now he's gonna hurt my Mom!" she said fresh tears spilling over.

"You always cope with it? He's done this before? This is why you couldn't be my mate, because you knew he'd hurt your Mom" I asked cupping her face making her look at me, realisation hitting me. He was hurting her and she was protecting her Mom by being with him, fresh sobs broke out of her, I put my forehead to hers wishing she'd told me, I could have helped her sooner. "Why didn't you tell me?" I asked desperately.

"He said he wouldn't ever let me go, he said he'd kill her if I tried to leave him" she said wiping her face with a shaky hand.

"Everything's ok now shortie, he won't hurt you or your Mom, I promise you, I'll protect you" I vowed.

"I can't see you get hurt either" she whispered looking into my eyes.

I smiled "I won't get hurt either" I said sternly.

"I can't believe Trey's a shifter, all this time" she asked looking shocked and scared, I nodded trying not to get angry again as I thought of him.

She ran her hand over my face slowly making me burn in need for her, "Oh god Jayden" she whispered. She whimpered slightly and crashed her lips to mine setting my body on fire, oh god I'm kissing her again! Waves of desire for her were crashing through my system, I'd dreamt of doing this every day since the party and now I've kissed her twice in one day. I pulled her closer to me kissing her for a couple of seconds before I pulled away.

"Call your Mom, tell her there's an emergency and that you're coming to pick her up, tell her not to go anywhere alone and if Trey shows up to call the police" I said easing her off of my lap and sitting her on the bed. I grabbed her phone from the floor and handed it to her, "Can you do that for me shortie?" I asked looking straight into her eyes, she nodded. I smiled and kissed her gently on her lips, "You have anything I could put on?" I asked slightly embarrassed that I was now naked. She moaned slightly as she looked me over and I could smell those damn hormones again, f*cking hell those hormones would be the death of me! I willed myself not to get turned on by it, that would be embarrassing as hell!

"Um I guess I have some of Trey's clothes here, if you want those" she said heading to the drawer and pulling out a pair of shorts and a t-shirt. I took them not really wanting to wear his clothes but as mine were now in shreds on the floor I guess I needed to.

I pulled them on "Are you ok shortie? That was a lot for you to take in huh?" I asked worried that she had just seen a fight between two full grown shifters, it's supposed to look terrifying to other shifters so I dread to think what it looked like to a human!

She nodded and bit her lip "I'm ok, I was pretty scared" she said, I wrapped my arms around her gently.

"I would never have let him hurt you" I said fiercely.

She shook her head "I wasn't scared for me Jayden, I thought you were gonna get hurt" she said pulling me closer to her. God she was so adorable!

"Are you hurt?" I asked trailing my fingers over her cheek again, it didn't look too bad but must have been sore.

She shook her head, "It's ok, I'm fine" she said squeezing herself to me making me so damn horny I could burst. Ok come on Jay make her and her mother safe!

"Call your Mom shortie" I said pulling away from her and hunting through the mess of mine and Trey's clothes for my phone. Finally I found it and dialled my father quickly, this was his pack, I needed his approval before I could make any plans.

"Jayden?" he said a little shocked as he answered the phone, I hadn't spoken to him for well over two years, I mean I saw him at pack meetings but I hadn't spoken to him for a long time.

"Yes Father, I need to talk to you it's important" I said quickly whilst stroking my hand down Brooks head gently, she was talking to someone on the phone asking for her mother, hopefully she would be able to leave, god I hoped she wasn't some damn surgeon or something and was stuck in an operation!

"Ok, what is it?" my father asked concerned.

"No I can't do it over the phone I need to come there" I said sternly.

"Well I'm home right now" he said.

"Ok, I just need to pick someone up and I'll come straight round" I said.

"Pick up who? Who are you bringing to my house?" he asked curiously.

"My mate and her mother" I said linking my fingers through Brooks.

"You mated?" he asked almost sounding proud.

"Yeah I did, I'll explain when I come there, I guess I'll be about an hour" I said. I walked to Brook's wardrobe and grabbed a load of her clothes and put them in the middle of her bed, I grabbed the drawers from their frame and tipped them onto the bed dumping all of her clothes into a pile.

"I'll see you then" he said ending the call, I grabbed another drawer and tipped all of her underwear into the pile.

She was watching me curiously, "Anything else you want?" I asked waving around the room, she was still talking hurriedly to her Mom about Trey. She ran to her closet and grabbed a couple of pairs of converse from the bottom throwing them onto the bed along with a teddy bear from her dresser. She nodded and I folded the corners of the quilt tying it in a knot. She was talking to her Mom now, hurriedly explaining there was an emergency.

I grabbed her hand and pulled her down the hall to the next room, I went straight to the wardrobe pulling out all of her mothers clothes piling them on her bed. Brook went to the drawers and pulled out armfuls of underwear and t-shirts, jeans, I grabbed a load of shoes from the bottom of the wardrobe. "Ok Mom, no I can't explain now, I'll be there in a bit, I love you" she said as she snapped her phone shut.

"Anything else?" I asked looking around, she looked around quickly and pulled open the bedside drawer grabbing a faded old photograph and two passports throwing them into the pile. I smiled sadly at her and tied up the corners of the quilt picking it up and carrying it to the hallway. It was really heavy, maybe I should have take the hangers off of the clothes. I smiled as I dumped it in the hallway and went to grab Brook's one from her room.

I put the two huge quilt parcels at the top of the stairs and turned to her, "Ready to go shortie?" I asked stepping to her side.

She wrapped her arms around me tightly. "Why are you doing this for me?" she asked looking at me gratefully.

I smiled "You're my mate, I'd do anything for you" I said. God she was so close I couldn't help but kiss her again. All my will to stay away from her was gone, Trey was gone surely there was nothing to stop us being together now, unless she just didn't want me. I touched my lips to hers gently, she squeezed herself to me tightly, my wolf wanted her, I was so f*cking hard it was unreal, I could smell how aroused she was too and the scent was filling my head making me slightly dizzy.

She traced her tongue along my lip and I opened my mouth eager to taste her again. As soon as her tongue touched mine my wolf growled, I pressed her against the wall kissing her deeply, bending my knees so our faces were at the same level as I ran my hands down her perfect body, the passion taking over. I broke the kiss to kiss down her neck pressing every inch of my body against hers, she was panting excitedly making me even hotter. Sh*t! We needed to go, I had to get her mother before Trey did, I didn't have time for this!

"We need to go shortie" I said reluctantly pulling my mouth from her perfect soft skin.

She looked at me torn, she didn't want to go I could tell, her hormones were raging and they were driving me wild. If we didn't stop right now I wouldn't be able to. "We need to pick up your Mom, she'll be waiting" I said tenderly.

She seemed to snap out of it immediately, "Ok, let's go" she said nodding. I grabbed her quilt bag and she went to get the other.

I laughed "You won't be able to lift it shortie" I said shaking my head. She didn't listen, she grabbed the knot and lifted with all her might, a sexy little grunt escaping her lips with the effort but it didn't even raise an inch off the ground.

"Crap! I'll take some stuff out" she said moving to untie it.

I smiled "It's ok shortie I got it" I said pushing her hands off of it as I picked it up in my other hand.

"Holy crap Jayden!" she gasped.

I smiled "Shifter remember?" I said teasingly as I winked at her.

She shook her head giggling, "Right come on then son of Alpha, let's go" she said heading towards the stairs.

"No Brook!" I ordered, she stopped immediately, "Behind me, just in case" I said nodding behind me, she moved to the side as I passed and stepped behind me. As we got to the front door I stopped. "Hold the back of my shirt shortie, don't let go, stay as close to me as you can, take the keys out of my pocket" I said nodding down to my front pocket, she grabbed them quick and I stepped out of the door with her hot on my heels.

"I need to lock the door Jayden" she said as we stepped over the threshold, I stopped and scanned the front while she locked the door behind us.

When I felt her grip my shirt again I started moving towards my car, she unlocked it and I threw the two quilt bags in the back of my car, lucky I brought the Chevrolet instead of one of my little old cars, otherwise her mother would never get in! I made her get in the drivers side as slide across to the other side. I pulled away as soon as her belt was on speeding to the hospital where her Mom worked with her giving me directions. She called her mother and told her to meet us in the back, I pulled right up and pulled Brook out of the drivers side again, holding her tight to my side.

Her mother was just inside the door looking totally panic stricken, they ran and hugged as soon as they saw each other, I smiled. Ok wow I would have preferred this meeting to have been under different circumstances!

"Brook, what happened to your face? Oh god my poor baby, let's get you inside and I'll have a look" she cried looking like she wanted to cry, Brook shook her head.

"It's fine honestly, we need to go" she said taking her hands and pulling her towards me, "Mom this is Jayden, Jayden my Mom" she said waving her hand between us, her mom looked at me confused, obviously wondering who the hell I was.

"It's nice to meet you Miss Mill's" I said holding out my hand to her, she smiled politely and I could see where Brook got her looks from, her mother was the complete opposite of Brook with blonde hair and grey eyes but their features were similar and the smile was exactly the same, I liked her already.

"You too Jayden, you can call me Beth" she said nodding at me politely.

"Thank you, we really need to get going, come on shortie" I said holding out a hand to her.

She came to my side immediately, "What's going on? You said there was some sort of emergency to do with Trey, Brook what's happened? Has there been an accident or something?" she asked curiously. Brook looked at me for help, ok I guess this is more my department than hers!

"Beth, I'll tell you everything when we get to where we're going, it's a long story and we don't have time for this right now" I said sternly. She didn't know of my dominance but people could usually sense an Alpha presence and not even realise what it was. Anyway she accepted my explanation with a small nod.

"Ok Jayden, let's go" she said as we walked to the car, I waited until both of them were safely in the car before climbing in and speeding away towards my fathers cottage.

CHAPTER 15

After about twenty minutes of driving I pulled up outside my fathers cottage. Beth gasped in the back as she looked at the house that I used to live in as a child. "God this place is beautiful" she said looking at the house in awe, I smiled I guess it is pretty nice, a stone cottage built right in the middle of the woods. It was quite a big with big bay windows either side ot the front door and a thatched roof, but all I had here were memories of my mother dying then my father rejecting me so it wasn't a happy place for me to be.

I stepped out of the car and headed round to get Brook's door, I opened Beth's too and waited for them to both be out. "Who's house is this Jayden?" Beth asked curiously, looking around at the little stream that ran down the side of the cottage.

"This is my fathers house" I said trying to keep the emotion out of my voice, Beth smiled "It's gorgeous" she said still looking around with wide eyes.

Brook took my hand as we walked up to the door making me feel instantly comforted, I squeezed it gently as we knocked.

"Crap I'm nervous about meeting your Dad" she said straightening her top.

I smiled "It's fine shortie, you look beautiful, he's gonna love you" I said proudly. Beth grinned behind me and I knew I'd just won her mothers approval, Brook grimaced and carried on fussing straightening her hair.

The door opened and my father stood there, he was a very dominant male, he radiated authority, even the way he stood was arrogant and I tried desperately not to challenge him. God it was so hard! Now I was of age, my body didn't like the way he was standing trying to be taller than me, looking at me like I was beneath him. "Jayden" he said holding out a hand for me to shake.

"Father" I said nodding respectfully but not taking my eyes from his like I was supposed to, I should have dropped my eyes to the floor. He noticed, his eyes tightened slightly but he let it go.

He looked at Brook and looking her over, I felt my body stiffen ready to protect her, he was Alpha, if he didn't approve of my mate I could be thrown from the pack and she would be killed. This hadn't happened for over two hundred years, no Philips Alpha had ever disowned a pack member because of choice of mate, but then again no shifter had ever mated a human before.

His eyes came back to mine and he nodded slightly showing his approval and I relaxed slightly. "Father this is Brook, and her mother Beth Mill's, Brook, Beth this is my father Richard Philips" I said politely.

Beth held her hand out to him "It's nice to meet you Mr Philips" she said smiling. I saw him stiffen, shifter's knew better than to touch an Alpha without them making the first move and I could see he was a little shocked.

He shook her hand and returned her smile with a tight one of his own, "It's nice to meet you too Mrs Mill's" he said.

"It's Miss, I'm not married, but you can call me Beth anyway" she said laughing, he nodded and his eyes snapped to Brook.

"So this is her?" he asked looking her over again, she pressed herself to me tightly.

"Yes" I said squeezing her hand reassuringly.

"Nice to meet you Brook, welcome to the family" he said nodding and stepping aside so we could enter the house.

"Thank you Mr Phillips" she said respectfully.

He nodded to the lounge so I led them in there motioning for them to sit down on the sofa. "Father can I speak to you in private?" I asked.

"Sure, let's go into the kitchen" he said looking at me curiously.

I kissed the top of Brook's head, "I'll be right back ok? Wait here for me?" I asked, she nodded smiling her sexy little smile making my heart melt and I followed my father to the kitchen.

"Ok Jayden, what's all this about? This isn't just you wanting my approval of your mate, but she certainly get's that, she's very beautiful even with the bruises, your pup's will be strong and healthy" he said proudly.

"She is beautiful, but no that's not why I came here today, I have a problem, something's happened that I need your help with" I said skirting around the issue slightly.

"What?" he asked leaning against the counter looking at me arrogantly, he liked to have power over me and the fact that I needed his help was amusing to him I could tell.

"When I mated with Brook, I didn't know she had a boyfriend, he's Alpha of The Tridents" I said watching his face harden.

"What the hell? Why the fuck did she let you mate her if she was with someone else?" he cried angrily. I moved slightly so I was in front of the door in case he went into the lounge where Brook was, I wouldn't let him near her if he was angry.

"She didn't know who he was father, but he's seriously pissed that we've mated, he wants both her and me dead, he's also threatened to kill her mother" I said trying to keep my voice down. I hadn't explained anything to Beth yet, I didn't want her to hear it like this.

He blew out a big breath and ran his hand through his hair, "Ok what do you want to do about this? Obviously you want something from me or you wouldn't be here" he said shaking his head.

"You're right father, I want your permission to kill him and any of his pack that get in my way, I won't allow him within a mile of my mate" I said clenching my jaw tight.

He raised an eyebrow "And how do you intend to do this? On your own?" he asked curiously.

I shook my head "I was hoping for the pack's help" I admitted.

He laughed "Right, you want me to ask my pack to protect your mate because she's too fucking stupid to realise she was already dating an Alpha when she mated with you" he said sneering.

My wolf burst forward and I slammed him against the wall my hand around his throat squeezing his soft neck that I could easily snap. "You WILL NOT talk about my mate like that" I growled.

He smiled "You wish to challenge for Alpha?" he asked looking amused, I let go of his throat and stepped back but didn't take my eyes from his. I didn't want Alpha but I would take it if necessary.

"I don't want to take Alpha from you unless I have to" I said honestly.

He laughed "You think it would be that easy, you want it you take it?" he asked his eyes twinkling with amusement.

I nodded, I could take it easily we both knew it, "Yes father, I could take it, but I don't want it, not yet, I just want to make my mate safe, but you WILL show her respect" I said sternly, showing him my dominance. His eyes flashed as he assessed my threat, he searched my face for the longest time before he looked away first. I had won, he conceded, he had just handed me the pack, I could demand Alpha right now without a fight and he would have to give it to me, but I didn't want it so I didn't say anything.

"Will the pack help me? If they come for her, will they fight with me?" I asked.

"How did she not know he was Alpha? Which pack is she from? I've not seen her before" he said not answering the question, ok great here's where it gets a little tricky.

"Father, Brook isn't from a pack, she's human" I said.

He laughed and shook his head, "Seriously which pack is she from? Is she a Trident?" he asked amused.

"Father this isn't a joke, Brook's human, I don't know how but I've mated her, I needed her, I mated her by accident, I couldn't control it, my wolf wanted her as soon as I laid eyes on her" I said watching his smile fade to be replaced by shock and then plain horror, he was horrified I had mated a human.

"You can't have, that's not possible" he said shocked.

"I did, it is possible, I don't know how, Trey Newton Alpha of the Trident's has tried to mate her too but it didn't work for him" I said my wolf growling again at the thought of his teeth on my angels neck, biting her hard enough to draw blood.

My father pulled up a stool and sat down looking a little shaken, "You mated a human? In wolf form?" he asked curiously.

I shook my head "No, in this form, I couldn't stop myself, the very second I saw her, smelled her even, I needed her, it wasn't a choice, I didn't even know her name when I took her" I said shrugging.

"God above" he said putting his head in his hands, I smiled and waited for him to take it in, I didn't know how to comfort him, I hardly knew the man.

"Ok, does she know what you are? Does her mother know?" he asked.

"Brook knows, I told her, but her mother has no idea, Brook had no idea until today that Newton was a shifter, they were just dating" I said.

He nodded and everything was quiet for the longest time, "Let's go talk to them, I think her mother needs to know, but if she won't keep our secret then she'll need to be dealt with" he said sternly. I nodded in agreement even though I knew we wouldn't be hurting a hair on Beth's head, I promised my angel I would protect her mother, and protect her I would.

Brook's POV

I watched him walk from the room, my Mom was looking around curiously, "This place is beautiful" she said looking around the lounge.

I smiled "It's cute" I said casually, trying desperately to hear what was going on in the kitchen. Jayden's father was very intimidating, I hoped he wouldn't hurt him, I couldn't hear anything. He was telling his father about me in there, about me being a human, about Trey wanting to kill the three of us.

How the hell could I have been so stupid as to start all of this? If I hadn't mated with Jayden then Trey wouldn't be threatening to kill my Mom and him now! But I couldn't blame the mating, I was happy I was mated to him, he was so adorable and kind and loving. I just prayed to god that I didn't get him hurt, or worse.

"So what's all this about? What's going on with Trey?" my Mom asked dragging me out of my little internal debate.

I sighed "Trey and I have broken up Mom, he's really angry, he wants to kill me and he's threatened to kill you too" I said grimacing slightly.

She shook her head not believing a word of what I said, "Trey wouldn't hurt anyone Brook, he's a good guy" she said looking a little amused.

I closed my eyes "He's not Mom, he's been hurting me since I was fourteen, I've been trying to break up with him for years but he wouldn't let me go, he said he'd kill you if I left him" I admitted not opening my eyes, I didn't want to see her reaction.

She gasped "He's been hurting you? As in physical abuse? Did he do this to your face?" she cried horrified as she grabbed me into a hug.

I nodded "Yeah, he's not who you think he is, the business he's in, it's not strictly legal" I said grimacing at the thought of her knowing he was a big time drug dealer.

She started to cry just as I heard a big bang come from the kitchen, I jumped up but she grabbed my arm, "Don't go in there, let them work it out, Jayden can take care of himself, I can tell that about him" my Mom said gripping me tightly.

I nodded and sat back down next to her, she was crying still so I wrapped my arms around her, "It's ok Mom, everything's ok, he won't hurt you, Jayden's gonna help us" I said confidently. God after seeing him fighting with Trey I had no doubt in my mind that he was a badass. I should have told him sooner, why the hell didn't I tell him?

"I'm not worried about myself Brook! Jeez you're always worried about me!" she said shaking her head disapprovingly.

I smiled and rolled my eyes, "So how do you know Jayden anyway?" she asked when she finally stopped crying, oh shit how the hell do I explain this?

"Um well, we err" I started but the door opened and he came in with his father following close behind. I breathed a sigh of relief and looked him over, he wasn't hurt there was no cuts or bruises on his perfect face, I felt myself relax slightly now that he was here.

He walked over and sat next to me taking my hand smiling his beautiful smile at me making me feel like the most important girl in the world. Jeez how the hell can he look at me like that?

He could have any girl in the world! "So Jayden I think maybe you should explain to Beth what we were discussing in the kitchen then we'll be able to move on" Richard said looking at him knowingly. His father's eyes came back to me as he looked me over again with a puzzled expression making me squirm in my seat. Was he looking to see if I was good enough for his son? Oh shit what if he say's I'm not? Would Jayden leave me, what the hell would I do without him now? I could feel the bond between us getting stronger by the second I don't even think I could live without him now, I needed to be in his life like he always says he needs to be in mine.

"Ok so Beth, try and hear us out ok? Keep an open mind, this may get a little weird for you" Jayden said looking at her reassuringly. My Mom nodded and I held my breath waiting fro him to say it, shit maybe he'd show her his wolf! The thought of him shifting again in front of me was scary but exciting at the same time, I wanted to see again, when he was fighting with Trey I was too scared to look properly, all I know is that it was huge, brown, loud and fast.

"Ok so my family, we're not like yours, we're well, we're shape shifters" Jayden said watching her for her reaction.

She took a deep breath and closed her eyes, "I knew there was something going on, but I didn't expect this" she said calmly. I stared at her in shock, why the hell is she not freaking out?

"Beth, do you know what a shape shifter is?" Jayden asked curiously, she nodded and opened her eyes and looked at me.

"Yeah, Brook's Dad's a shape shifter" she said smiling at me sadly. I felt Jayden stiffen next to me, my Dad? I looked at her too shocked to speak, how? When? Who? Questions were buzzing through my head so fast I could barely even focus on each one.

"Her father's a shifter?" Jayden asked his hand tightening on mine, I felt tears stinging my eyes, how could she not tell me? All this time?

My Mom nodded and looked at me apologetically, "I'm sorry honey, I should have told you, I was afraid you'd think I was crazy, that I'd made it up, hell sometimes I even think I made it up" she said shaking her head sadly.

"How is this possible? Are you human?" Jayden asked looking like he was struggling to speak.

My Mom nodded "Yeah I'm human, he was my boyfriend, we dated for about three years then one day he told me he'd mated with someone else, his parents forced him into a mating that he didn't want" she said looking really upset. She loved him, she still loved him I could tell.

"But how the hell did you get pregnant? He would have been infertile, shifter's can't produce children until they mate" Jayden said shaking his head in confusion.

"I know, when we dated he told me I couldn't get pregnant, then he mated with this girl, when he came to tell me it was over between us, we ended up sleeping together and I got pregnant, obviously he could have children with me after he mated with her" she said crying again now.

I wrapped my arm around her shoulder. "No, that's not possible, if he was mated he wouldn't have had sex with you, he couldn't, he couldn't be untrue to his mate!" Richard said sternly.

My Mom looked at him and smiled sadly, "Well he managed, he was devastated after about it though, I can still see the look on his face when he told me how much he loved his mate and how he would do anything not to hurt her and how she could never find out, it almost killed him I think, it broke my heart seeing him like that" my Mom said struggling to stop crying.

"Oh god, Mom I'm sorry" I said honestly.

She hugged me tight, "It's ok honey, I got the best daughter in the world from that man, I'll always love him for that" she said tucking my hair behind my ear.

"So Brook's a half shifter, that's why I could mate her!" Jayden said as if this was the answer to some really exciting question.

My Mom looked between the two of us, "You two mated? Your together like how your father was with his mate?" she asked shocked, Jayden nodded looking at me lovingly, his eyes sparkling with joy making my heart speed up uncontrollably.

"This is just too much to take in" she said putting her head in her hands, "You never showed any signs, he came back and tested you a few times to see if you were a shifter but he said you weren't, he said you were human" my Mom said.

I looked at her in shock "My father? You're talking about my father? I've met him? Who is he?" I asked confused, I don't remember ever meeting him.

"I told you he was a friend of mine, you know him quite well actually, it's Dominic Logan" she said.

I gasped and jumped up from the chair "Holy shit! Dom's my Dad? No! He can't be!" I cried, I knew him. He was a nice guy, he was a friend of my Mom's and probably came over about once a month to hang out with us. He taught me to swim, he bought me my favourite teddy, he taught me to add up for christ sake. And all the time he was my father? Shit I even had his name, Logan was my middle name!

"He is honey, I'm sorry I didn't tell you, I couldn't, it would have ruined everything for him, then as time went on I couldn't tell you after I had lied to you for so long" she said quietly.

"Dominic Logan? As in Alpha Logan of Bane's Creak?" Richard asked, I looked at him confused, he was deep in thought. My Mom nodded and Richard's eyes snapped to Jayden.

"You mated with an Alpha's daughter Jayden" he said looking at him proudly, I looked at Jayden who just looked shocked.

"What difference does that make?" I asked confused.

"It means Jayden now has the right to challenge for Alpha of Bane's Creak too, bring the pack's together, Dominic Logan has no other children, his mate died before they could conceive" Richard said looking at him in awe.

"I don't want Alpha of either pack, I just need my mate safe, will you help us or not father?" Jayden asked sounding truly menacing.

Richard nodded frowning, "Yes, under the circumstances, knowing who she is, I don't see how we can't help you" he said nodding. Jayden relaxed next to me. "This is a great mating, you should be very proud" Richard said.

Jayden laughed, "I am proud, I was proud when she was just human father, I don't care in the slightest who her father is" he said smiling at me tenderly.

"But to mate a bloodline Alpha female, it doesn't happen very often, there aren't very many pure bloodlines left" Richard said smiling happily.

"I'm not an Alpha female" I said confused.

"Technically you are, Alpha Logan is your father, you have his Alpha blood, he never had any more children which means that you, illegitimate or not, would be next in line to lead his pack, but as your female that would be up to your mate, which is now Jayden" he said confidently.

I looked at Jayden who nodded, ok this just gets more and more complicated! But what are they talking about bloodlines? "What does that mean when you said about not very many pure bloodlines left?" I asked curiously.

Jayden gasped, "That's why Newton couldn't mate her but I could!" he cried shocked.

His father nodded with wide eyes, "That certainly makes sense" he said. "Some Alpha females can only be mated by true Alpha's, true Alpha's have it in their blood, they pass it down through their children, Jayden's blood holds the Philips Alpha, this is why he could mate you but the Trident Alpha couldn't, because this Newton guy has taken Alpha by force not by blood" Richard said trying to explain. "This would also explain your need to mate her Jayden" Richard said smiling.

I looked between the two of them totally lost now, "How?" Jayden asked a little confused.

Richard smiled "Her Alpha blood, it called to you, Alpha Logan is a third generation Alpha, so he's a bloodline Alpha too, her blood would have been calling to you to mate her, I've heard of this before, a long time ago when there were more true Alpha's around it used to be more common, it ensures the survival of the packs and ties them together to make them stronger" he said confidently.

Jayden nodded slightly taking it in, "I guess that makes sense" he said squeezing me gently. "I bet that's why Newton wanted her too, so he could challenge for Alpha of Banes Creak" Jayden said angrily, "Brook said he was twenty when they got together, that's when he was of age, I bet he was setting up to take over" he said his fists clenching slightly. Richard nodded in agreement, I just sat there not really knowing what the hell to say or do, I mean my father was a shifter? And I had known him my whole life, this was just crazy!

I had a feeling I had a lot to learn about this whole shifter thing that I seem now to be very much a part of, Jayden hugged me tight. "None of this is important shortie, so father, you'll call a pack meeting?" he asked curiously.

Richard nodded "I'll call it for tonight" he said standing up. Jayden stood too, Richard looked tired, he looked like he had aged ten years since I first met him at the front door. "Where will you be staying?" he asked nodding his head towards me and my Mom.

"They're coming to stay at mine" Jayden said confidently.

"Err, that's not really possible, I have to get back to work" my Mom said from next to me.

"No Beth, I'm sorry, Trey Newton wants you dead, he know's I've mated with Brook, he's threatened to kill you, I've promised Brook I'll keep you safe and I won't break that promise, you'll stay at mine until this is over, no discussions" he said sternly. He said it with so much authority my Mom flinched back behind me slightly.

Richard started to laugh "She really has Alpha blood, look at her, you just used your full force and she didn't even blink" Richard said pointing at me.

Full force? What's that about? Jayden smiled at me proudly, "Full force of what?" I asked confused again.

"His full Alpha command, you should have bowed to him, even just being half a shifter you should have bowed to that, even humans can feel it, right Beth?" Richard asked smiling, my Mom nodded with wide eyes. Ok Jayden just scared my Mom with some Alpha command?

"What the hell's an Alpha command?" I asked throwing my hands up in exasperation, "God I'm getting more and more confused" I cried.

Jayden grabbed my hand and pulled me up against his body, "It's just a tone of the voice or sometimes even a look that people respond to, you didn't respond to mine because you have Alpha blood too, that's all" he said shrugging, god that's just stupid!

"I didn't get scared of you because I know you wouldn't hurt me Jayden, not because of some Alpha blood" I said dismissive-ly.

"Actually I've used the Alpha on you a couple of times and you didn't bat an eyelid" Richard said grinning sheepishly.

Jayden's face snapped in his direction, "That had better be a joke old man, you WILL respect my mate" he growled angrily.

Richard flinched slightly but tried not to show it, "Go, I'll arrange the meeting" he said changing the subject.

Jayden nodded and took my hand, "Come on then shortie, Beth, let's go back to mine, you must be hungry" he said leading us back out to the car again.

CHAPTER 16

W e pulled up outside Jayden's house, it looked different in the daytime, last time I was here it was already banging with a wild party. Now it just looked like a really cute log cabin set against a gorgeous back drop of tree's. Jayden opened the door's for us and grabbed the two extremely heavy quilt's filled with mine and my Mom's clothes. How the hell is he lifting that? I watched the muscles in his tanned arms ripple as he carried them, one in each arm and I started to feel hot. God he was so powerful, it was turning me on really bad.

He took a deep breath and looked over his shoulder at me making my whole body tingle, he smiled a sexy little smile as if he knew what I was thinking and I wanted him so bad I could barely stand it. He nodded into the house and we followed him upstairs, I couldn't keep my eyes off of his ass, it was tight and pert and so hot it was unreal. He went into one of the bedrooms and put one of the quilts on the bed, "We brought you some clothes and stuff Beth, you can stay in here, hopefully it'll only be a couple of days" he said apologetically. "Bathroom's through there, make yourself at home ok?" he said smiling warmly at her.

She nodded and immediately started untying the knot on the quilt, Jayden grabbed my hand and pulled me out of the room closing the door behind us. As soon as the door shut he pushed me against the wall, his body pressing into mine, his mouth so close to mine I could barely stand it. "Stop getting turned on, please, I can't stand it, you're killing me" he whispered sounding so sexy I whimpered.

"How do you know I'm turned on?" I asked breathlessly, god that was such a stupid question it must have been showing on my face!

He rubbed his nose along my jaw inhaling deeply, "I can smell the hormones, they're coming off of you in waves, I'm surprised they haven't knocked me off of my feet they're so strong" he said running his fingers through my hair making my heart throb. My whole body was starting to ache for him, "God, it's getting worse!" he growled pressing against me tighter, I could feel he was trembling slightly. He was so aroused his rock hard erection was pressing into my stomach.

"Stop turning me on then! This isn't helping!" I breathed as he ran his hands down my back.

He took a deep breath and pulled away, he was looking at me hungrily, he wanted me just as much as I wanted him. As I looked into his eyes they started to relax slightly. He stared at me for a minute or so and I worked desperately to calm my hormones. "So I'll put you in the bedroom down the hall, next door to me" Jayden said grabbing my makeshift suitcase and started walking off quickly. Next door to him? Did he not want to sleep in the bed with me?

"I'm not sharing a room with you?" I asked trying to hide my disappointment.

His eyes snapped to mine. "You want to?" he asked shocked but hopeful at the same time, I bit my lip and nodded trying desperately not to think of sleeping a bed with him and how close he would be to me, his hard body in the bed next to me all night, his arms wrapped around me. "Stop please" he said closing his eyes looking like he was in pain, my hormones obviously attacking him again. Now that Trey was out of the way I could be with Jayden properly, if he still wanted to be with me after all the trouble I've caused him and his pack, maybe he didn't. I walked up and took his hand pulling him down the hall to the bedroom I went to last week at the party when I went to use the bathroom.

I stopped outside the door, "Is this your room?" I asked quietly, he groaned and nodded "Don't you want me to sleep in with you?" I asked a little hurt.

He groaned again and looked right into my eyes "I want you to sleep in my room, I want you with me every night for the rest of my life shortie, but you didn't want me" he said looking hurt. I wrapped my arms around his neck, god I had hurt him so much!

"Jayden, that was because of Trey, I tried to break it off before, he wouldn't let me, that's why I said I didn't want to be your mate, that's the only reason, I promise" I said honestly.

He smiled a heart stopping smile and bent his knees, picking me up with one hand under my ass, his other hand still holding all of my clothes and shoes. I wrapped my legs around his waist as he fumbled with the door handle and carried me into his bedroom kicking the door shut behind him.

"So your saying you DO want to be my mate?" he asked as he dropped the quilt on the floor with a loud bang and wrapped his other arm around me. God that is a really silly thing to ask.

"I thought you could smell that I do" I said teasingly, he smiled happiness clear across his face and I pressed my lips to his. My whole body started thrumming in need, I pulled him closer to me desperately wanting to feel every part of him on me.

He made a small growling sound as he moved us to the bed climbing on top of me kissing me deeply running his hands down my body massaging my breasts. He pulled out of the kiss just as I was starting to get a little light-headed and started kissing down my neck, I tipped my head to the side wanting him to kiss lower, he was so close to where I wanted his mouth. Suddenly my body started to throb as his mouth touched where his mark was on my neck, I gripped my hands into his hair holding him there as my body started to bump through the gears as he licked and kissed it.

I pulled his head away quickly as it became too much, "Enough, Oh god that's enough of that" I panted looking into his beautiful green eyes. He looked at me amused as his hands travelled down to the buttons of my jeans, I ran my hands down his hard chest gripping the bottom of his t-shirt pulling it up slowly over his head. God he was so beautiful! His chest and ab's were perfectly toned, he shivered slightly, I gripped his ass pulling him closer as I ground against his erection making him moan quietly.

Just as he had undone the buttons on my jeans his phone started to ring, I pulled out of the kiss and smiled. "Ignore it" he said as he crashed his lips back to mine.

I giggled against his lips and pushed him back, "It could be important Jayden" I said watching his face grow frustrated.

He sighed and sat up pulling out his phone, he glared at it before snapped it open and putting it to his ear, "This better be important Scott, I'm busy" he said sounding annoyed. I couldn't help but laugh, he looked so pissed. "No man, it's ok she's here with me, yeah come on over, I guess I should explain what happened before the meeting tonight" he said running a hand through his hair. "Ok see you in a bit then" he said nodding, he snapped his phone shut and groaned, "Scott's coming over, I'm sorry" he said tucking my hair behind my ear.

I took his hand and pulled him back down on the bed, "It's ok, I'll let you make it up to me later" I said teasingly.

"Oh god Brook, you're killing me! I don't think I can cope with this" he said almost pleadingly as he wrapped his arms around me, what the hell does that mean?

"Cope with what?" I asked confused, oh shit he means cope with me! He thinks I'm too much trouble and he doesn't want to be with me! I started to panic, he pressed his body to mine.

"Cope with this" he said running his hand down my body, hitching my leg over his hip, "I want you so bad, I swear I've never wanted anything more in my life, it's almost painful, and it's all the damn time" he whined. Oh thank goodness for that!

I let out a breath I didn't even realise I was holding and snuggled closer to him, "God Jayden, I thought, oh never mind" I said pulling his mouth to mine kissing him deeply.

He pulled away after a couple of minutes and looked towards the window, "Scott's here" he said pouting at me slightly.

"How do you know?" I asked glancing towards the window but I couldn't see out, all I could see was sky.

He smiled "I can hear his car" he said shrugging, wow this shifter stuff really is crazy! He was looking at me lustfully inching his head back towards mine, I turned my head away at the last second so he kissed my cheek.

"Go let Scott in" I said giggling slightly, he really did look frustrated! He groaned and climbed off of the bed. Wow it felt like it would kill me to wait too!

He held out a hand to help me off of the bed, "Come downstairs with me, I need to tell Scott what's going on ready for the meeting tonight" he said frowning slightly. We started heading down the hall hand in hand.

"So all of your pack will be at the meeting tonight?" I asked curiously.

He nodded "Yeah don't worry, they'll love you" he said smiling at me proudly.

I stopped, holy shit I was going too? "I'm coming to the meeting?" I asked shocked.

He smiled "Well of course you are, you're my mate shortie, when I claim Alpha, you'll be Alpha female, they'll want to meet you, you've already met a lot of the younger members of the pack at Seth's this afternoon" he said shrugging.

I gasped, holy crap I wasn't an Alpha female! I pulled him to a stop, "Jayden seriously, I can't be this big strong woman that you think I am, I'm not an Alpha female! Honestly crap you're just gonna embarrass yourself if I go and get introduced to your pack" I said horrified.

He smiled and shook his head "Brook, even if you were just human like I thought, you would still be my Alpha female, we're mated, I gave you that title when I marked you, but on top of that you are already that through blood anyway so you have two claims on it" he said looking at me amused.

"Jayden, I don't think I can go, what if I freak out seeing all those shifters?" I asked starting to panic at the thought of sixty families worth of huge wolves.

He shook his head and pressed his forehead to mine, "I want you to come with me, nothing will hurt you I promise, I need to introduce you to my pack, but I guess if you really don't want to go you don't have to" he said running his fingers through my hair tenderly. Oh jeez he is so sweet! He wants me to go so I can't really say no can I?

I sighed and grabbed his hand making us start walking again, "Come on then let's go talk to Scott" I said rolling my eyes. Wow I am already under the thumb I can feel how whipped I am! We walked down the stairs just as Scott let himself in.

He smiled at me warmly "Hey Brooklyn" he said suddenly his face turned hard, "Shit what happened to your face?" he growled.

"It's fine Scott, don't worry, no Mel?" I asked looking back at the door.

"No I needed to talk to Jay" he said nodding at him, they gave each other the man hug thing and Jayden looked really happy probably because Scott seemed to have forgiven him for mating me. "So there's a meeting been called for tonight, some announcement to do with your mate" Scott said his eyes flicking to me for a second.

Jayden nodded "Yeah man, a lot's happened since I left Seth's, let's go sit down and I'll tell you" he said motioning for him to the lounge.

"Um I'll be in the kitchen then" I said a little uncomfortable, I mean I wasn't in the pack and they obviously wanted to talk about me.

"Brook, this involves you too, besides I'd rather not have you out of my sight at the moment" Jayden said looking at me a little pleadingly. I smiled and took his hand again ignoring Scott looking at our intertwined fingers, with a confused expression across his face.

"I thought you two were being friends" Scott said as we got to the lounge, Jayden smiled and beamed at me happily.

"No Brook's agreed to be my mate now, some stuff's happened, the situations changed" he said his face turning hard slightly towards the end obviously thinking about Trey.

"Ok so what's going on?" Scott asked shaking his head confused, Jayden took a big breath before he started to speak.

"It turns out that this Trey Newton guy's a shifter" he said.

Scott jumped up out of his seat looking shocked "What the fuck? Seriously?" he cried.

"Sit down man, it gets worse" Jayden said sadly, "He's Alpha of the Tridents, and he knows we've mated and he is pissed" Jayden said sounding murderously angry.

Scott's mouth dropped open as he looked between the two of us obviously checking to make sure this wasn't a joke. "Alpha of the Trident's? Shit, this is bad" he said running a hand through his hair.

Jayden nodded, "It's fine man, but he's really not happy, he thinks he's gonna kill me and Brook and even her Mom" he said looking slightly amused like this was a ludicrous idea.

Scott jumped up again his eyes black looking extremely angry, "He won't" he growled.

Jayden nodded "I know man, don't worry, I'm gonna kill him first" he said casually as if we were discussing the weather or something.

Holy shit he's gonna kill him? No way! "No! You can't do that Jayden! I don't want you anywhere near Trey, please you don't know what he's like, he's crazy his boys are crazy too" I said trying desperately not to cry at the thought of Trey hurting Jayden.

"Brook, I need to kill him before he comes after you, there's nothing else I can do, I won't let him near you and therefore I need to kill him before he tries" he said shrugging.

"I'll come with you" Scott said his eyes still black and angry looking, Jayden looked at him gratefully.

"That's what I was hoping you'd say man thanks" he said smiling.

I gasped "No! Please! Don't do this please!" I begged a tear forcing it's way out.

Jayden groaned and wiped it away quickly, "Please don't cry shortie, I can't stand it" he said pleadingly as he pulled me closer to his side.

I willed myself to calm down as he continued to talk to Scott, "It turns out that Brook's not entirely human" he said excitedly.

Scott gasped and looked at me accusingly, "Why the hell didn't you say Brooklyn?" he asked looking a little hurt.

"She didn't know man, she's just found out today, her father's a shifter and got her human mother pregnant after he had mated with someone else" he said still trying to make sense of it himself.

Scott shook his head "He can't have" he said sternly.

"He did, that's why I could mark her" Jayden said nodding reassuringly, Scott looked shocked as hell. "Her father's Alpha Logan of Banes creek" Jayden continued.

Scott's eyes snapped back to me, "Alpha female" he whispered.

Jayden nodded "Bloodline Alpha female, my father thinks that's why I had to claim her, he says her blood was calling for my bloodline" he said giving me a reassuring smile.

"Holy shit" Scott whispered still staring at me.

"I think Trey wanted to be Alpha of Banes creek, he tried to mate her" Jayden growled angrily.

"That fucker!" Scott said just as angry, "When do we go?" Scott asked looking at Jayden again now for guidance.

Jayden shook his head, "I'm not sure, we'll see what my father says at the meeting tonight, I guess I need to speak to her father, this concerns him too if Newton wants his pack" he said glancing me. Oh shit he wanted to meet my father? I didn't know how to feel about that, I mean I really liked Dom, he was a really good guy and when I was younger I always wished that he would get with my Mom. But now I know he's my father, jeez I just don't understand how he couldn't have told me!

"The meetings been called for nine" Scott said still watching me closely, "What happened to your face?" he asked tenderly. I felt Jayden stiffen next to me and his hands went into tight fists.

"Trey" I whispered rubbing Jayden's leg reassuringly as his teeth snapped together sharply.

I heard Scott curse under his breath, "Scott?" my Mom said excitedly from behind me.

He smiled and jumped up, "Hey Beth, long time no see" he said hugging her tight.

"I haven't seen you in about a year and a half, still a heart-breaker huh?" she said teasingly patting his cheek making him laugh.

"I guess so" he said grinning.

They started chatting about Scott's college and I took the opportunity to look at Jayden. He pulled me closer to his side his fingers trailing over my sore cheek and lip, god I bet I look a right state! "This sore?" he asked quietly.

I nodded "A little, it's not too bad though" I said honestly, I'd definitely had worse!

He sighed "Beth, do you think you could have a look at Brook and see if there's anything you could do for her face?" he asked not taking his eyes from mine.

"Yeah of course, come on honey" she said standing up holding her hand out for me. I stood and let her lead me to the kitchen area, she grabbed a bowl and went to the freezer grabbing some ice and putting it in the bowl.

She dragged over a stool, "Sit down, is it just your face?" she asked grabbing a tea towel from the side and filling the bowl with cold water so the ice would melt slightly. I groaned internally, I had to tell the truth, Jayden would probably see later anyway, I already knew there would be wicked bruises there tomorrow.

"Um no, my back and side" I said quietly.

"Take your top off honey" she said trying to appear professional even though I could see she was trying not to cry. I sighed pulled my top off over my head holding it close to my chest covering myself, I didn't want her to have to look at me. I closed my eyes as she gasped, ok maybe I wouldn't have to wait until tomorrow for the bruises. "Oh god Brook" she groaned, I knew she was crying now but I couldn't look, I didn't want to see her face while her heart broke. She loved Trey, they were close, it was probably hard for her to see this knowing that this was going on under her nose.

She applied the damp towel to my back as she prodded my side gently, there was no broken bones, I could tell, I'd had broken ribs before and that was definitely a lot worse than this. I knew it was only bruises but if it made Jayden feel better then I guess I could get checked out. "I don't think there are any broken bones honey" my Mom said through her tears.

I nodded "Yeah, it's just bruises, it'll be fine, I'll take some painkillers, it'll be fine in a couple of days" I said honestly. She sniffed and swiped at her face as Jayden came in, I knew he was watching from the doorway trying to go unnoticed.

"Everything ok?" he asked leaning on the counter next to me taking my hand.

"Yeah, nothing's broken" Beth said nodding.

"Good" he said looking into my eyes, his eyes were tight with worry and concern so I squeezed his hand reassuringly. "Beth I need you to do something for me" Jayden said dragging his eyes from mine, she nodded looking at him curiously. "Would you call Alpha Logan and ask him to come here? I need to talk to him, before the meeting tonight if possible" he asked.

She nodded "Yeah ok, what time shall I ask him to come?" she asked grabbing her phone from her bag.

"I don't know, whenever he can, the meetings at nine" he said rubbing circles in the back of my hand, "Scott can give you the address and directions" he said nodding to the living room.

"Ok" she said walking out to the living room quickly.

Jayden turned to me looking at me sadly, "This looks bad shortie" he said tracing his fingers down my side.

I smiled "It's fine I promise, I've had worse" I said sighing, his body stiffened and he squeezed his eyes shut tightly. I raised his hand and kissed it gently rubbing the back of his hand across my sore cheek. It felt so nice to have him touching me, he relaxed slightly and bent down next to me moving my arm and planting little kisses across my sore ribs as if he was trying to kiss the pain away.

I closed my eyes enjoying the sensation of his lips on my skin as he moved round kissing over my back gently. "It hurts here too Jay" I said pointing to my neck, he chuckled quietly and I felt him kissing up my neck, "And here" I said pointing to my cheek. I couldn't help but smile as he moved to kiss me there, "Here" I said pointing to my nose, "And here, it hurts a lot right here" I said teasingly pointing to my mouth. He groaned and crashed his lips to mine with such a force that it almost knocked me off of the stool I was sitting on.

He wrapped his arms around me holding me against him as he kissed me deeply. I wrapped my legs around his waist clinging to him tightly, god I was totally crazy about this boy. I had known him exactly a week but I knew I couldn't be apart from him now. Now that there was nothing in our way I needed to be with him. By the time he pulled away to kiss down my neck I was totally breathless and I was more than up for heading upstairs to his room.

"Oops, sorry" my Mom said from the doorway, Jayden stopped immediately and turned to look at her smiling a little sheepishly.

"Sorry, my bad" he said looking at her guiltily making me laugh.

She grinned and rolled her eyes, "I've phoned Dom, he'll be in an hour, that ok?" she asked changing the subject.

"That's great Beth, thank you" he said smiling affectionately at her. Shit I can't believe I'm gonna be seeing Dom again knowing that he's my father and that he's a shifter, I always thought my father didn't want me as I was the product of a one night stand and now I find out he's been in my life the whole time. Wow this is gonna be awkward!

CHAPTER 17

Jayden's POV

After we had a quick bite to eat I grabbed all the plates and started stacking the dishwasher. This was going to be hard seeing Brook's father, he was an Alpha and I had broken a rule by mating his daughter without asking his permission. I mean he was supposed to asses me and see if I was worthy of an Alpha female, but hopefully he'll understand once I explain about the bloodlines and my need to claim her. If not then this was probably going to end in a fight and I couldn't afford to lose, I had to kill Trey first.

Brook hovered behind me looking stunningly beautiful even with her bruised face, she was watching me with a lustful expression on her face so I tried not to breathe through my nose. I couldn't cope with smelling her raging hormones again, not today. God I can't believe she agreed to be my mate, I was honestly so happy I could do a little happy dance but I didn't want to embarrass myself. When I was done with the dishes I wrapped her in my arms being extra careful of her back and side, shit those bruises looked bad they must have been painful. I felt my blood start to boil again as I thought about that asshole hurting her, I glanced at the clock, it was only seven thirty and I was so impatient to get to the meeting. I needed to have a plan in place to finish this, I didn't like sitting around and waiting, it felt like I wasn't doing anything about it.

"You ok shortie?" I asked kissing the side of her head and trying my best to ignore the blast of desire I felt for her. This was just crazy, the feeling of pure need, it wasn't want, I literally needed her like I needed air to breathe and my body was yearning for hers. All I could think about other than killing that asshole, was ripping her clothes off of her perfect body and making her scream.

"I'm fine Jay, I'm just a little nervous about seeing Dom, I mean all this time I always thought he was just a family friend" she said shaking her head frowning.

I smiled and pulled back cupping her face in my hands, "Shortie, just do me a favour and remember he was there for you when you were growing up even though his mate died, when your mate dies it's supposed to feel like your insides die too, the fact that he still cared for you after that means he's a really good guy, so cut him some slack ok?" I asked quietly. She looked at me curiously and I knew I needed to explain more, "I've had first hand experience with this, when my Mom died my father just abandoned me, he wasn't in my life like your father was, just try to think about this from his point of view ok? I know it's hard shortie but just keep that in your mind and let him explain ok?" I asked looking into her beautiful hazel eyes.

She smiled and pulled me closer, "Wow you're a wise one huh?" she said rolling her eyes.

I nodded grinning at her playfully, "Oh yeah I'm the wisest that there is, and as your mate you need to do everything that I say" I said trying to look stern. Wow if she knew that our mating made that the other way around I would be in seriously deep shit!

"Oh really, and what if I don't? You going to spank me or something?" she asked raising one brow looking so unbeliev-ably sexy that I almost lost control of my wolf and took her on the kitchen counter in front of her mother and my best friend. I gritted my teeth and didn't say anything.

Luckily the doorbell rang snapping me out of my horny wolf state, she gasped and looked towards the door. I turned her away from the door, as I kissed her softly, "Everything's ok, I need to get the door" I said as I pulled away kissing her forehead. She nodded so I reluctantly let her go and went to meet the man who technically had every right to rip my throat out.

I quickly opened the door to see two men standing there, I knew the one at the front was Brook's father, I'd met him once, at my mothers funeral. He had come to pay his respects and the respects of his pack. He actually looked a little like Brook, he had the exact same colour hair and eyes as hers but Brook's features were her mothers. The guy behind him was taller than me, probably about six foot five, he had light brown hair and blue eyes, both of them wore the same expressions, confusion, curiosity and annoyance.

"Alpha Logan, thank you for coming" I said nodding respect-fully.

He put out his hand and I shook it quickly, "What's all this about? Your Jayden, Alpha Philips son right?" he asked frowning slightly.

I nodded "Yes sir, come on in, I'll explain" I said opening the door wider.

The guy at the back held his hand out to me as he walked in, "Pete Jacobs" he said nodding, this must be the Alpha's second in command if he's brought him along too.

"Nice to meet you" I said closing the door and motioning for them to go into the lounge. I followed them in and introduced them to Scott who insisted on staying here to meet Brook's father in case he was angry about the mating, maybe he thought I'd need help taking down and Alpha if it came to that.

Beth was standing there looking uncomfortable, "Hey Beth, what's going on? Why the cryptic phone call?" he asked smiling warmly at her. She looked at me.

"I asked Beth to call you, I need to talk to you about a few things which your not going to like" I said frowning hoping he would hear me out before he tried to kill me.

Brook walked in and Dom's face snapped in her direction, "What the hell happened to your face Brook?" he asked angrily as he stepped closer to her.

"Jayden will explain everything" she said quietly looking at me for help, Alpha Logan's face was so angry as he looked at me that I had to fight with my wolf who wanted to challenge him for dominance. Wow did he think I did that to her?

"I didn't do that" I said quickly, his face relaxed slightly as he turned back to her.

"You got a hug for your Uncle Dom?" he said holding his arms out to her.

She laughed and shook her head amused, "Sure Uncle Dom why not" she said sarcastically as she hugged him.

"I missed you kid, haven't seen you in a month" he said kissing the top of her head, she pulled away and came to stand next to me taking my hand.

"Ok let's get this done" I said nodding for him to sit on the sofa, I waited until he sat down before sitting opposite and pulling Brook down next to me. I tried my best to ignore the glare I was getting from her dad at our close proximity. "Ok so I'll just start at the beginning I guess" I said running a hand through my hair, he nodded looking at me curiously. "Well Brook and I have mated" I said.

He sprung out of his chair, I jumped up too and stood in front of Brook protectively. "You mated her? How the hell could you mate her? I didn't want this life for her! She doesn't need to be involved with shifter stuff!" he roared. I held up my hands innocently, ok better explain quickly before he goes for my throat!

"I needed to claim her, it's the bloodlines! Her blood called for me, I couldn't help it" I said defensively, trying desperately not to react to his anger, I didn't need to make another accidental challenge for Alpha, this one wouldn't be as easy I could tell. He squeezed his eyes shut and took a deep breath, ok so far so good, I'm still alive.

"I forgot about the bloodlines" he said sadly as he sat back down putting his head in his hands. I watched him to make sure he was calm before I moved my body from the protective place in front of my mate.

"I'm sorry Alpha Logan, I should have asked your permission, I know that but I couldn't help it, we met at a party, it was an accident" I said honestly. He looked at me, anger still on his face but he accepted my reasons, ok issue number two. "Sir there's more, Brook was dating someone who turns out to be Alpha of the Tridents pack" I said trying to control my anger.

His eyes snapped to Brook, "Trey's a shifter?" he asked shocked.

She nodded, "Apparently" she said pressing herself against me as if she was trying to disappear.

"He tried to mate her, I think he wants your pack" I said.

He frowned "He wants my pack?" he asked even more shocked.

I nodded "Yeah, and he is seriously pissed that I've mated with Brook, he wants us all dead, he did that to her face, he's been hurting her for years, but he's gone too far this time, he's threatened my mate so I'm going to kill him and any of his pack that get in my way" I said sternly.

He jumped up again his hands shaking his eyes black, he was so close to shifting, "He's been hurting you? Why the hell didn't you say?" he growled angrily looking at Brook.

"Why would I say anything to you Uncle Dom? I didn't know who you were, why the hell would I confide something like that to you?" she asked angrily doing air quotes around the words Uncle Dom. I took her hand squeezing it gently trying to calm her down, she shouldn't speak to an Alpha like that, even if he is her father.

"For Gods sake! Beth did you know about this?" he cried turning to her mother.

She gasped "If I'd known anything like this was going on do you think it would have still been happening?" she said crying.

"I know that this is a lot for you to take in, but I needed to make you aware in case he comes to try and claim your pack, he won't hurt her again, you have my word" I said desperately trying to control my anger, I couldn't talk about Trey without my wolf trying to get out and smash everything to pieces.

He looked at me, "He's threatened to kill Brook?" he asked his face hard.

I nodded "And her mother" I said.

He clenched his jaw tightly, "And you're going to kill him first?" he asked, Brook stiffened next to me.

"Yes sir, we have a meeting tonight with my pack, I need my fathers permission before I can act, but no matter what he says tonight, Trey Newton is going to die" I said honestly.

He nodded "I'll come with you when you go after him" he said looking at me intently.

"I will too" said the other guy he brought with him. I smiled, ok I wasn't expecting that!

"Thank you" I said gratefully, I knew that I needed more backup than just Scott, not that I doubted either of our abilities but there would be a lot more than just two of them.

He nodded at me before turning back to Brook, "So you know who I am now?" he asked quietly. She nodded and he looked at her sadly, "I'm sorry Brook, I couldn't have people find out about you, it would have ruined everything for me, this way I still got to be in your life, please forgive me" he asked her pleadingly.

Wow he was a nice guy, I could see he cared for her deeply, it was a direct contrast to how my father looked at me.

"Jayden said that it would have been hard for you to have a relationship with me" she said playing with her watch uncomfortably.

"It was hard, especially after Emily died, but you're my daughter Brook, I'll always love you even if it's not as much as you need, and for that I'm sorry, but I've always been here for you" he said looking like he was struggling to talk.

"I understand" she said nodding, she smiled "I've always liked you" she said rolling her eyes.

He grinned happily, "Well I've always liked you too" he said teasingly. "I guess now it's gonna come out about Brook being my daughter, I don't think we can keep it secret anymore" he said looking towards Pete. Pete nodded slightly looking deep in thought, "Once people find out I had a daughter out of mating I'll be banished from my pack" he said frowning looking like he was thinking hard about something.

Brook gasped, "No! I don't want that to happen, that's not fair!" she cried her eyes filling with tears.

Alpha Logan smiled "It's ok Brook, I knew this day would come, I don't mind, you're worth it" he said looking like he was telling the truth.

"Well then Jayden, I guess I should be calling you Alpha Philips" he said smiling warmly at me. What the hell? Everyone looked at me, Pete dropped his eyes to the floor and nodded respectfully. No fucking way!

"No, I don't want Alpha" I said honestly shaking my head fiercely.

Alpha Logan smiled "Please, it should be yours, it should pass to my daughters mate, you're the only one I could give it to, if I have to step down and leave the pack without an Alpha then Trey could come in and make the challenge for my pack anyway, this is the only way I can protect them, Alpha should be yours next anyway" he said looking at me intently.

I looked at Brook, I didn't want Alpha of any pack, al I wanted was for her to be safe, I was only twenty, she was only seventeen and in school. We couldn't have the responsibility of running a pack! Brook looked at me shocked, "I can't take it, I'm sorry, we've only just mated, we're too young, I won't put that respon-sibility on Brook" I said turning to back to him.

He looked at me pleadingly, "Please Jayden, I can see your ready, I can sense your Alpha presence it's very strong, I can't let Trey take my pack, I won't let my pack turn like the Tridents" he said shaking his head fiercely. I looked at Scott who shrugged and looked torn, "Jayden, please, you're my daughters mate, the pack should be yours, either way I'm stepping down as Alpha as I'll be banished anyway, if you take over it will still be passing down through my family, if I step down the pack will be in turmoil until a new Alpha is found, you are the only one I can hand Alpha to, please" he asked begging me with his eyes.

I closed my eyes, shit I didn't want this! But he was right, Trey would join the challenge for the new Alpha and Bane's Creak would end up just like the Tridents, a lawless badass pack that didn't respect the rules. I looked at Brook again, I hated this, I didn't want this at all, but I already felt responsible for his pack, I couldn't let them end up like the Tridents either. "What do you think shortie?" I asked needing to know how she felt about it.

She smiled "I don't know Jay, you should do what you thinks best" she said taking my hand, god she was so damn beautiful!

"But if I take his pack then it will mean responsibility for both of us" I said brushing her hair away from her face.

"Jayden, you do what you think, I trust you to make the right choice" she said making my pride swell immensely. I loved that she trusted me, that she would do whatever asked her to do. I looked into her eyes as I thought about it. I couldn't see any other way to do this, he was right, I didn't want Trey to have his pack either and at least if I took the pack for a while I could step down in a few months and let them fight over it once I had taken care of Trey.

I turned back to Alpha Logan, "Ok" I said quietly. He immediately got down on one knee bowing his head to the floor, so did his lieutenant. Oh shit, what the hell have I done?

"Thank you Alpha Philips" he said still on his knees, wow I did not like the sound of that at all!

"It's ok, you don't need to bow to me like that" I said quickly waving for them to get up, I looked over at Scott to see he had an amused smile on his face, I gave him a warning glance making his smile get even bigger.

They both got up and sat back on the sofa, if I'm Alpha now does that mean I have the power to banish people? "Alpha Logan, as new Alpha of Bane's Creak I guess I'm supposed to banish you for not being true to your mate" I said trying not to smile. He nodded sadly and Brook gasped her grip tightening on my hand, "However, on this occasion I've decided that your experience and knowledge would be useful in the pack, I'd like to keep you on as a special adviser if your willing to take the role" I said smiling.

His eyes snapped to mine, relief clear across his face, "Seriously? Can you do that?" he asked shocked.

I shrugged "I guess I can do whatever I want, I'm Alpha now" I said wrapping my arm around Brook pulling her close to me. I can't believe I've brought all this on her already, she really didn't need all of this extra pressure.

"Thank you" Alpha Logan said gratefully.

I laughed "Well thanks for not killing me for mating your daughter without asking permission" I said a little sheepishly.

He grinned "Well she seems to be happy which is all I could ask for" he said shrugging. I rubbed my hand up and down her back affectionately, that was all I could ask for too.

"So I guess we should get going to the meeting Jay" Scott said standing up, I nodded glancing at the clock, it was almost eight thirty now.

"I'll talk to you tomorrow Alpha Logan about meeting your pack" I said.

He laughed "You can call me Dom and it's not my pack now, it's yours" he said smiling. I groaned internally, this was something I was going to live to regret I could tell.

"Right ok, I need to go and sort out this Trey thing then I'll arrange a time to come to meet your, sorry my pack" I said stumbling over the word.

"Do you think we could come to the meeting with you? I'd like to know what's going on, if we're coming with you when you go to the Tridents then we'll need to know the details, there will be others from your pack that will want to come with you too, Bane's Creak is very loyal" he said smiling fondly.

"Ok I guess you can come to the meeting, I'll talk to my father about it before it starts if we get there quickly" I said grabbing my keys from the side before taking Brook's hand again.

"Beth I'm going to need to you to come too, I don't want to leave you here on your own" I said apologetically, she nodded and slipped on her shoes walking close to Dom, he put his arm around her reassuringly. They seemed to have a good relationship, it was weird to know that what I thought was completely normal with my father was actually not the case if the person works hard enough. The trouble was seeing him act like this just made me resent my father that much more, if he'd wanted to he could have been in my life like Dom was in Brook's. "Come on then shortie, don't worry about anything, they won't be in wolf form" I said squeezing Brook's hand gently as I led her towards the door.

CHAPTER 18

When we pulled up to the little field I could see there were already a lot of cars here even though there was twenty minutes left until the meeting. I pulled up close to the trees and walked round to get Brook's door for her, I couldn't help but roll my eyes when she let herself out of the car without waiting for me. "You not used to being treated like a lady?" I asked shutting her door.

She smiled "What's a lady?" she asked teasingly as she wrapped her arm around my waist.

I sighed, she'd get used to it, eventually she'd forget how that asshole treated her. "Not gonna get my door?" Scott asking jokingly as he climbed out of the back.

"Sorry, I forgot you ARE used to being treated like a lady" I said laughing.

"Damn right" Scott said winking at Brook making her laugh, I smiled she seemed to really like him which was nice. I could see he still wanted her but she had absolutely no interest in him in that way, which made me feel a hell of a lot better, I think that if I had any competition for her affections it would be Scott. I just prayed that the mating had worked enough for her to stay interested in only me, she wasn't a full shifter so technically the mating had only worked on her shifter side, hopefully that would overpower her human side and she would never want anyone else.

Alpha Logan pulled up next to my car, well technically he wasn't Alpha anymore so I guess I should be thinking of him as just Dom now. He got out followed by Beth and Pete who I guess was now my second in command, I'd have to speak to Scott about that. I always planned on Scott being my second when I took Alpha, he would take the position from his father who was my fathers second, but I guess now that I was Alpha of a different pack I couldn't really do that.

"Hey, you ready?" I asked pulling Brook closer to my side as we turned and walked towards the tree's. I could feel she was trembling slightly, she was nervous about meeting the pack, I think maybe she thought there will be over a hundred wolves running around or something. As we stepped out into the clearing I spotted my father at the top of the field. People were staring towards us knowing that Dom and Pete and Brook and her Mom didn't belong here.

"I'm going to go speak to my father, Scott look after Brook for me ok? Don't let anyone giver her shit" I said sternly, glaring at a couple of girls who were still looking at her jealously. He threw his arm over her shoulder and I felt my wolf want to rip his arm off, I forced him away and kissed the top of her head, "Be right back ok?" I whispered. I turned to walk off but she grabbed my hand making me stop, as I looked back at her she threw her arms around my neck and kissed me hard. Oh my fucking god, is she kidding me right now? Everyone is watching and she makes me get a fucking boner? Damn this girl!

I pressed myself to her making the most of the kiss before I pulled away, "Sorry, but the girls were looking at you" she said apologetically. I laughed and shook my head amused, how the hell could she be jealous of these girls? She knows I don't want any of them!

"Jealous?" I asked teasingly.

She rolled her eyes, "Now why would I be jealous? You're not that hot" she said smiling her sexy little smile. I kissed her again trying not to breathe in her raging hormones, I didn't want to have to drag her off into the trees and, oh shit I don't even want to finish that thought as I'll have to go and do it!

"I got go shortie" I whispered against her lips, she groaned but let me go pulling the most adorable little pouting face that I had ever seen in my life. I pulled my top down making sure no one could notice how aroused I was and ran off to the top of the field to speak to my father.

As I approached he stiffened and dropped his eyes to the floor, oh shit I forgot I challenged him, he obviously hasn't! I nodded "Father, I need to speak to you before the meeting starts" I said motioning for him to come away from the group of people he was standing with, they were all this high ranking members of the pack.

Paul Porter, Scott's dad grinned at me "Hey Jay, congrats on the mating, Brook's a really great girl, your lucky to have her" he said holding out a hand to me.

I shook it grinning proudly, "I know I am, and thanks" I said nodding. I followed my father a few feet away, "Dominic Logan is here, he wants to come with me when I go after Trey, I said it would be ok for him and his second to come to the meeting" I said nodding in the direction I left them in.

He nodded "It's probably a good idea, this involves his pack and his daughter" he said frowning, his pack yeah right!

"Well actually I needed to talk to you about that too, he's handed me his pack" I said trying to go for casual but not quite pulling it off.

His face turned to utter shock as he stared at me with his mouth hanging open, "How are you going to manage two packs and still go to college?" he asked sounding concerned for the first time in fifteen years. Two packs? What the hell's that about?

"Two?" I asked confused, he nodded and stepped closer to me looking around to see if people were listening, it was pointless really, people from the other end of the field could listen to this conversation if they wanted to.

"Jayden, we both know that you're Alpha of Willow Creak now, I was going to announce it at the meeting" he whispered. Fuck no!

"NO!" I cried loudly then looked round quickly as everyone stopped talking to look at us, shit! "What I meant was, that's not very appropriate at the moment, but thank you for the offer, I don't want you to do that, not yet" I said trying to get my point across without actually saying it. People were listening now but pretending not to.

He looked at me and frowned "You don't want me to do that?" he asked confused.

"Not yet, maybe in a year or two, it's not really something that's possible at the moment what with what I just told you, two is out of the question, I don't even want one" I said honestly. He squeezed my shoulder, I looked down at his hand not really knowing how to react to it, if it was anyone else I would take it as affection or support but from him I just had no clue.

"Ok you let me know when, I better call the meeting, you should bring Brook and her parents to the front, people will want to see her" he said nodding his head respectfully asking for my permission to leave. Fuck it old man stop with the being submissive to me! I nodded and turned on my heel running as fast as I could to Brook.

Mel was there with her and the two of them were talking at once seeming to have no trouble talking and listening at the same time. How the hell do girls do that? "Hey shortie" I said as I wrapped my arms around her from behind.

She jumped a mile into the air. "Jay, shit you scared me" she said putting my her hands on top of mine on top of her stomach. I bent my head and kissed her neck just once, as I spread my fingers wide so I could feel her whole stomach under my hand. I couldn't help but think about my pup growing inside there one day, her belly all swollen, part of me growing inside her, fuck me that's a turn on.

"Come on then, let's go up to the front, the meetings about to start" I said guiding her to the top of the field, "Come to the top" I said to Brook's parents and Pete as we walked past.

As soon as we were at the top of the field my father called the meeting to a start. "Ok thank you for coming to this meeting, I know it was last minute and I apologise, we have a situation that

I need to make you all aware of" my father said loudly. It was so quiet you could hear a pin drop, people had been told this was about my mate and were obviously very interested in it. No one knew she was human apart from Scott's family and a couple of close friends so this was going to be fun, not.

"My son Jayden has chosen a mate, her name is Brook Mills" he said nodding in our direction, I heard Brook curse as she stood up straighter as every single shifter at the meeting looked at her. I wrapped my arm around her and pulled her as close as I could. People started clapping and cheering and I smiled proudly, "Enough!" my father called making everyone silent in an instant. "Brook's not a full shifter, her mother is human, her father is a shifter" he said, people immediately started whispering and staring at her shocked. I groaned, fuck it that wasn't really the best way to put it!

"Her father is Alpha Logan of Bane's Creak" he said making the whispers grow louder, Dom stepped forward to her side. "Brook is Alpha female by blood, and now she is also Alpha female through mating, Jayden has taken over as Alpha of Bane's Creak" my father said looking at me almost proudly. People immediately started clapping again, Dom smiled at me and bowed slightly, I nodded. Ok enough of the announcements, get to the Trey part I need to get this sorted!

"Ok, if I could just have your full attention again, there are some important things I need to share with you" my father said. Slowly people stopped watching us and focused on him, "There's a shifter that wishes to do Alpha Philips and his mate harm" he said, people gasped and shouted in outrage. "Alpha of the Trident pack wanted to mate with Brook too, he is very unhappy with this pairing and has vowed to kill them both" he said. "Obviously we can't let that happen so Jayden has proposed a pre-emptive strike, Jayden could you come up here and tell us what exactly it is you want?" my father asked.

I nodded, "Wait here for me" I said kissing Brook's forehead and stepping onto the little wooden step that my father used so the people in the back could see him. "Right, obviously I'm not sitting around here waiting for him to come for my mate, I want to move tomorrow night, I think it would be best to go in the dark give us more cover and hopefully they would be less prepared" I said looking over the sea of faces, most of which just looked plain scared. Most of the shifters were families, couples that just lead their normal lives and just so happened to be shifters, it was only really the higher ranking males that really got involved in anything. Occasionally fights would break out with rival packs over territory but this was rare.

"Scott Porter, Alpha Logan and Pete Jacobs from my new pack have volunteered to come with me, I plan on killing Alpha Newton and any other shifter that gets in my way" I said sternly. "If there is anyone that would be willing to help me I would be very grateful, I'm sure there will be more of them than three or four" I said almost apologetically, I didn't want to have to ask people to risk their lives for me and Brook. A few hands shot up immediately as I knew they would, most of them were my group of friends, Paul, Seth, Anthony, Rick and three adult shifters that were all higher ranking members of the pack. "Thank you, if you want to help then I'd be grateful, maybe you could see me after, but I'm warning you now this is going to be dangerous, we all know what the Tridents are like" I said frowning.

"I would like to speak to Christian, so if you wouldn't mind seeing me after the meeting Christian I'd appreciate it" I said looking through the crowd until I found him.

"Yes Alpha Philips" he shouted nodding.

I smiled gratefully, "That's all I have to say, if anyone would like to meet Brook I'm sure she'd be more than happy to talk to you after the meeting" I said smiling fondly at her. She nodded and smiled a tight smile, I knew she'd probably kill me for that, but she needed to get it out of the way sooner or later.

"Are the Tridents coming here?" a female shifter shouted from the crowd sounding scared, I shook my head firmly.

"No, you don't need to worry, this is why we're moving quickly tomorrow night, I won't let them anywhere near here, you don't need to worry" I said sternly watching her relax as she believed me.

"Ok so if there are no more questions then this meeting is adjourned" my father said gripping my shoulder again, ok what the hell does that mean? Maybe he was proud of me now I was Alpha, I doubted it, that would mean he actually had some feelings towards me.

I moved quickly back to Brook as a huge crowed of older female's started to approach her. I stood protectively by her side, but there was no need, they were all speaking to her warmly, welcoming her to the pack and shaking her hand smiling. I relaxed slightly and saw the crowd of about twelve males all standing in a group waiting for me off to one side. "Mel, stay with Brook ok, if she needs me then shout" I said pushing her a little closer to Brook as I jogged over to the rapidly expanding group. By the time I got there, there was seventeen male shifters.

"Ok guys, are we all volunteers?" I asked looking around at my friends and former pack members, I smiled at Scott's father, I knew he would come, he'd want to protect Brook too.

"What about Bane's Creak? Will you be asking for their help too?" Dom asked, I looked around at everyone, we didn't need anymore help surely eighteen fully grown males would be enough?

"I don't think that will be necessary, I don't want my first task as Alpha to be asking them to fight for me" I said shaking my head grimacing slightly.

I turned to Christian, he used to be a member of the Trident pack but he left four years ago when the new Alpha took over as he didn't like that way the pack was run so he joined Willow Creak instead. "Christian, what can you tell us about Trey Newton?" I asked looking at him hopefully.

He shrugged, "He's a bad guy, he has guns, run's drugs, he blackmails people and uses physical violence to get what he wants, he controls his pack by fear, everyone I spoke to when I was there hated him but was too afraid to do anything about it" he said frowning.

I heard growls coming from the guys around me, "How many high rankers does he have?" I asked.

He thought about it, "He has about eight that he keeps close to him, but I think he only really trusts two or three of them, they live with him" he said turning his nose up.

I nodded "Will you come with us?" I asked hopefully.

He nodded quickly, "Yeah absolutely, I hate that guy, I want to see him get what he deserves" he said his fists clenched, I had a feeling he had seen some of the physical violence he spoke about.

"Great, so you can show us where he lives, we'll meet as soon as it's dark, so we'll meet here at ten and go to their territory, we can get the lay of the land and then move in around midnight, I want it quick and easy, in and out, and boys, Newton is mine" I growled angrily. They all nodded, "Ok, tomorrow night, here at ten then, and thank you guys, this means a lot to me that you've volunteered for this" I said honestly.

"Congratulations on the mating" one of the guys said, he was an elder member and didn't usually get involved in the fighting, I was actually surprised he volunteered at all.

"Thank you David" is said smiling, he nodded looking a little uncomfortable, "David you don't have to do this, just because you volunteered doesn't mean you need to go through with it, I'm sure your wife wouldn't want you involved in the fighting" I said giving him the option to back out.

He smiled sadly, "Thank you Alpha Philips, but I want to" he said still looking uncomfortable as hell.

"Ok well thanks again guys, I'll see you tomorrow, any problems you have my number right?" I asked, a couple of the guys said no so I gave them my number just in case.

I headed back to Brook who was now on her own with Mel and her mother, when I got to her she wrapped her arms around me pressing her face into my chest tightly. I smiled and kissed the top of her head, "Ok shortie?" I asked leaning back to look at her.

She nodded "I'm so glad that's over" she said shaking her head.

I grinned, "It's done now, I'm sorry I left you getting swamped" I said honestly pushing her hair behind her ears gently, she rolled her eyes.

"The older ladies were ok, I don't think the younger girls liked me much, they all want you" she said pretending to be annoyed but a smile was playing on her lips.

"Well that's too bad for them, because I'm yours" I whispered as I kissed her softly, she moaned in the back of her throat and I pulled her tighter against me possessively, not wanting any space between us at all.

Someone cleared their throat behind me, I almost growled at being interrupted. I didn't want to be away from my mate, I'd only been with her once and she was driving me wild. I looked behind me angrily and saw it was her father, shit! I shook my head a little trying to clear it of the thoughts I was having about Brook and stepped back making her whimper and cling to me tighter as she stepped with me refusing to allow any space between us.

"Alpha Philips, we're now leaving, when do you want me to introduce you to your pack?" Dom asked, shit I was so not used to being called that!

"Tomorrow day time?" I offered.

He nodded smiling, "How about lunchtime? I could arrange a barbeque or something, you could get to know them for a few hours" he suggested.

I nodded "Yeah ok sounds good" I said trying not to grimace at the thought of actually having a pack and meeting them.

He handed me a card with his address and number on it, "About twelve?" he offered.

I nodded "Great, and thanks for everything" I said holding out a hand to him. I meant it, he didn't need to be helping with Trey, he didn't need to give me his pack, he didn't need to announce to everyone that he had an illegitimate daughter.

"You're welcome son" he said shaking my hand firmly, I shook hands with Pete and watched as Brook and her mother hugged him and said their goodbyes.

Scott came over, "Want me to take Beth back to mine so you two can have some private time?" he offered smirking at me, oh shit I would love that! The thought of Brook and me in a house alone was just way too tempting.

"I'm not sure that either of them would go for that, maybe you should suggest it and see what they say" I said nodding towards them. He smiled and punched my shoulder, Scott knew how hard this was for me, I'd spoken to him a lot this week about how hard it was to be mated and be so far away from your mate.

I tried not to listen as he spoke to them, Brook glanced over at me almost looking shy as she smiled at me making my whole body tremble slightly. A few minutes later they all walked over to me, "Jayden, you don't mind if Beth stay's at ours tonight do you? We thought she'd be more comfortable there, my parents would love to have her" Scott said smirking at me.

I could feel my wolf rejoicing inside, "No I don't mind, if that's what you want to do Beth" I said playing along that I had no idea.

She nodded "I'd love to catch up with Rachel and Paul" she said happily.

"Ok well would you like to come to Alpha Logan's barbeque with us tomorrow lunchtime?" I asked curiously.

She smiled "Sure, if that won't be a problem for him though" she said frowning.

"I'll check with him in the morning, but I don't think it will" I said honestly. We walked back to the car, Scott had left his car at mine so we all piled into my car heading for my house. I could barely contain my excitement at the thought of having Brook all to myself.

CHAPTER 19

Brook's POV

I couldn't keep my eyes off of him as we drove, he was so damn sexy, he was Alpha now too and it seemed to turn me on all the more. The thought of him being so powerful and strong was actually making my mouth water. "You sure your parents won't mind me staying?" my Mom asked Scott for the hundredth time.

He smiled affectionately at her, "Of course not Beth, I told you it was my Mom's idea in the first place" he said shaking his head amused.

"I just don't want to impose" she said wringing her hands nervously.

"You're not imposing" Scott said sternly.

When we pulled up Jayden looked at me, "Wait there please" he said grinning as he got out and jogged round to my side opening the door for me and taking my hand helping me out of the car.

"Oh so that's what a lady feels like" I said jokingly.

He smiled and kissed my hand "Yep" he said tugging me to-wards the house. He went to the kitchen to make us a drink and I headed to the lounge flicking on his TV for a bit of background noise, I hated it when it was dead quiet.

My Mom headed upstairs to pack an overnight bag and I started to get nervous, Jayden and I were mated now, but what happens if he doesn't like my body? I know last time we slept together he said I was beautiful but maybe he was drunk or something. I squeezed my eyes shut and plopped onto the couch trying not to imagine him taking my clothes off and turning his nose up like Trey always did. I don't think I could see that look of revulsion on Jayden's face, it would be ten times worse because I wanted to please him. I was going to be the only one he would ever want, what happens if he didn't even want me?

He sat down next to me and took my hand, I just looked at his perfect angels face, looked into his beautiful green eyes. God I could just look at him forever and never get bored of it. Scott sat down in the armchair, "Can't you two hold off the lovey-dovey stares until we've left?" he whined making me laugh, Jayden rolled his eyes looking slightly frustrated.

My Mom came down a few minutes later with a little bag, "Ok I'm ready" she said smiling at me.

I got up and hugged her tight, "I'll see you tomorrow, don't stay up all night gossiping with Rachel" I said jokingly as I kissed her cheek.

She laughed "Yes Mom" she said hugging me tighter. She brushed my hair behind my ear, "You look really happy Brook, it's weird what with everything going on, but I've never seen you look so happy and contented before" she said looking at me happily. I nodded, I'd never felt so happy and contented before, but at the same time I'd never been more afraid of anything in my life. "Be safe" she whispered winking at me.

I laughed "Yes Mom" I said rolling my eyes.

"Bye Jayden, I'll see you tomorrow" she said watching as Scott grabbed her bag, he kissed me on the forehead and gave Jayden the man hug thing before walking out of the door after my Mom.

I bit my lip and turned back to Jayden feeling sick with nerves, "You want to watch TV or something?" he asked. Oh God he's not feeling it like I am! Then again why the hell would he? He's like a freaking God and I'm just plain old Brook Mills.

"Um yeah sure" I said heading back to the lounge. I grabbed the wine that he had poured for me and downed half the glass before he even sat down next to me.

"Shall I put on a DVD?" he asked, I downed the last of my wine and put my glass on the table before turning to look at him. Ok I guess we needed to talk, I needed to find out exactly what he wanted from me, because I wanted everything from him.

"Jayden, do you really want to watch a DVD?" I asked curiously, not really sure of how to word, 'hey want to take me to bed?'. He shook his head his eyes locked on mine, my breath caught in my throat at the expression on his face. It was pure lust, pure want. "What do you want then?" I whispered not trusting my voice to speak normally.

"You" he growled his voice sounding so husky and sexy that I whimpered.

"Take me then" I said breathless with excitement. Before I even knew what happened he was out of his chair picking me up. I pressed my body to his wrapping my legs around his waist as he ran so fast to his room that all I could see around us was a blur. Unless it just felt like that because I couldn't see anything other than his eyes.

The passion had taken over my body as I crashed my lips to his roughly, I heard a little growl coming from his chest making me even hotter for him. My whole body was almost vibrating with need for him, he laid me down on his bed and climbed on top of me pressing his whole body to mine but somehow not putting any of his weight on me. I ran my hands down his back and gripped hold of his t-shirt pulling it off over his head before gripping his ass and pulling him closer. He was rock hard already, I raised my hips grinding against him as he kissed down my neck.

Oh God this was taking too long, I couldn't wait any longer I needed him now! "Please, Jayden please" I begged desperately, he pulled back, his hands going for the buttons on my jeans, he didn't undo them just ripped them open the buttons flying off. I bit my lip at how incredibly hot that was. He pulled my jeans and panties off in one smooth movement throwing them on the floor. I unbuttoned his jeans quickly, almost frantic with need now.

He gripped hold of my top and started pulling it up tracing his fingers across my stomach. I grabbed his hand panicked, God I needed him, I didn't want him to get turned off at the sight of me and not want to be with me. "Can't we leave that on?" I asked holding his hand stopping him from removing my top.

He looked at me shocked, "This is about what that asshole said to you isn't it? When he said you were fat and that no one would want you" he asked looking murderously angry.

I bit my lip, "It's just, I don't want you to look at me" I said quietly.

"Why?" he asked frowning angrily his jaw tight, I looked away from him.

"Because I'm horrible, my body, it's not nice and" I started but he put his hand over my mouth stopping me from talking and sat up pulling me up with him.

"Come here" he said tugging me gently off of the bed and pulling me over to a full length mirror that was hanging on the wall. I didn't look in it, I couldn't, he gripped my top and before I could stop him he pulled it off over my head so I was just standing in my bra. I gasped shocked and wrapped my arms around myself trying to hide away from him. He unclasped my bra pulling it off and dropping it at my feet, "Stop that" he said sternly taking hold of my wrists and forcing them to my sides.

"Jayden please" I begged feeling tears stinging my eyes, he turned me to face the mirror and I closed my eyes. I hadn't seen myself completely naked for about a year and a half and I couldn't look now.

"Open your eyes shortie" he said resting his head on my shoulder from behind me, still holding my fists to my sides.

"I don't want to see, please Jayden, I don't want you to see either, please" I begged. I felt so sick, I tried desperately to squirm out of his hold.

"Brook even with the bruises you are the most beautiful girl in the world, every guy I've spoken to thinks you're so hot it's unreal, your legs are perfectly toned and long" he said softly. He let go of my wrists and run his hands over my thighs making me get goose bumps from his touch but I still couldn't open my eyes. "They're so soft and delicate, and your hips are perfect curves leading to your tiny little waist that I can almost wrap my hands around, look" he said putting his hands around my waist, I opened my eyes slowly and looked in the mirror, his fingertips were a couple of inches from touching across my stomach.

"Your stomach is perfectly flat and toned, which leads me to these" he whispered trailing his fingers over my breasts making me moan quietly, he was driving me crazy with desire. "These are perfect, soft, perky, and they fit in my hands like they were made for me" he said his voice husky and filled with lust.

He turned me around slightly and one hand skimmed down to my ass, "And your ass, my God Brook, this is the most perfect peachy ass I have ever seen" he said squeezing it gently as he moaned quietly. He turned me back to face myself in the mirror. "Your body is perfection, your skin is flawless, everything about you is beautiful" he whispered in my ear as I looked over my body.

I could feel the tears building, I didn't look that bad, all this time I was convinced I was some sort of hideous ugly freak and it wasn't true. "He lied to you Brook, he wanted you to himself so he made you think no one else would ever want you so that you would stay with him, he was manipulating you shortie, you are nothing less than a goddess, I swear to you on my life, you are so beautiful it's almost painful, and you need to start believing it" he said sternly.

He wiped the tear that fell down my face, he had his chin resting on my shoulder as I looked in the mirror, his eyes were shining with love and affection. His hands were skimming over my hips and the tops of my thighs, I tipped my head to the side and looked at the red bite mark on my neck. He moaned quietly as he looked at it, "That's my favourite part of you" he said blowing on it gently making me shiver.

I smiled "Yeah? Not my perfect peachy ass?" I asked teasingly using his words.

He pulled back slightly and looked down to my ass, "Mmm maybe your right" he said grinning making me laugh and blush. "Seriously though, my mark on your neck is the single best thing I have ever done in my life, nothing in this world will ever compare to seeing that and knowing that you're mine" he said looking at me with total honesty clear across his face. God he was too adorable.

I turned and wrapped my arms around his neck, "Thank you" I said gratefully.

He smiled "For what?" he asked curiously.

"For mating me, and wanting me, for what you just said about my body, for protecting me and my Mom, and most importantly, for making love to me again" I said smiling teasingly at the last part. He laughed and picked me up quickly moving us back to the bed, he kissed me softly, tenderly making my heart melt. He moved down trailing little kisses over my chest and stomach, he moved to one side and I felt him trailing his fingers across my bruises tenderly.

He moved my arm out of the way pinning it above my head as he ran his tongue over my sore skin and blew on it softly making me get goose bumps. Oh God he is seriously good at this! I bit my lip and moaned as he slipped his hand down between my legs massaging me gently as he continued to kiss over my sore ribs. I closed my eyes concentrating on the fire he was starting between my legs, as I moaned and gasped for breath.

He kissed his way back up to my mouth, I kissed him hungrily, savouring his taste. He kissed down my neck and I gasped as he blew on his mark teasingly, is he doing this on purpose? "Stop teasing me please, I can't take it" I begged pulling him closer, he smiled at me lovingly as I pulled his clothes off trailing my fingers over his chest just marvelling at how perfect he really was.

My heart was crashing in my chest, I was so excited I could barely breathe. He crashed his lips back to mine making me moan as his tongue slipped into my mouth and massaged mine. God he was such a good kisser! I wrapped my legs around his waist, he gripped my thighs looking at me, "I could get you pregnant now that I've mated you" he said watching for my reaction.

"I'm on the pill" I said breathless with anticipation.

"I don't know if that'll work" he said honestly.

I moved under him rolling him to his back as I sat up on top of him, "I don't care Jayden, please" I begged almost crying with need.

"Ok shortie" he said tenderly running his hands up over my thighs, I looked down at his smiling face, he was so handsome, and he was mine. He was just watching me sitting on top of him, the look on his face was complete and total adoration. "I love you shortie" he whispered, I couldn't speak, the happiness was bubbling up inside me. I crashed my lips to his, he made a growling noise deep in his chest and flipped me onto my back so fast I barely knew what happened. I laughed breathlessly as he kissed me with so much passion my body was tingling.

When we had finally finished exploring every part of each others bodies, I smiled and wriggled closer to him, enjoying the feel of his body against mine. His eyes were raking over every part of my sweaty body with a small satisfied smile on his face and I felt my heart skip a beat. He really meant what he said, he really thought I was beautiful I could tell by his eyes. I felt my heart trying to break out of me chest because he found me attractive, that I didn't have to feel self conscious around him. Looking at him just looking at me with total adoration and love, I felt so beautiful, I could feel all the shame and hurt and disgust that I'd felt for myself for so long just sliding away.

"Oh and by the way, I love you too Jayden" I said looking into his eyes, he smiled a heart stopping smile, and moaned quietly.

"Thank God" he said pressing his forehead to mine closing his eyes, I tangled my hand into his hair hugging him tightly. He kissed me softly, "I love you so much Brook, I'd do anything for you, you know that right?" he said brushing my hair away from my face looking at me tenderly.

"Yeah I know you would" I said honestly, how the hell could I doubt that after what he was already doing for me and my Mom, what he was going to do for me tomorrow.

He bent his head kissing over my stomach softly, "Think maybe I've put a pup in here?" he asked against my skin.

"Damn it, a pup? Like puppy?" I cried sitting up, oh God I didn't want to give birth to a wolf!

He laughed and pulled me back down next to him. "It's just a word, I meant baby, a normal little baby, that could maybe shift, or maybe not, depending on who it took after" he said grinning.

I breathed a sigh of relief, "Shit I though you meant I'd give birth to a wolf!" I said shaking my head at how stupid I was sometimes, I really had a lot to learn about shifters.

He shook his head amused, "No shortie, don't worry, you may not even get pregnant, you're half human so maybe you being on the pill will work, I don't know" he said shrugging but looking at my stomach a little hopefully. Was he hoping I'd get pregnant?

"Do you want me to have a baby Jayden?" I asked curiously.

He smiled happily, "Of course I do, I want you to have my pup's, you're my mate, I want you to have a hundred pups, as soon as you're ready" he said teasingly as he kissed over my sweaty stomach again, I smiled happily, he was so adorable.

I laid there watching him tracing his fingertips over every square inch of my body looking like he was trying not to miss any part of me. God he was Alpha of his own pack now, I watched my father bow on his knees to him. "Jay?" I said.

"Mmm" he mumbled against my stomach.

"What does being Alpha mean?" I asked curiously. He sighed and pulled himself up next to me wrapping his arm round me tightly as if he was scared I was going to leave him or something. Not much chance of that happening I thought with a small smile.

"Well, I don't know how big Bane's Creak is or anything but basically, I'll need to hold pack meetings each month, keep the peace between pack members, make any decisions that need to be made, sort out any disputes, make sure the rules are adhered to, that kind of thing" he said frowning. Rules? Damn I don't even know the rules!

"What kind of rules?" I asked snuggling closer to his chest. Wow he is so warm.

"Well there aren't many rules really, humans can't find out about us, we're not allowed to encroach on another packs territory, we're not allowed to use our extra abilities to gain anything from the humans, so we can't enter the worlds strongest man competitions, that kind of thing" he said laughing slightly.

I smiled, ok that didn't sound too bad, "Didn't you already break the rules by telling me though?" I asked teasingly.

"Hmm yeah your right, maybe I should banish myself" he said smiling cockily at me.

"You like the power" I said nodding.

He laughed and shook his head, "No not really, I didn't want this, not yet, but I guess in a way I knew I would be Alpha one day, my body wants to be Alpha, it's the bloodline, it makes me more dominant even if I don't want to be, I don't respond well to authority I never have" he said a little sadly.

"Jay if you really don't want to be Alpha then why did you take it?" I asked curiously, I was glad he took it, what he did for Dom was incredible and I would always be grateful to him for looking out for my father.

"I don't want Trey getting it and turning the pack like he has with the Tridents" he said simply, I frowned at the thought of Trey.

"Are you really going after Trey?" I asked quietly feeling the tears welling up in my eyes.

He looked at me curiously, a sad expression on his face, "You don't want me to hurt him? Do you still love him shortie?" he asked his voice rough and tight. Love him? Crap did he think I was in love with Trey? Stupid Brook, of course he does, you told him you were.

I pressed myself to him tighter and felt the tear escape down my face, "No I don't love him Jayden, I haven't loved him for over three years" I said honestly.

He looked at me confused "Then why are you crying shortie?" he whispered brushing my tears away.

"I don't want you to get hurt Jayden, I know Trey's boys, they're not like you, they're mean and ruthless, I don't want you anywhere near them, I don't want anyone near them" I said my voice breaking slightly at the thought of him, Scott, his father, and my father all fighting.

He sighed "It needs to be done, you won't be safe until he's dead, your mother won't be safe" he said quietly looking slightly pained. I know it needed to be done, Trey wouldn't stop, once he set his mind to something he didn't stop until he got it, if he wanted us all dead, we'd die.

"Are you sure you can do it without getting hurt?" I asked trying not to imagine him injured or worse.

He smiled confidently, "I'm sure shortie, don't start worrying" he said kissing my nose, but I couldn't help it. He looked at me and sighed, "Brook honestly stop worrying, we'll have the element of surprise on our side, he won't have time to group or anything, most likely he'll be asleep and I'll be back within the hour" he said confidently as he brushed my hair away from my face gently.

I nodded, he looked so confident it was hard to doubt him, "Can I come with you? I could show you his house" I said hopefully.

His teeth snapped together his face hard. "No way, you're not going anywhere near him ever again" he growled angrily.

I frowned "But I could help you, I know where his boys live, I know the way in" I said quietly.

"We're not talking about this" he said sternly, ok wow conversation over then!

I sighed and nodded deciding to change the subject, he still looked murderously angry and I would imagine he was thinking about killing Trey again. His face got hard like that whenever Trey was mentioned. "What happens when you go back to college? How can you be so far away and still be Alpha?" I asked running my fingers down his chest.

He smiled "I'll have to transfer here somewhere, I was going to do that anyway" he said kissing my forehead his body relaxing now he wasn't thinking about Trey.

"You were? How come?" I asked barely able to contain my excitement that he wasn't leaving me to go back to college, I didn't want to be away from him now.

He laughed and rolled his eyes at me, "We're mated silly girl, as if I could be that far away from you" he said gripping my ass tightly biting my ear lobe and making me giggle.

"Well then Alpha Philips of Banes Creak I'm very glad you'll be sticking around" I said honestly.

He groaned "I really hate that you know" he whined making me laugh, he was a badass Alpha wolf but he could still whine like a little girl.

"Hate what? Being called Alpha Philips?" I asked curiously.

He nodded "Yeah, it's just too weird" he said shuddering slightly.

I grinned and decided to tell him the truth, "Well personally I think it's super sexy, and the sound of it actually turns me on" I whispered.

He moaned and pulled me closer to him, "Oh it does huh?" he asked, I nodded and bit my lip, oh hell yeah it did. "Well would it turn you on even more if I told you I'm technically Alpha of two packs now?" he asked smirking at me. Two packs? What the hell does that mean?

"Two?" I asked confused.

He nodded, "Technically I'm Alpha of Willow Creak now too, but I haven't actually claimed it" he said grimacing slightly.

"You are? How come?" I asked confused.

He sighed sadly, "Well, when I went to talk to my father in his kitchen today, he said something I didn't like and I accidentally got mad and threatened him, he backed away so technically he's handed me the pack, he was going to make the announcement at the meeting tonight but I've told him I don't want it yet, he's going to run the pack until I'm ready for it" he said shrugging.

"Holy crap Jayden, can you run two packs?" I asked shocked.

He smiled sadly, "Yeah, maybe in a couple of years, but I'm thinking that once I've taken care of that as$hole Trey, I'll step down as Alpha of Bane's Creak and let them have a competition for it" he said shrugging. I frowned, I didn't want him to step down, this was my fathers pack, he asked him to take it personally to hand down through the family, but it wasn't my choice I guess.

"If that's what you want to do" I said nodding.

"We'll see how it goes, you and I can talk about it in a couple of months" he said casually, yeah ok, he's all powerful Alpha and he wants my opinion? As if he would listen to me anyway!

He smiled his $exy little smile at me, I still couldn't quite get my head around the fact that this boy was mine, that he was looking at me as if I was the only girl on the planet, he was just so God damn perfect! How the hell could someone like him want me? I kissed his hard chest feeling his hot skin under my lips, his body was touching every inch of mine and I could feel the my desire for him building again, my body was starting to tingle.

He ran his nose along the edge of my jaw inhaling deeply, he groaned "Damn it Brook, those damn hormones of yours are attacking me again" he whined. I smiled and raised an eyebrow at him, they were attacking me too.

"Do something about it then Jayden" I said seductively as I pulled his mouth back to mine again.

"You're gonna kill me shortie" he whispered against my lips, I smiled and pulled him closer ending the conversation.

Trey's POV

"He's on the phone" Dan said handing me his cell, I grinned and took it, finally!

"Well?" I asked into the phone.

"It's been arranged, they're coming for you tomorrow night around midnight" he answered his voice shaking through fear.

"Midnight? You're sure?" I asked sternly.

"Yes, they're meeting at the field at ten then coming over to your territory and Jayden wants to go in around midnight" he said quickly. I felt the growl trying to rip it's way out at the mention of his name, that little $hit stole my girl and mated her! I could feel my hands were shaking so I took a deep breath willing myself to calm down, I'd already shifted three times tonight because I couldn't control my temper I didn't want to ruin another set of clothes.

"How many of them are coming?" I asked angrily.

"About seventeen" he answered his voice shaking again. Damn it seventeen? "There's something else you should know" he said quickly.

I sighed "What now?" I asked bored of speaking to this little shit, he was such a pussy, how he ever expected to be able to protect his mate I don't know.

"Jayden is Alpha of Bane's Creak now, he mated with the Alpha's daughter" he said.

"NO!" I shouted my whole body shaking as I punched my hand through the table, f*cking as$hole stole my girl and now he's stolen my pack! They were mine, both of them!

"Alpha calm down" Simon one of my high ranking pack members said putting his hand on my shoulder. I span round and punched him in the face as hard as I could, taking my anger for that prick Jayden out on him. He's f*cking ruined everything for me! I had the perfect girl, the perfect plan, I was with her for four years trying to get that pack and that ass could mate her and I couldn't!

I could feel the rage building and building the more I thought about him. I loved Brook and that as$hole took her away from me! She would never have mated with him willingly, he must have forced her somehow. Once he was dead she'd want me again and I could finally claim Bane's Creak. That had been my plan as soon as I found out Dominic Logan had an illegitimate daughter, I found her and pursued her until she agreed to go out with me. I never expected to actually fall in love with her, but Brook was special, she's incredible, and she's mine.

"Trey!" Dan said sternly, I snapped out of my rage and looked down at Simon's lifeless body on the floor, $hit I didn't even realise I was still hitting him!

I wiped his blood off of my hands onto my t-shirt, "If he's not dead then take him to the hospital" I said nodding at him. Dan nodded grimly and bent to check his pulse. I put the phone back to my ear to see if he was still there, watching as Dan nodded at two of my boys, they came in and carried Simon's bloody limp body out of the room. "You've done a good job David, you can come and get your wife now, your both free to go, but I suggest you leave your pack, they won't be too pleased when they find out you passed this information on to me now will they?" I asked teasingly.

"I can come and get her?" he asked hopefully, I smiled stupid prick as if I could really let them live and run off to tell him I knew he was coming for me.

"Absolutely, she'll be where we met earlier" I said rolling my eyes at how idiotic he was.

"Thank you Alpha Newton, oh God thank you" he cried happily.

I snapped the phone shut and threw it to Dan. "He's coming for his mate, wait until he sees her then slit her throat, make him watch her bleed before you kill him, that will teach him not to betray his pack" I said grinning. I turned to the rest of my boys sitting in my living room, "They're coming here at midnight tomorrow, they want to take out all of the high rankers and replace them with their own, I told you they'd make the move quickly" I said looking at them individually as their faces got harder and angry. "Therefore we'll move on them before that, if we take out Jayden then they'll stop their move on us, he's the one driving this plan" I said angrily. I had told my pack this was a coo, and that the Willow Creak high rankers wanted our pack for themselves. If they knew they were just coming for me they might not fight for me and I needed help, that f*cker Jayden was strong, too strong for me on my own.

Some of them growled, "Tell the boys we'll go to his house at around five, I want him, I want my girl and her mother, everyone else that's there dies, understand?" I growled angrily. If he's slept my girl I'm gonna rip his balls off first, I gritted my teeth as my wolf tried to break free again. "He's tough, the toughest I've fought so don't try and take him down alone, we need to stop him shifting, once he's shifted that's it, it's over, so drug him before he gets the chance" I said frowning at the thought of him fighting me earlier. He was going to be hard to take down, especially if Brook was threatened, my shoulder and back were still aching even though I'd spent most of the day shifted so I could heal.

"And no one touches my girl, anyone lays a finger on her and I will personally rip your head off, got it?" I growled angrily.

"Yes Alpha" the chanted.

"Good, go get some sleep, meet here at four" I said nodding for them to leave.

Dan hung around at the back of the pack, "Is Simon dead?" I asked not really bothered with the answer, he knew better than to touch me when I was angry he brought it on himself.

Dan shook his head, "No, he should be fine if he can shift to heal" he said smiling looking amused.

I grinned "Guess I need to work on my temper, it's just the thought of that prick makes me so f*cking angry, he's stolen my life and tomorrow he's gonna pay for it" I promised.

Chapter 20

Jayden's POV

I woke up in the morning with Brook wrapped tightly in my arms, I grinned and pressed myself to her naked body tighter wanting her closer to me. I had been dreaming about waking up with every day since the mating. She looked so beautiful this morning, her hair was all knotty and splayed over the pillow, she was fast asleep and looked so peaceful, just like a sleeping angel. I looked over her shoulder at the clock knowing it would be 6am, I always woke at the same time.

I pulled away from her slightly wanting to look at her, she was just perfect. I can't believe she has all those hang ups about her body, that fucker Trey would pay tonight I would make him beg before he died. Maybe I'd find out exactly how he's hurt her in the past then do that to him first see how he likes it. I could feel the anger boiling up inside me at the thought of him so I stopped thinking about him. Today was going to be a long day, I didn't need to be thinking about that as$hole all day, I'd think about him when the time comes tonight.

Brook shivered and clutched the sheet tighter, I didn't usually bother with any covers at all, my body ran hotter being a shifter so I didn't feel the cold. I scooted closer to her again letting my body warm hers while I watched her sleep. I know I'm a freaking weirdo but I just couldn't look away from her, I could look at her forever and never get bored.

After a couple of hours she stirred pressing her face into my chest as she sighed slightly, I ran my hands down her back savouring the feel of her skin on mine praying that she would never want to be away from me again. Now that I had woken up to her once I wanted to do it everyday, scratch that, I needed to do it everyday. Once all of this Trey stuff was over I'd ask her to move in with me, or maybe she'd rather I'd move in with her so her mother wouldn't be alone, I wasn't too sure her mother would go for that though!

She pulled her head back and smiled sleepily, "Hey you" she mumbled rubbing her face slightly, I grinned at just how $exy she was this early in the morning, god she was turning me on so badly and all she did was smile! I really am in some deep $hit with this mating.

"Hey shortie, you sleep ok?" I asked brushing her hair away from her face, she nodded and pressed herself closer to me.

"Yep, you?" she asked grinning happily.

I nodded "Best nights sleep ever" I said honestly.

She laughed "Yeah did I wear you out?" she asked teasingly, I grinned, wear me out? Yeah ok, I didn't tell her that I could have kept going all night, she really had a lot to learn about shifters!

"Yeah shortie you wore me out" I said kissing her gently, she kissed me back wrapping her arms around my neck pulling me closer. $hit I just can't get enough of her! I really need to remember that she's half human and I needed to take it easy with her body, it was so hard to let her rest when all I wanted to do was ravage her twenty four hours a day!

After another hour in bed we got up, I pulled on my boxers and she threw on my t-shirt and her panties, I groaned, damn she looks sexy as hell in my clothes! "I'm hungry, do you have any food in the house Jay?" she asked looking at me hopefully.

I grabbed her hand and pulled her downstairs, "What's your favourite breakfast?" I asked curiously praying that I had whatever it was.

She shrugged "I don't usually eat much breakfast so anything you have will be fine" she said casually.

"Yeah you don't like to eat in the mornings?" I asked as I led her to the kitchen pulling out a stool for her to sit on.

She laughed "You're such a damn gentleman Jay, opening car doors, pulling out chairs, what's next? Laying your jacket in a puddle so I don't get my feet wet?" she asked teasingly.

I shook my head, "Why ruin a jacket? I'd just carry you over" I said shrugging making her laugh. I made French toast for breakfast and she ate three slices, so much for not eating much in the mornings!

"So what do you think it's going to be like meeting your pack today?" she asked.

"Our pack" I corrected.

She laughed "Yeah ok, Alpha Phillips, I'm sure I'll have a lot to do with a pack" she said sarcastically. I frowned, she had no idea how a mating worked, part of me was glad that she didn't realise the power she had over me but the other part of me felt guilty, maybe I should explain it to her. I didn't think she was one to start demanding things or changes but whatever she asked for she'd get, in a way this was really her pack more than it was mine. I'd be the one to make the decisions and run it, but if she needed something then it would be done end of story.

"Shortie, it's your pack too, I need your help and support to run it, your opinions matter to me" I said honestly. She smiled looking at me tenderly, my heart was starting to beat faster at the soft loving look she was giving me right now, it made me feel like the only guy in the world.

"Well what do you think it's gonna be like meeting our pack today then?" she asked looking at me curiously cocking her head to the side, instinctively my eyes dropped to the collar of the t-shirt she was wearing and the red mark on her neck, I shivered slightly. $hit that mark was so freaking $exy!

$hit Jay she's waiting for an answer, stop staring! "Um I have no idea, hopefully it'll be ok, I just hope that your father doesn't get too much of a hard time for not being true to his mate" I said honestly. She got up out of her chair and walked round the counter to me, I twisted in my chair to face her as she climbed up onto my lap wrapping her arms around my neck.

She buried her face in my neck, "I hope he's ok" she said quietly, I kissed the side of her head as I rubbed my hands down her back.

"He'll be fine shortie, don't worry, and by the way, OUR pack is gonna love you" I said honestly.

How the hell could they not love someone like her? Full shifter or not, she was just so damn adorable and kind, and she was so strong, typical Alpha female, not physically strong like a shifter but emotionally strong. She let Trey do that to her for years to protect her mother, she would have stayed with him forever to save her mother, she'd have to be strong to not be a broken wounded girl right now. "Our packs going to love you too Alpha Phillips" she mumbled as she bit my shoulder making me moan. She really did know how to tease the crap out of me!

I finally managed to prise myself off of her at 11am and we drove over to Scott's to pick up Beth ready to go to the barbeque. I'd phoned Dom and he said it was probably a good idea that she go in case people wanted to meet her being as she was the one he cheated with. I gripped Brook's hand as we headed into Scott's to get her Mom.

"Hey Jay, I was thinking I'd come to yours about half past six tonight in case there's anything you need help with before we go to the field" Scott said looking at Brook who went stiff when he mentioned tonight.

She didn't want us to go, she was worried about us getting hurt, but to be honest there wasn't much chance of that. We had surprise, numbers and skills on our side. Trey was gonna be easy to take down, I should have just finished him off at Brook's yesterday when I had the chance. I should have just ignored her clinging to me and begging me like that and jumped out of that window and ripped him to pieces, it would have been easy.

I wrapped my arm around her "Yeah great man, half past six is fine" I said nodding, Scott really was the best friend a guy could ask for. I really wish I could ask him to be my second, he deserved it, he wasn't even of age for another month but he was ready for it. When I took Willow Creak from my father I would definitely make him my second.

Beth was saying her goodbyes to Scott's parents, Brook was chatting with Mel in whispers and my god I wanted to know what they were talking about, I wondered if they were talking about me. If I listened would that be an invasion of privacy? I laughed at myself, I really am obsessed.

"What's funny?" Scott asked grinning.

I shook my head "I am so whipped" I admitted laughing.

He punched me on the shoulder rolling his eyes, "Jayden Phillips pus$y whipped, never thought I'd see the day" he said laughing.

I grinned, "Me either" I said shrugging.

When Beth was finally ready we left making our way over to Dom's house, luckily Beth knew the way as we were short on time and getting lost and being late to my own introduction wouldn't be a very good impression! We pulled up and ten to twelve but there was already a lot of people here, probably at least a hundred, crap this pack was bigger than I thought! It must be almost the same size as Willow Creak. I held Brook tightly to my side as we walked in through the house, people we smiling and nodding respectfully as we walked past. Damn this was so freaking weird!

I spotted Dom in the kitchen pulling out plate after plate of meat to put on the barbeque. "Alpha Phillips, Brook, Beth" he said nodding respectfully.

"Alpha Logan, how are you?" I asked holding out my hand to him.

He laughed "I'm good, and it's just Dom now" he said grinning as he shook my hand. He kissed the girls and turned back to me, "I told them this morning, I asked everyone here from eleven to get it out of the way before you came, I hope that's ok" he said almost apologetically.

I nodded "I would have helped you, did everything go ok?" I asked curiously, I knew his pack would give him shit for cheating on his mate and I wanted to be here to help him and calm the crowd if needed.

He laughed "Alpha, Bane's Creak is an awesome pack, we're very close, more like a family, families forgive mistakes, everything was fine, they're excited to see you" he said looking pleased.

I grinned and breathed a sigh of relief, I thought I would be fighting with them to banish him from the pack, I thought they would challenge my decision. "Dom, you can call me Jayden or Jay" I said laughing at just how ridiculous Alpha sounded when applied to me, I just couldn't get used to it. I actually liked the sound of it from Brook's mouth though, but only because she told me it was a turn on.

He grinned "I guess I should if you're mated to my daughter" he said shrugging, I kissed Brook trying my best to ignore the taste of her on my lips and the way her mouth fitted perfectly against mine.

Pete came over grinning, "Alpha Philips, good to see you, I know you said you didn't want to ask for the help of your pack but I was speaking to few of the high rankers and they want to come with us tonight" he said almost apologetically.

Shit, they did? "Really?" I asked a little shocked, maybe this was a good pack.

He nodded "Yeah, they want to protect their Alpha and his mate" he said smiling at Brook warmly. She smiled back, I sighed I really didn't want them to have to do this for me, I'd been Alpha for less than a day and already they were having to risk their lives!

"Ok well I'll talk to them later, see how it goes" I said trying to think of a way I could say 'thanks but no thanks' without hurting anyone's feelings or anything.

"Come on, Pete why don't you put this food on the barbeque I'll introduce Jayden to everyone" Dom said holding out a huge plate of sausages and burgers.

Beth grabbed another one off of the side, "I'll help you put it on, I'm not needed right Jay?" Beth asked hopefully. She was nervous at being the 'other woman' she said in the car she didn't want people to hate her, but it was a long time ago, and technically she didn't do anything wrong anyway.

"Yeah, your not needed Beth don't worry" I said smiling reassuringly at her, she sighed seeming to relax as she followed Pete out of the back door into the garden.

Dom smiled "Ready?" he asked, I nodded and grabbed Brook's hand as we followed him out into the garden. His garden was huge, it backed right onto the woods and he's taken down the fences so people were just milling around everywhere. The were so many people, probably close to a hundred and fifty men, women and children all standing watching our every move. Holy crap this is a big pack! Brook stiffened next to me, her hand squeezing mine so tight I was a little worried she'd hurt herself. I shook her hand lightly trying to get her to loosen her grip as we walked behind Dom to the little patio area.

"Calm down shortie" I whispered, she nodded and put on a fake smile.

"Ok guys, so after my announcement earlier, I'm proud to introduce you to your new Alpha, Alpha Jayden Phillips" Dom said loudly grinning at me. Oh f*ck my life! People started clapping and cheering, I held up a hand to stop them and everyone was quiet instantly. $hit that was awesome! I smiled a little overwhelmed at the power I had over these people that they would just instantly stop talking like that with the raise of my hand.

"Hey it's nice to meet you all, I look forward to talking to you all individually, I know you're probably worried about what having a new Alpha will mean for you, but basically I don't want to change anything, Alpha Logan and I will sit down and talk about how he ran the pack and I'll try my best to stick to the things that work for everyone" I said honestly. I didn't want to come in and disrupt everyone's lives.

I pulled Brook a little closer to me, "This is my mate Brook Mills, your Alpha female, I want everyone to know that although Brook isn't a full shifter she is still Alpha female by blood and by mating and I expect people to respect that" I said sternly.

"Jayden don't" Brook whispered gripping my arm blushing like crazy, I smiled at her, I needed to get our pack to respect her. No one would dare disrespect a normal Alpha female but I didn't want people thinking they could get away with anything because she couldn't shift.

"Ok shortie, I'm done" I said nodding reassuringly at her. I turned back to the crowd "So Alpha Logan's laid on some awesome food and stuff, and Brook and I will be happy to meet anyone, but I am really bad with names so please forgive me if I have to ask you a couple of times what your name is" I said grimacing slightly, people chuckled in the crowd. "Does anyone have anything they want to ask or anything while we're all together?" I asked curiously. It would probably be easier to get this all out of the way instead of repeating it a hundred times.

A couple of hands went up in the crowd, I smiled and pointed to a guy in his mid thirties, "Yeah um, I was just wondering, if you'll be staying in the area, Alpha Logan mentioned you were in college" he asked.

"Yeah I'll be transferring closer to here so I can be near my pack and my mate" I said nodding, I pointed to a lady who had her hand up.

"Will you still be running monthly meetings?" she asked.

I nodded "Yeah monthly meetings, I'll probably call the first next week after I've spent a little time with Alpha Logan" I said looking at him.

"Dom" he said grinning.

"Right" I said laughing, I keep forgetting that!

"Will you be changing the high rankers? Bringing in some people from your old pack?" a guy asked curiously.

I shook my head, "No, as long as the people that were Dom's high rankers are happy to be mine then I don't see there will be a problem" I said frowning. I really needed to speak to Scott and make sure that this was ok with him. I know that he always thought he would be my second too and I didn't want him to be disappointed or angry with me.

There were a few more questions, people wanted to know how old we were, how long we had been mated, they wanted to know about my father and my Alpha blood and lots of other tedious questions. I answered everything honestly, it was easier to just get this all out of the way now. After about twenty minutes the questions were done and I was starving! "So guys, let's eat and we can start to get to know people better" I said eyeing the barbeque longingly.

I smiled at Brook as people started to talk amongst themselves, "Did I do ok shortie?" I whispered wrapping my arms around her tightly.

She grinned, "You did excellent Alpha Philips" she whispered back making a shiver run down my back. I kissed her gently pulling away before I couldn't.

"Lets get some food, I'm starving and maybe your Mom will need a hand" I said looking over at the crowd of people all milling around her getting food. She nodded and I led her towards the food eagerly. We didn't get very far, we were stopped every foot of the way to meet people, it seemed like every single person was just taking it in turns to talk to us.

After an hour of talking we were still only half way to the food, Dom came over and handed me and Brook a burger each slapping me on the back amused. Oh thank god! We continued to talk to people while I inhaled my burger making Brook laugh at me. Everyone seemed really nice and were really welcoming and friendly.

A little girl of about four ran over and tripped in front of us, Brook immediately bent down and picked her up. "Hey, you ok sweetie?" she asked rubbing the little girls knee. The little girl started to cry and shook her head. "Does you knee hurt?" Brook asked soothingly, the little girl nodded. Brook smiled and kissed her fingers before rubbing the little girls knee. "There all better right? That was a magic kiss, I learnt it from my Mom" Brook said smiling at her as she sat down next to her.

"Really?" the little girl asked wiping her face, Brook nodded smiling making the little girl smile back.

I could see her parents looking at us unsure whether to approach or not, probably intimidated thinking she was in trouble or something. They made their way over timidly, "What's your name sweetie?" Brook asked as she plopped herself in Brooks lap.

"Isabelle" she said playing with Brooks hair.

"That's a pretty name" Brook said smiling happily, God she'll make a good mom!

"I'm sorry" Isabelle's Mom said looking horrified.

I sat down next to Brook, "Don't be sorry, it's fine, don't worry" I said honestly. "So Isabelle how old are you?" I asked.

She grinned "Four and a half" she said proudly.

"Really? Is that all? I would have said you were at least five" I said jokingly, she grinned at me proudly. We chatted with her parents for a while and in the end a group of about twenty kids and mom's were all hanging around chatting to Brook.

I glanced over to Pete who waved me over and pointed to a group of guys standing near him, I nodded and turned back to Brook. "Shortie, I just need to go talk to some people ok?" I asked, she nodded and gripped the front of my shirt pulling me closer so she could kiss me. I kissed her back softly very aware that my new pack were all watching so I didn't want to get too into it. "I'll be right back, you want anything? Drink? Food?" I asked.

"I'd love a soft drink" she said smiling her $exy smile, I couldn't resist kissing her again before I got up.

I made my way over to Pete, dodging people and promising to be right back when people stopped me. "Hey, everything ok?" I asked him as I grabbed another burger eating it in four bites.

"Yeah, the high rankers want to talk to you about tonight" he said nodding over to the group of about ten guys sitting down chatting. I sighed and nodded making my way over to them, Pete followed me over.

"Hey guys" I said sitting down with them. Then all bowed their heads respectfully but to be honest I was getting used to it now, people had been doing it to me since we arrived a couple of hours ago. "I'm sorry I haven't had a chance to come and talk to any of you yet" I said honestly, they all smiled.

"We kinda hung back so you could meet the rest of the pack, there'll be plenty of time for us to get to know each other" one guy said.

I grinned "Thanks, I appreciate it, so you guys want to tell me your names and rank?" I asked looking round at them.

They were all a lot older than me, mostly in their early forties, I tried my best to memorise their names as I went round them. The most important were my top four, I already knew Pete pretty well and he seemed like a nice guy. Rick was my third, Spence my fourth.

"So about tonight" Rick said raising his eyebrows at me expectantly, I shook my head, I didn't want them to come, I couldn't ask that of them on my first day.

"It's fine guys, I have seventeen coming with me from Willow Creek, I can't ask you guys to do that for me" I said sternly.

They all looked a little pis$ed off, "Alpha, we're your high rankers, if your going to fight we need to be with you" Rick said fiercely, I looked round at them all, they all had the same expression, determination and annoyance.

"Guys I appreciate the offer, but I don't want to ask you to do that, I don't want my first responsibility as Alpha to be to come in and ask you to fight for me and my mate, none of this is your problem, I can sort it" I said honestly.

"Alpha, it IS our problem, were a close pack, we want to come with you, you don't need to ask for support for it to be there, it will always be there" Spence said sternly. I smiled, they really were nice guys, I looked at Pete, he nodded in agreement. I couldn't really say no to that.

"Ok well thanks, we're meeting at a field in Willow Creek territory at ten, maybe you could travel with Pete and Dom, they know where it is" I said.

Pete nodded, Dom came and sat down next to me, he'd been hovering on the edge of the group looking like he didn't want to intrude or something. "Actually Alpha, I was thinking I'd come back with you when you leave, maybe spend some time with Brook and Beth" he said looking at me hopefully.

"Sure Dom, that'd be fine, and I told you to call me Jayden, you can all call me Jayden" I said smiling, they all nodded. "I better get back to Brook, thank you guys, I'll see you tonight and then we can maybe have a meeting in the week so I could get to know you all better, sort out anything that needs sorting" I said standing up, they all stood and bowed their heads again. "I'll see you tonight" I said a little uncomfortably but trying desperately not to show it, I thought I was getting used to the whole bowing thing but apparently not!

I grabbed two cokes from the cooler and headed back over to my angel who was still sitting there chatting happily with a bunch of women whilst making a daisy chain with Isabelle. God I loved that girl so much, watching her with that little girl I couldn't help but hope she was carrying my pup, but I knew that it would be better for us to wait a couple of years. She hadn't even finished school, I didn't want to take any opportunities away from her because she was pregnant or anything. I sat down behind her scooting forward so her back was pressed against my chest and breathed in her beautiful smell.

"Hey, everything ok?" she asked pressing into me.

I wrapped my arms around her "Mmm Hmm" I mumbled against the back of her head. Everything was fine now that I was back at her side.

After another hour the barbeque started to wind down, by the time everyone left and I had passed out my number to everyone in case of emergencies it was almost five thirty. "We better go shortie, Scott's coming in a bit" I said brushing her hair away from her face.

She nodded, "I'm ready when you are" she said nodding.

"Dom, I better go, Scott's coming at half past six" I called.

He nodded "I'm now done, I'll finish this tomorrow" he said throwing the last of the rubbish in the bin.

I led Brook out to my car opening her door for her, "Hey you waited" I said laughing as she stood there waiting for me to open her door.

She grinned "I remembered" she said rolling her eyes.

I shut her door, "You coming in my car or following?" I asked Dom.

"I'll follow in a couple of minutes, I'll bring Beth I just want to put the rest of the food in the fridge and stuff " he called heading into the house with a plate of food.

I held Brook's hand on the way back to mine, I was really happy, the pack were great, they seemed to love her to pieces which was the most important thing in the world to me. When we pulled up I jogged round to get her door, she was so breath-taking, honestly the most beautiful thing in my world. "Thank you Alpha Philips" she said teasingly biting her lip, I stopped breathing, I knew her hormones were raging, I could tell by the look on her face. I didn't need to smell it to know what she was thinking right now.

I felt my wolf rejoicing at the thought of her naked body. I pressed my body against hers and pushed her against the car gently as I kissed her. God she tasted amazing, kissing her seemed to get better and better every time. I heard Dom's car pull up but I couldn't break the kiss, I could have a few more seconds. I felt a sharp pain in the back of my neck, "Ow $hit" I said pulling back and rubbing my neck. There was something there, at the back of my neck, I pulled it off and looked at it. It was a little silver thing, no bigger than a thimble with a needle point at one end.

"What's that?" Brook asked looking at it curiously, my head was swimming. What the hell IS that? My throat was getting dry, I glanced up to see Dom walking towards us, I saw him flinch and clutch the side of his throat pulling his hand away looking at something confused.

Suddenly it dawned on me. Oh my f*cking God! Trey's here! I shoved Brook against the car roughly spinning around, someone had shot me with something. I tried to shift but I couldn't. F*cking $hit! I tried again but I definitely couldn't shift. My head was swimming, my vision getting a little blurry, I was vaguely aware of Brook squirming behind me, "Jayden what the hell's going on?" she asked scared. I needed to get her the hell out of here, he was here, he'd shot me with something to stop me shifting. I couldn't protect her, I could barely stand. I was going to watch her die and there was nothing I could do about it.

I grabbed my keys from my pocket with shaky hands, my whole body was getting weak, I fought with everything in me to stay upright. I glanced at Dom just as he collapsed to the floor. "Go Brook, go now" I gasped trying to stay on my feet. I was so damn tired and dizzy, she was holding me tightly I could tell she was crying.

"Jayden? Oh god please, are you ok?" she asked desperately. I used the last of my strength to turn around and wrenched open the car door.

"GO NOW!" I shouted throwing the keys at her leaning against the car for support. Oh God shortie please get away, please. I tried again and again to shift but I couldn't even feel my wolf, it was like it just wasn't there. "GO!" I shouted fiercely knowing I couldn't protect her, I was going to pass out any second.

"Wow you are a strong one huh? I shot you with enough tranquilliser to take down a small elephant yet you're still on your feet" Trey said laughing, I spun around and pushed myself away from the car willing myself not to fall over. My legs felt like jelly, I was so f*cking angry but I couldn't do anything, he was grinning from ear to ear.

"I'm gonna rip you to pieces" I growled. I couldn't stand anymore, I fell to my knees vaguely aware of Brook screaming, everything was closing in around me, my whole body was going numb.

He laughed "You don't seem to be in a very good position to be making threats" he sneered at me. I tried again to shift but nothing, this was it, she was dead. I watched as his foot came up and smashed into my face, I didn't even have time to feel it before I was unconscious.

CHAPTER 21

Brook's POV

Jayden let go of my hand grinning as he jumped out of the car and ran round to my side to get my door, God he is so damn adorable, I wonder how long he'll be like this. I mean Trey was great to start with, I wonder how long he'll think I'm the most special girl in the world for. He smiled his sexy smile as he opened the door for me. Jeez he did it again, how the hell does he keep making me want him like this? The physical attraction for him was just crazy!

"Thank you Alpha Philips" I said trying not to think too many lustful thoughts, my parents were due here any minute we didn't have time for me to get all hot and steamy so I didn't want him to know how I was feeling. I didn't like to tease him, I knew he could smell my hormones when I was aroused.

It was too late, he already knew, a look of lust crossed his handsome face as he pushed me against the car pressing his whole perfect body to mine. He kissed me softly making my heart beat faster, I gripped his shirt so he couldn't pull away, oh God I loved him more than anything. Suddenly he pulled out of the kiss, "Ow shit" he said rubbing his neck, I looked at him curiously as he pulled his hand away from his neck and looked at it. There was a little silver thing in his hand.

"What's that?" I asked. Where the hell did he get that from? He just looked at it confused, he looked over and I saw Dom walking towards us suddenly I was slammed against the car with Jayden's back pressing against me so hard it was actually hurting.

I squirmed trying to get out from behind him, god he was so heavy! He was looking round tense but seeming like he was unsteady on his feet, what is he doing? "Jayden what the hell's going on?" I asked getting scared as he swayed slightly. I wrapped my arms around his waist trying to help him, was he sick or something? I could feel the panic rising in my chest, something was wrong with him, he needed a doctor. I looked over at my Mom about to shout her to help him when I noticed she was looking at Dom worriedly, he way swaying on his feet too, clutching his knees for support. What the hell is happening? Dom collapsed and I couldn't keep the tears from falling, shit something bad has happened and I didn't even know what!

I turned my attention back to Jayden trying to push him away from me so I could help him but he'd trapped me against the car, I couldn't move an inch. "Go Brook, go now" he gasped his voice husky and scared. Go? What the hell is he talking about?

"Jayden? Oh God please, are you ok?" I asked trying to hold him up as he seemed to be on the verge of falling over.

He pulled away from me quickly and yanked open the car door, "GO NOW!" he shouted as he threw the keys at me, I was too shocked to catch them so they fell to the floor, the look on his face scared the shit out of me. He was terrified, he was pale and sweating slightly, his whole body was shaking.

What the hell is he talking about, go? Go where? Why? "GO!" he shouted again when I didn't move.

Then I saw him, Trey was walking out of the trees with three of his boys. Oh shit! I could feel the panic trying to take over. Trey was going to hurt Jayden and Jayden was sick! He couldn't defend himself, shit what the hell do I do? I desperately tried to think of something but Jayden was just getting paler and paler leaning against the car looking like he was struggling to stand. He was begging me with his eyes to leave him, he wanted me to go on my own, he knew Trey was here that's why he said go. I was frozen on the spot, I wouldn't leave him, I'd never leave him.

Trey smiled at me before turning his attention to Jayden's back, "Wow you are a strong one huh? I shot you with enough tranquilliser to take down a small elephant yet your still on your feet" he said laughing. Jayden stiffened and turned around quickly moving back in front of me again, the silly boy was trying to stay between me and Trey but he was swaying looking like he was going to fall over.

"I'm gonna rip you to pieces" he growled menacingly, oh God why isn't he shifting to protect himself like last time?

He fell to his knees and I stopped breathing, I was going to have a heart attack, if Trey hurt Jayden it was going to kill me. Trey took a few steps towards Jayden's unsteady figure, I didn't even realise I was screaming until my throat started to hurt. Trey laughed and the sound of it made my blood run cold, he sneered at Jayden like he was a piece of trash, "You don't seem to be in a very good position to be making threats" he said angrily. I knew this was bad by the look on Trey's face, we were all going to die, the only thing I could do was try and get him to let Jay go somehow. He raised his foot and kicked Jay full in the face making him slump to the floor instantly.

I looked up at Trey my heart breaking, he drew back his foot and kicked Jay in the stomach hard.

"TREY!" I screamed pushing myself away from the car, oh god please stop this! He kicked him again before his face snapped up to mine and softened slightly, "Please stop" I whispered. I heard my Mom screaming at me to stay away from him, but I couldn't, I needed to help Jay, I couldn't let him hurt him. "Please Trey, please" I begged as I reached him, I tried not to look at Jayden's limp and lifeless body on the floor, I needed to stay strong. If Trey knew how much I loved Jay he'd be dead, no doubt about it.

He reached out his hand and touched my face softly, "Hey baby" he said stepping closer to me.

"Hey" I whispered not trusting my voice to speak, I could feel the bile rise in my throat as he touched me. His hand pulled away and he slapped me so hard that I thought my head had exploded. I fell to the floor next to Jayden, I almost screamed when I looked at his face, it was covered in blood, a cut across the bridge of his nose. Oh God Jay please be ok! I could see his chest rise, he was still breathing, I reached for his hand.

Trey grabbed me and pulled me up, I could barely see him through the tears in my eyes, my face was throbbing. "I'm sorry baby, are you ok?" Trey asked pulling me to his chest hugging me tightly, he's sorry, is he fucking kidding me?

"Are we ready to go?" Dan asked Trey, he nodded.

"Yeah, call Lee and Jason and tell them to bring the cars" Trey said stroking the side of my head. Cars? He's taking us somewhere? Oh God please let him just leave Jay and my Mom here! I heard Dan talking on the phone but all I could focus on was the sound of my Mom screaming at me. I looked over at her, one of Trey's boys was holding her tightly while she kicked and screamed trying to get free.

A van and a car pulled up skidding to a stop a few feet from us, a couple of Trey's other boys jumped out of the back heading towards Jayden's body on the floor. I stiffened, they were taking him?

"Trey, just take me, leave them please, I'll come with you, please" I begged watching as they pushed my Mom towards the car.

He laughed "Ok baby, whatever you say" he said laughing as he nodded at his boys, two of them searched Jayden's pockets taking his cell then picked him up and threw him roughly into the back of the van.

"Please!" I begged clinging to him tightly, he just ignored me.

"Take Logan too" Trey said nodding towards Dom.

"Why are you taking them?" I asked desperately.

He sighed and turned back to me, "Because you need to learn not to disrespect me and to do as you're fucking told, you're mine, you're supposed to be mine" he growled angrily as he gripped my arm tightly shoving me towards the car. "Get in" he said sternly, how the hell am I gonna save Jay if he won't even listen to me?

"Trey please, I won't disrespect you again, please I'm so sorry, just take me and leave them alone, please I'll do anything" I begged sobbing.

He grabbed me and kissed me hard hurting my lips with how much force he put into it, I squeezed my eyes shut trying not to heave. He pulled out of the kiss and pushed me towards his car so hard that I fell and slammed my chest into the seat knocking my breath out of me. "Brook get in the fucking car NOW!" he shouted making me flinch.

I nodded and climbed in scooting over to my Mom who was crying hysterically. "It's ok, everything's gonna be ok" I lied soothingly as I hugged her tight. I couldn't think of a single plan, not a single thing that would help us all out of this situation. Jayden, my Mom and Dom were all gonna die because of me and by the look on Trey's face it wouldn't be painless and quick either.

After twenty minutes of driving we pulled into Trey's drive, my Mom was still sobbing, I kept my eyes firmly fixed on the van in front of us watching for any signs of Jayden. I couldn't see him get hurt, this was killing me and it was all my fault. Trey came to my door and gripped my arm pulling me out of the car roughly, I grabbed my Mom's hand keeping her close behind me as he led me through the familiar house. It felt like I hadn't been here in years but in all honesty I had stayed here on Friday night so that was only two nights ago.

"Sit down Beth" Trey ordered pointing to a chair that one of his boys had brought from the dining room and placed in the middle of the living room. She looked at me desperately, I nodded, we needed to go along with whatever he said for now, I needed to keep him sweet until I could think of something.

"Why are you doing this?" she asked angrily, he took a step towards her.

I stepped in front of him quickly "Please don't hurt her, please" I begged pushing her towards the chair.

He sighed "Fine, now get in the fucking chair Beth or I swear to God I'm gonna hurt you, I don't care what Brook says" he growled angrily making my Mom flinch. She wasn't used to seeing that face, he was always nice to her, it was probably a shock to her seeing him like this.

She sat down just as four other guys came in carrying Jayden and Dom, they were both still unconscious. My Mom started crying hysterically again and I tried desperately not to react, I couldn't let Trey know how much power he had over me. I watched horrified as they tied them to a chair, Jayden was slumped over blood dripping slowly from his chin, his lip was split and I would imagine that was from being thrown into the van roughly. They tied their wrists to the arms of the chairs with leather straps.

My Mom was wailing loudly, Dan slapped her hard across the face. "Shut the fuck up! You're making my head hurt with all that fucking crying!" he shouted. She bit her lip and closed her eyes trying to calm herself, I heard Trey laugh quietly.

I looked at him horrified. Suddenly he pushed me against the wall bending his head and running his nose along my jaw. "You smell like that fucker" he growled angrily, he grabbed my hair and yanked my head to the side making my whimper as pain shot through my scalp. He pulled my top to the side and growled as he looked Jay's mark on my neck, he ran his finger across it and I tried not to flinch as I started to feel sick. "Why could he mate you and I couldn't?" he asked angrily.

I gulped "The bloodlines, he said something about Alpha blood" I gasped as he pulled my hair harder.

He growled again, "Bloodlines? Like when an Alpha is passed down through generations?" he asked frowning. I tried to nod but his grip tightened on my hair making me yelp.

"Yes" I croaked.

"So you're mated to a bloodline Alpha" he said turning his nose up, I tried desperately to think of something, the only thing I could think of was to play up my human side.

"No not really, Trey please, your hurting me" I said holding his wrist trying to get him to let go of my hair, he looked at me interested and finally let go.

"What do you mean not really?" he asked, I pressed myself to him, hating myself but I'd do anything to keep Jay safe, anything.

"It didn't work, not properly, I'm not a full shifter, I don't love him Trey, I love you, I'll always love you" I lied pulling him closer to me. He looked at me and I tried to look like I wasn't disgusted with myself right now, that I wasn't feeling sick saying these words to him. I was so glad Jayden was unconscious so that he couldn't hear these lies I was saying.

"You still love me?" Trey asked looking at me hopefully as he put his hands on my hips.

I nodded "Of course I do Trey, we've been together for four years, I've always loved you, always" I said pulling him closer.

He pulled my hips against him, "I was ready to kill you if you said you loved him" he growled, my breath caught in my throat.

"He's nothing to me Trey, you should just let them all go, you don't need to prove anything to me, I promise I'll never do anything like this ever again, you should just punish me if you need to, but please don't hurt them, none of this is their fault, it's mine" I begged running my hands down his chest and hooking my fingers in his belt loops trying to look seductive. I think it was working, his face softened and his eyes flicked down to my lips, my heart started to beat faster as I started to hope. It was working, he was gonna let them go!

"Hey! The son of a bitch is waking up already!" Dan said sounding shocked, I flinched as Trey's hands tightened on hips digging his fingers into me. He turned to look and I stepped to the side so I could see too, Jayden had his eyes squeezed shut, his hands in fists, looking like he was concentrating really hard on something.

Trey started to laugh, "You can't shift if that's what you're trying" he said, Dan laughed too. Jayden opened his eyes his face still looking a little dazed, he looked like he was having trouble staying awake. His gaze slid to me and a pained terrified expression crossed his face. Maybe he was hoping I'd got away, knowing him he was probably hoping I'd left him to die on his own, stupid damn overprotective boy!

"Brook, go please" Jayden begged his voice sounding croaky and husky, he was fighting to get out of his chair that he was tied to, but the straps they used were like leather strips, he wasn't getting them undone anytime soon.

Trey bounded forward and punched him repeatedly in the face, I ran forward and grabbed his arm, I couldn't see anymore, every blow felt like he was cutting my heart out. He span round and slapped me hard across the face again, it hurt worse than before because my cheek was already sore. I fell to the floor as Trey turned back and started punching Jay in chest and stomach making him grunt and groan with each blow.

"You don't talk to her again you little shit" Trey shouted angrily in his face. I looked at my Mom she was staring with her eyes wide, maybe she was in shock or something, Dom was still unconscious. There was no hope, no one was coming to help, no one even knew there was anything wrong. We were all going to die.

Trey stepped away from Jay and gripped my wrist yanking me to my feet making pain shoot up my arm where he pulled it so hard. He shoved me towards Jayden gripping the back of my hair shoving my face inches from Jay's. "Tell him you don't love him" he growled his hand tightening in my hair making me yelp and grip his wrist trying to relieve the pressure. I looked at Jayden, his beautiful face was covered in blood, it was bruised, his lip and nose were split and swollen. God I loved him so much, he was killing me, looking at him like that was killing me inside. I couldn't say it, I clamped my jaw tight, I couldn't say it right in his face like that, he nodded slightly urging me to do it pleading me with his eyes.

I closed my eyes not wanting to watch his face as I said the words that were the biggest lie anyone had ever told. "I don't love you Jayden, I love Trey" I said.

Trey yanked me up by my hair, "Don't fucking hurt her!" Jayden shouted angrily squeezing his fists so tight his knuckles went white as bone.

Trey sneered at him, "I told you, you can't shift, the drug I shot you with is something we've been working on, it's a paralytic, it's very effective on shifters, you can't even feel your wolf right now can you?" Trey asked smiling a wicked smile.

Jayden started thrashing in his chair again, his wrists turning red as they rubbed on the straps. "I'm gonna fucking kill you, I swear to God, I'm gonna rip your heart right out of your chest and show it to you before you die" Jayden growled angrily. Trey punched him hard in the face making his head snap back, I couldn't watch this anymore. I needed to get him the hell out of here before he pissed Trey off so badly that he'd be dead. I couldn't watch him die.

"Trey hon, just stop, you've made your point, he doesn't matter" I said dismissively, I wrapped my arms around his waist, he took a deep breath and stepped back puling me with him. He kissed me hard biting my lip hard enough to draw blood, when I gasped he shoved his tongue in my mouth holding the back of my head so I couldn't get away. I squeezed my eyes shut and kissed him back pulling him closer. I heard Jayden groan but I didn't stop, when Trey pulled back I pulled his face back to mine again. By the time he pulled back a second time we were both breathless, I didn't look in Jay's direction, I couldn't see the look of devastation and jealousy that I knew I'd see there.

"Let them go Trey and take me upstairs, I've missed you" I said fighting the urge to be sick. I heard Jayden struggling in his chair again and I prayed to God that he just stayed quiet this time and let me try.

"How about I take you upstairs right now? I've missed you too" he said running his hands down my sides gripping my ass.

I shook my head, "Not like this, I don't like this, please, just let them go and I'll do anything you want, anything" I said raising my eyebrows suggestively on the word anything.

A small smile crossed his face, "How about I make you a deal, I'll let one of them go, you can choose" he said shrugging. That's easy, Jayden.

"Why not all of them?" I asked gripping his shirt.

"One, choose now" he said sternly, Jayden definitely, I loved my mother so much but if I had to choose it would be Jayden, there was no other option for me, that was the only choice I could live with.

"Let Jayden go" I said shrugging.

Trey laughed and rolled his eyes, "I can't let that fucker go, he'll run straight to his pack and come back to rip my head off" he said amused by the thought.

"But you said I could choose" I said trying not to panic, he cupped my face in his hands.

"If you don't love him then why do you want me to let him go?" he asked his face turning hard making me flinch. Shit that backfired! Think Brook, think!

"Because I don't think you'll hurt my Mom or my Dad, I think Jayden's the only one that's in danger here and I don't want anyone to get hurt because of me, I don't love him Trey" I lied hoping my voice sounded true. He pulled out a gun pointing it at Jayden whilst watching my face. I stopped breathing, my heart crashing in my chest. I kept my face neutral, at least I hope I did. Please let this be a bluff, please let this be a bluff, please let this be a bluff. I shrugged, my eyes not leaving Trey's.

He smiled and lowered his gun, I must have passed the test, I felt the panic start to recede slightly. "Choose either your Mom or Dad to go free" he said quietly.

"My Mom" I said quickly, Dom was still unconscious, I prayed he would understand when he woke up and found out I had chosen my Mom's freedom over his, I think he would.

Trey smiled and raised the gun again, "Say bye to Daddy Brook" he said grinning. What the hell? He wouldn't. He turned to look at Dom and shot him right in the face.

CHAPTER 22

Scott's POV

I pulled up outside Jay's a little before half past six, his car was there so at least he was back from the barbeque already, mind you I had a key anyway so it's not like I would have been waiting outside for him. I jumped out and walked to the door, it was open already. "Jay? Brook?" I called as I let myself in. Jay's stuff was everywhere, literally, everything that should be in a cupboard or drawer was now over the floor, his sofa was on it's side the table smashed up. What the fuck? I tensed ready to shift, I backed up against the wall listening to see if there was anyone in the house, I couldn't hear anything at all.

I snapped open my phone and called him quickly, what the hell's happened? Had he been robbed or something? I ran round the house as I listened to his phone go straight to voice mail. "Jay, what the hell's happened at your house man? Seriously call me as soon as you get this" I said snapping the phone shut, I tried Brook then her Mom but they all went straight to voice mail. The house was empty, there was a smell I didn't recognise, I didn't know the person that had been here.

I made my way outside, "JAY" I shouted hoping he would hear if he was in the woods or something. His car was here he couldn't be far, I glanced up at his car and noticed the passenger door was open, I'd parked on the other side so I didn't notice before. Why the hell would he leave his door open? I jogged over to see that he'd even left the keys to his house and car just lying on the ground.

This was seriously weird, had something happened? SHIT! Trey's been here I'd bet my life on it! I grabbed my phone and called my Dad, as I ran back to my car, I had no idea where this Trey guy lived. My Dad answered just as I was about to give up, I pulled out of the drive and sped back down the road, "Dad, something's happened, I've just been to Jay's and he's not there, the place is a mess, I think Trey's been there, I can't find Jay or Brook" I said desperately as I floored the gas pedal.

"What? Shit! We need to go there, where are you now?" he asked.

"I'm going to Christian's I don't think where this fucker lives, I'll pick up Christian and I'll come and get you" I said snapping the phone shut. Shit this was bad, this was really bad. If Trey had Jay and Brook, they'd probably be dead already from what Jay said he was threatening to do to them. But we needed to try, he was my best friend. I pulled up at Christian's praying he'd be home.

Jayden's POV

"Say bye to Daddy Brook" Trey said sneering at her as he raised the gun to point at Dom, she was looking at him shocked, she didn't think he would do it. He looked round and shot Dom right in the face, the sound of the gun made me jump slightly and I started thrashing in the chair again. Brook screamed a shrill agonising scream that ripped my heart out, she was killing me, why the hell did she not get in the car and drive away when I said go? How the hell could she make me watch this now?

I looked round to see Beth was pale and shaking, blood was splattered across her face, she was staring at Dom's lifeless body. I was thankful that his head had slumped forward so Brook couldn't see the mess that would be his face. If by some miracle we lived through this I didn't want her seeing that when she closed her eyes. Blood was seeping down his body soaking into his shirt and starting to pool on the floor.

"Why Trey? Why would you do that?" Brook screamed beating her fists against him crying hysterically. Oh God stop it shortie, he's gonna hurt you again, please stop! He turned and shoved her hard against the wall making my body go cold at the sound of the thump, she gasped and held her head. I squeezed my hands tight trying again to shift, I could feel my wolf now but I had no hold on it, I couldn't do anything!

"Because he gave away something that should have been mine, Bane's Creak was supposed to be mine! You're supposed to be mine" he shouted at her making her flinch. I was so fucking angry my whole body was shaking.

"I am yours" she said quietly, oh God please don't kiss him again shortie, please, I can't see that again! He slammed his fist against the wall inches from her head and I couldn't help but growl, it missed her by inches. I looked around the room, there were five other guys in here, all of them looked totally fucking badass, these must be his high rankers. The one standing closest to Beth was more relaxed than the others, they were slightly more tense that meant that he was ranked higher than them, he was probably Trey's second. I'd have to take him down quickly too, he'd be a good fighter, if I could only shift! My wolf was getting closer with every second as the drugs left my system.

"You can't be mine if you're mated to someone else!" Trey shouted making her flinch again.

"Hey asshole, why don't you just untie me and we can sort this out ourselves, or do you just like fighting girls because they can't fight back?" I said angrily, if he could untie me maybe I could keep him distracted long enough for the drugs to leave my system, if I could last long enough against a wolf!

"Just shut the hell up Jayden!" Brook screamed, what the hell? Does she think she's actually getting somewhere convincing him to let me go? He had no intention of letting me or her mother go, I think he wanted Brook himself though, I don't think he would kill her but that wouldn't stop him from hurting her badly.

Trey started to laugh, "You tell him baby" he said brushing her hair away from her sore looking face.

"Trey, I'm not mated to Jayden, it didn't work for me, it worked for him but I don't feel anything for him, maybe you should try again" she said gripping her hand round the back of his head. Try again? What the hell does that mean? Try what?

"It'll hurt you" he said running his hands down her body making me feel sick that he was touching my mate. I wanted to break every single bone in his hand so he'd never be able to touch her again.

"I don't care hon, please, please try again" she said guiding his face to her neck. Oh hell no! She wants him to try and mark her?

"NO!" I screamed yanking and twisting my arms to try and get them free. I looked over to Beth to see if there was any way she could get free and untie me or something but she had passed out, she was all sweaty and pale. I turned my attention back to Trey who's face was inches from my angels neck. She yelped and squeezed her eyes shut gripping his shoulders so hard she was probably drawing blood as he bit her hard on the opposite side of her neck to my mark.

He pulled back "FUCK IT!" he shouted punching and kicking the wall over and over again, "It didn't fucking work!" he screamed angrily. He turned back to me and I growled at the sight of her blood on his lips, he punched me over and over taking his anger out on me. I clamped my jaw tight and tried not to make a sound, I didn't want Brook to worry any more about me that she already was. I sucked in a ragged breath as I felt my ribs and nose snap. He was breathing heavy when he pulled away and my eyes were stinging, pain shooting down my whole body, making it hard to breathe.

"Maybe I should kill him first, then try" he said to his second, I looked over at Brook, she was sat on the floor crying blood trickling down her neck from the bite. I saw red, I couldn't watch anymore, I don't care if I can't shift, I'm killing Trey! I pushed my feet along the floor quickly scooting my chair back to the wall, then I stood up awkwardly and threw myself back at the wall smashing the chair against it as hard as I could. I felt something hard dig into my back piercing the skin and I clamped my teeth tight. I moved forward and slammed back against the chair harder, it worked, one of the arms snapped off so I could get my wrist free. Oh shit this was gonna work, I couldn't help but get excited. The broken chair was still tied to one of my arms, I glanced up in time to see three of the guys shift including his second. Fuck.

All six of them were advancing on me, I didn't have time to free my other hand, one of the wolves launched themselves at me. I gripped the broken chair in my hand and swung it hitting him hard in the face with it sending him shooting back. I wrenched my arm free and picked up one of the metal chair legs, it was all I had, I tried to shift but nothing, my wolf still wasn't close enough.

"You really are a tough one" Trey said looking at me shocked.

"Tough enough to kill you" I said honestly, but this wasn't a fight I could win, there was two other wolves, three shifters who were in human form and the other wolf that I had hit with the chair was picking himself up off of the floor. I couldn't win this fight, I had no chance at all.

Trey nodded and another of the wolves launched at me, I moved to the side I grabbing hold of his throat and slammed him against the wall, I heard a sickening crack and he made a yelping noise as he slumped to the floor, his legs limp, he obviously had a broken back or hip. I turned back too late, the one I had hit with the chair jumped on me his teeth sinking into my arm making me drop the only weapon I had, blinding pain shot up my arm. His weight knocked me to the floor with him on top of me, his teeth snapping inches from my face as he tried to go for my throat. Shit!

I reach my hand out trying to grab the chair leg I'd dropped whilst trying to keep his mouth away from my body at the same time. My finger tips grazed it, come on! I squeezed my eyes shut, I refused to die before that fucker did! I shoved him hard off of me and rolled to grab the metal chair leg. As he lunged for my throat again I thrust it up at the same time and drove it straight through his chest, his eyes locked on mine as I felt his blood running down my arm where I was still gripping the metal bar.

He shifted back to his human body as he died, I threw him off of me and jumped up just as Trey's body slammed into mine knocking me back off of my feet again. He hadn't shifted which was a surprise, I would have thought that he would have used my lack of shifting to his advantage like the fucking pussy that he was. I smiled, if he wasn't gonna shift this was gonna be too fucking easy. I ducked my head to the side as he went to punch me in the face making him hit the floor, I heard his knuckles or fingers break. I shoved him hard off of me and rolled so I was sitting on top of him and smashed my fist into his face as hard as I could over and over listening to the satisfying cries of pain he was making.

Suddenly I was on the floor again, another wolf on top of me, I was pinned on my front unable to move, I felt his mouth go around my neck, his teeth about to sink in, this was it, I was dead. Suddenly he was gone, I shoved myself up looking back to see a light tan wolf locked in a fight with an almost black wolf. Shit that's Scott! Oh thank fuck for that, Scott was here, he could get Brook the hell out of here! They were fairly even matched, I ran over to the body of the guy I had killed earlier putting my foot on his shoulder and grabbing hold of the metal bar pulling it out of his chest. I knew that if I lived through this I would be thinking about the way his body rose off of the floor slightly as I pulled, how the bar slid out of his body covered in blood with a slight sucking sound, that sound would stay with me forever.

I grimaced and turned back to kill Trey but he wasn't there on the floor where I left him. I looked around wildly for him just as another wolf ran at me, I jumped to the side and smashed the bar into his face, he shook his head making blood splatter on the floor. Shit where was the rest of the help? I needed to get to Brook so I could keep her safe. Another wolf was advancing on me from the other side. I couldn't protect myself from both sides at the same time, I backed up trying to get my back against a wall so they would have to approach from the front.

I glanced up to see Scott with his teeth round the throat of the black wolf, the sounds of their fight was deafening, this was probably scaring the crap out of Brook! He pulled his face away quickly and the black wolf slumped to the floor shifting back to his human form clutching at his throat blood seeping through his fingers as he made a gurgling sound drowning in his own fluids.

Scott turned back and ran towards me to help, the other wolf's blood dripping from his snout. There was a loud bang and Scott fell to the floor mid-stride blood seeping from his chest. What the fuck? I looked round to see Trey standing there with a gun, he'd shot Scott. I felt sick, the only sound I could hear was Brooks piercing scream.

CHAPTER 23

"Trey, I'm not mated to Jayden, it didn't work for me, it worked for him but I don't feel anything for him, maybe you should try again" I lied still desperately tying to think of a way out. He wasn't going to let Jayden go, I was going to watch him die. I gripped my hand around the back of Trey's head.

"It'll hurt you" he said his eyes raking over my face lustfully as he ran his hands down my sides gripping my thighs making my skin crawl. Oh God I know it'll hurt, I remember the last time he tried but I didn't have a clue what he was doing then I just thought he bit me.

I pulled his head forward towards my neck, "I don't care hon, please, please try again" I begged. Oh shit I didn't want to be mated to him but if it worked and he felt even half of what I felt for Jayden then I might be able to convince him to let him go, if I told him I needed him to do it for me, if he loved me enough he would do it. Scott said that male shifters would do anything for their mates, if this worked I could make him let Jay and my Mom go.

"NO!" Jayden screamed I could hear him thrashing around in his chair again, please be quiet Jay please! I clenched teeth and squeezed my eyes shut as I felt his lips touch my neck. Please work, please! His teeth sank into my neck and blinding pain shot down my shoulder and up towards my ear, I could feel the blood dribbling down my neck and I couldn't help but cry out a little. He pulled back slightly his face was murderously angry, shit it didn't work!

He slammed his fist into the wall near my face making me whimper slightly, "FUCK IT!" he shouted getting angrier and angrier as he punched and kicked at the wall, "It didn't fucking work!" he screamed angrily. A small part of me was relieved that I wasn't mated to him, but most of me was so devastated that I could barely breathe. It would have been so much easier, I might have been able to save him. Trey turned away from me and my legs wouldn't support me anymore, I slumped to the floor my neck burning and still bleeding. Trey turned to Jay and started punching him over and over. My heart sank, this is it, this is where he dies and I couldn't even help him.

"Maybe I should kill him first, then try" Trey said breathlessly as he turned to look at Dan. I prayed to God that he would kill me too, I didn't want to live without Jay, there was no life worth having if he wasn't in it, he was everything to me. I closed my eyes crying silently, suddenly I heard a crash, I panicked and opened my eyes to see Jay throw himself at the wall on the other side of the room, the chair broke and he got one of his arms free. Holy shit! What the hell is he doing?

I jumped up, Trey and his boys all started moving towards him, three of them shifted into their wolves and I pressed against the wall terrified, these things were fucking huge and I had only ever seen Jayden and Trey when they were fighting. One of the wolves jumped towards him and Jay smashed him in the face with the chair.

"You really are a tough one" Trey said a little shocked.

"Tough enough to kill you" Jay growled angrily his face the picture of rage.

I looked around wildly for help but there was nothing, he was facing six of them on his own! Where the hell did Trey leave his gun? I couldn't see it anywhere, he must still have it on him, fuck it! I took the chance to run over to my Mom's chair and frantically started to untie her arms. She'd passed out and was slumped in the chair but I needed to untie her in case we could somehow make it out of here. I didn't see much chance of that happening Jay couldn't fight six shifters on his own and I was no fucking use at all! God why did I have to be so damn pathetic?

I glanced over to see Jay was now on his back with a wolf on top of him, he was struggling to reach something. I panicked as the wolfs teeth snapped inches from his beautiful face. Suddenly he pushed up and rolled at the same time grabbing what looked like a metal bar and shoving it deep into the wolfs chest. My heart was crashing in my ears, did he just kill someone? Oh God. The wolf shifted back and I realised it was Ed, bile rose in my throat as I saw the blood seeping out of his body. Oh God five left, come on, someone help us please!

Jay jumped to his feet but Trey slammed into him sending them both sprawling to the floor again, I saw Jay flip Trey over, his face was hard, he was so angry he actually looked like a different person. He was winning, seriously Trey was gonna be beaten to death any second how hard Jay seemed to be punching him in the face. I couldn't help but get my hopes up.

My Mom stirred and I looked down at her, "Mom, Shh everything's gonna be ok, you need to be quiet" I whispered quickly as I looked around to see if anyone had seen me untie her or anything, she looked at me terrified then looked at Dom and started crying again. "Shh Mom" I said stroking her face reassuringly. I saw a black wolf move from the corner of my eye and was just about to shout Jay when he launched at Jay's back sending him sprawling to the floor, my breath caught in my throat as the wolfs mouth went around the back of his neck. I felt the scream about to rip itself out when a light tan wolf shot past me and slammed into the black one. They were snarling and snapping at each other and the sound was deafening, my Mom was wailing again now, I was terrified. Who the hell is the tan wolf and why is he helping? Oh God please tell me helps here!

I was so focused on watching Jayden push himself up, scanning his face and body for signs of injuries that I didn't even notice Trey until he grabbed my arm and jerked me away from my Mom. I winced at how tight his grip was on my arm, I could feel the bone giving, he was gonna break my arm! I looked around wildly for Jay he was backed against a wall with two wolves advancing on him, he still hadn't shifted, the drugs still stopping him from defending himself. All I could hear was growls and snarls, I saw Trey grab his gun from the waistband of his jeans, he sneered at me. "Now he dies" he said pointing his gun at Jay.

I squeezed my eyes shut, I was so angry, I had never been so angry in my life, I literally felt like my blood was boiling in my veins, it was almost painful. I heard the shot. Oh my God, Trey shot Jayden! My anger doubled, I couldn't think of anything else other than ripping everyone to pieces. Suddenly I felt like I was being stabbed with a thousand knives at once, I felt like my skin was melting, like I was being submerged in acid. I had never felt any pain like this in my life, I screamed and clenched my hands into fists as my whole body shook, oh God I'm dying.

Suddenly the pain was gone, I opened my eyes and looked over to Jay expecting to see his dead body lying there on the floor. Instead he was staring at me with wide eyes, "Holy shit" I heard Trey say, I turned back to him my anger still bursting over. He hadn't shot Jay but I wouldn't give him the chance again, he'd missed but he wouldn't get another shot.

Trey was looking down at me horrified and actually a little scared, suddenly he exploded into a wolf and I flinched back slightly, I heard Jay shouting at me to run but I couldn't. I wouldn't let him get hurt, I don't care if it killed me I was going to do everything I could, all I could think about was ripping Trey's throat out and watching him bleed. My Mom was screaming.

Jayden's POV

Brook was screaming, I looked over and saw her shaking, her eyes squeezed shut, she looked like she was in pain. What the hell has he done to her? I'm gonna fucking kill him! I felt the growl ripping it's way out of my throat, I could feel my wolf now trying to push his way out, oh thank God! I was just about to shift when Brook exploded into a wolf, her clothes ripping and falling to the floor in tatters. What the fuck? Oh my God Brook just shifted! How the hell did this happen?

Her head looked in my direction and all I could do was stare at her, she was a little smaller than a normal female shifter which must have been because she was half human. Her fur was a dark brown, "Holy shit" Trey said looking at her shocked the same as I was. Her head snapped round in his direction a growl creeping from her lips, I was so proud of her I could burst.

The two wolves were advancing closer but I wasn't worried now, I could shift, the drugs finally gone from my system, this was gonna be easy. Suddenly Trey shifted, shit he was so close to Brook, I started to panic, I needed to kill these two before I could get to her. "Brook run!" I shouted desperately, she didn't, instead she lunged at Trey. Fuck it this is bad!

I shifted and jumped towards the wolf closest to me throwing my body against his smashing him into the wall, the other one bit into my back hard making pain shoot through me, I threw him off and turned towards him. I didn't have time to waste I could hear growling and snarling coming from Brooks direction and I just prayed that Trey loved her enough not to hurt her. The wolf lunged at me, I moved to the side and gripped his shoulder tearing through his flesh, he whimpered and laid down submitting. Fucking pussy.

I looked at the other one that I had slammed against the wall, he whined and shifted back to his human body. "Please, please don't" he cried holding his hands up innocently, I looked at him he was laying on his side his leg twisted and awkward. He wasn't a threat, I turned and looked for Brook, she was backed up against a wall, her hackles up, snarling fiercly. I ran as fast as I could to her putting my body in front of hers, she was still going mad behind me, I could smell her blood, he'd hurt her.

My wolf went crazy, all I could see was Trey, my pulse was drumming in my ears I was so fucking angry I thought my anger would kill me. I lunged for him raking my claws down his face, he jumped back, I heard a commotion and another wolf came in the house. Fuck it! I glanced to the left to see another tan wolf, shit it's Paul, Scott's father! He ran straight over to Scott who was lying on the floor, he let out a howl which distracted Trey for a split second. I lunged for him again biting deep into his neck, pushing him down to the floor pinning him there with my jaw clamped tight.

He was yelping and trying to struggle free, I bit down slightly harder ignoring the rancid taste of his blood in my mouth. I didn't want this to end too quickly, I didn't want him to get let off too easy, I wanted him to suffer like he made my mate suffer. I twisted my head slightly making him yelp louder, his feet trying desperately to push me off. I hope that hurts you asshole. I heard Brook starting to go crazy again, she was snarling and growling, shit she's probably scared! I needed to kill him, I almost didn't want to, the fight was over way to quickly for my liking but I needed to go to my mate. I squeezed my jaw tight crushing his larynx and pulled away ripping his throat out. I didn't even spare him a second glance as I turned back to Brook.

She had backed herself into a corner, a wolf that I recognised from my pack was walking towards her stalking her, he was going to attack her. I ran and jumped in front of her growling warningly at him, he stopped immediately and looked at me. I looked around the room, the two that had surrendered were still over by the wall in human form, another wolf was against the other wall where I had slammed him against the wall earlier, he was probably mending his broken back. The black wolf that Scott was fighting was dead and so was Trey.

There were no others in here, Beth was leaning over a now shifted Scott and was examining a hole in his chest that looked really bad. There was no danger to my mate here. I shifted back and held a hand out to the wolf in front of me, he shifted back too. It was Christian.

"Who's that?" he asked looking behind me confused and slightly angry that I wouldn't let him attack her.

"That's Brook, go watch those two" I said nodding to the two guys that had punked out of the fight.

Christians eyes went wide as he looked at her growling like crazy in the corner, "Brook? Your mate?" he asked shocked.

I nodded "Go watch them" I said again. I looked at Beth and Paul desperately working on Scott, "Is he gonna be ok?" I asked quickly.

Beth looked at me her face was grim, "I'm not sure, the bullet went into his lung I think, there's a lot of blood" she said grimacing with tears in her eyes. There was nothing I could do, they would call for an ambulance and have him taken to West Bridge, a shifter hospital, I just prayed to God that he would be ok, I turned back to look at Brook.

She was terrified, her hackles were raised, her teeth bared as she assessed my threat level. She was crouched slightly ready to attack me. It was hard the first time you shift, the wolf takes over and because you don't know how to gain control, it can be hard to get back. Some shifters have lost themselves to their wolf, this is why the first shift is always controlled, why you learn how to do it before you do so that you can get back to your human self as your wolf won't want to go back. Come on shortie you can do this.

"Shortie, it's ok" I sad taking a step towards her, she slapped her front feet on the floor growling louder.

"Careful Jay" Paul warned behind me.

I nodded and took another step. "Brook, you need to calm down, try to relax shortie, come on you can do this" I said pleadingly. Please let her be able to do this! I didn't really want to spend the rest of my life as a wolf but I would, I would do anything for her, if she couldn't shift back then we'd have to go wolf full time I guess.

I took another step holding up my hands innocently, she lunged forward and snapped at my hand, I just jerked it back in time. I just needed to get close enough, she wouldn't let me any closer. I shifted into my wolf too and jumped on her quickly pinning her to the floor with my weight. She was snarling and snapping at me trying to throw me off, persuasion wasn't working maybe I needed to try something else.

I was still Alpha male, maybe I could make her calm down by getting her to submit to me. I felt sick for doing this, I ignored her thrashing and wrapped my teeth around her throat applying no pressure at all. I couldn't hurt her, she'd be able to kill me before I could even hurt a hair on her head but I was hoping that the warning would do the trick. I growled loudly as I pinned her to the ground with my mouth around her throat. She whimpered and stopped moving, shit it was working! I stayed there for a few seconds letting her calm and know that I was in charge, yeah right in charge my ass but she didn't know that!

I shifted back still pinning her to the floor, "Calm down Brook, shift back" I ordered trying to sound stern with her. She didn't move, just laid completely still under me, shit maybe I was hurting her I literally had all of my weight on her! I moved slightly hovering above her, "Shift back shortie, everything's fine now, you did great but you need to shift back now, please, for me, can you do that for me?" I begged. I stroked my hand down her side a couple of times. She couldn't do it. She was lost. I looked right into her beautiful brown eyes and resigned myself to the fact that I would never have another conversation with her, that we would never sleep in a bed or do anything human again.

Suddenly she shifted back, she looked at me shocked and terrified. I gasped, oh thank God! I stroked her face, "It's ok shortie, are you ok?" I asked, she was struggling to breathe, she nodded slightly. She made no moves to touch me or move, oh shit she hates me for what I did to her! "I love you shortie, please forgive me, please, I'm sorry, I just needed you to calm down, you wouldn't let me near you, I'm so sorry" I whispered. Silent tears were falling down her face.

"Jayden" she whispered wrapping her arms around my neck.

I breathed a sigh of relief as I sat up, pulling her up with me, sitting her on my lap rocking her gently. "You did so great, I'm so proud of you" I said as I discreetly checked her whole body, she had a fairly deep cut on her upper leg but it didn't look too bad, her neck had stopped bleeding now but looked sore and angry. Now that she could shift it wouldn't even leave a scar if she healed as a wolf. She tangled her hands into the back of my hair pressing her whole body into mine as she sobbed onto my shoulder.

"I couldn't help it, I'm so sorry" she said her voice hitching as she cried harder. I pulled her closer to me needing every inch of her skin to touch mine.

"Couldn't help what shortie?" I asked a little confused, what the hell has she got to be sorry about?

"I tried to hurt you, I wanted to kill you, I couldn't stop" she wailed squeezing me tighter almost choking me she was holding so tight.

"Shh Brook, it's ok, that wasn't you, that was your wolf, it's ok you just couldn't control it that's all, you'll learn how, I'll teach you" I said soothingly.

She pulled away shaking her head fiercly, "I don't ever want to do that again, please don't make me Jay, please" she begged.

I cupped her face in my hands, "You don't have to shortie, it's your choice, shh" I said softly.

I looked at her beautiful face and ran my fingers through her hair, I was so scared I'd lost her. "I love you so much Jay, I didn't mean what I said to Trey, you know that right?" she asked looking at me pleadingly. I smiled and pressed my lips to hers, they tasted salty from her tear streaked face, I kissed her as if I could devour her soul, I wanted it all to myself, I didn't want to share it. I pulled out of the kiss and pressed my forehead to hers looking into her eyes.

"I know you love me shortie, don't worry" I said honestly.

She smiled sadly then looked at something over my shoulder, "Is that Scott?" she cried as she pushed herself out of my arms.

"Yeah, he got shot" I said trying to stand in-between her and the two male shifters blocking her from view. She was still my mate at the end of the day and I didn't want them looking at her naked body if I could help it.

"Is he gonna be ok?" she asked desperately crying again now.

"Your Mom's looking at him shortie, let's go get some clothes and stuff for everyone and let them help him ok?" I asked pulling her away. She nodded and made her way to the stairs in the hallway her eyes not leaving Scott.

I followed her upstairs to what I assume was Trey's bedroom, she went over to the dresser and started pulling out a pile of clothes and laid them on the bed. She pulled on a t-shirt and a pair of his boxers, nothing else would probably fit her. I pulled on a pair of his shorts and t-shirt grabbing extra stuff for Paul and Christian. We didn't speak, I had no idea what to say, she'd just seen me kill three people, maybe she thought I was some kind of monster now or something.

I grabbed the stuff from the bed and went to the door waiting for her, she walked up to me and stopped. "I love you more than anything in the world Jayden" she whispered melting my heart, I brushed my hand over her face lightly.

"I love you too shortie" I said honestly. "Come on, let's get these clothes downstairs and see if we can help" I said grabbing her hand and pulling her quickly down the stairs.

Beth was still working on Scott, pressing on his chest trying to stop the bleeding, he was unconscious and so pale, it didn't look good. Maybe once the bullet was out, if we could wake him up enough to shift back he could start to heal. "Have you called the ambulance?" I asked throwing the clothes to Christian and Paul.

"Yeah it'll be here any minute" Paul said quietly, he looked so stressed, him and Scott were really close, this was probably killing him inside.

"I'll go wait outside for it" I said needing a little fresh air, I grabbed Brook's hand not wanting any space between us, I couldn't let her out of my sight, not yet, not after that. I pulled her out of the front door with me and froze, standing there on the front lawn was about twenty five to thirty wolves from the Trident pack. Holy fuck this is bad. I yanked Brook behind me and prepared myself to shift.

CHAPTER 24

I took a couple of steps back forcing her against the wall keeping my body in front of hers, "Paul, Christian" I growled my eyes not leaving the wolf standing closest to the house, he was obviously in charge of this little posse. I heard them move up behind me one to either side, Brook wrapped her arms around my waist whimpering slightly. "We don't want any trouble, you WILL stand down" I growled using my full Alpha command, the guy at the front shifted back and looked at me his face stern.

"Where is Alpha Newton?" he asked trying to look past us into the house. Oh $hit here comes the fight, I just need to push Brook into the house then take as many as I can, Paul was an awesome fighter, as long as they didn't come at us more than two or three at a time each we should be ok.

"Your Alpha is dead" I said unwrapping Brook's arms from my waist letting my wolf come to the surface ready.

The guy looked at the wolf next to him who shifted back as well, "What do you mean dead? Who killed him? Where are our high rankers?" he asked looking a little nervous.

"I killed him, most of his high rankers are dead too, two of them have surrendered" I said not breaking eye contact with him, he looked at the other guy and then turned back to me.

"Well who are you?" he asked, I noticed a couple of the other wolves shift back too.

Brook was gripping the back of my shirt for dear life, her whole body pressed against mine, I could feel she was shaking so I put one hand back rubbing her hip reassuringly. "I'm Alpha Philips of Bane's Creak" I said sternly, it was the first time I had actually said anything like that out loud, it still felt a little weird.

"If you killed our Alpha then wouldn't you be Alpha of our pack too?" the same guy asked.

A few more shifted back moving closer to each other looking nervous and possibly a little excited. Why the hell would they be excited? Are they glad he's dead? Wait! Shit, did that mean I was Alpha now too? I swallowed a groan and turned to Paul, he nodded slightly. Damn it! Three damn packs, are you kidding me?

"Technically as I've killed you Alpha and you have no high rankers I guess so" I said trying not to show how annoyed I was at the moment, maybe I should have said Paul killed him or something! The two guys at the front spoke in whispers, I tried my best not to listen to them, instead I focused on the sound of Brook's ragged breathing behind me. I can't believe this has happened, for God sake, I didn't even want one pack and now I have three?

The two guys at the front turned back to me and bent down on one knee, oh for Christ sake I hate it when people do that! The rest of the pack shifted back and went to their knee too,

Paul chuckled slightly next to me, probably at my horrified expression I'm not sure. "You can stand up it's fine" I said calmly, "Paul go back to Scott" I said slapping his shoulder gratefully. He nodded and disappeared back into the house quickly.

"We have an ambulance coming from West Bridge any minute, one of my pack are hurt" I announced as they all seemed to be standing there waiting for me to speak. "I need to go to the hospital, my mate has been injured, maybe we could arrange a meeting for tomorrow about Alpha" I suggested looking at the two guys at the front in particular, they seemed to be in charge more than the others.

One of them nodded eagerly, "I'll arrange it, what time?" he asked, I groaned internally, three packs was impossible, I couldn't have this one as well, in a year or so I would have Willow Creak too.

"About 12" I said I turned to Christian, "You can show me where the meeting site is right?" I asked, he nodded grinning happily. He was probably happy that Trey was dead, he said that this pack hated their Alpha and the way the pack was run, he probably had a lot of friends that would benefit from him being dead.

They were all standing around still, "It'd be great if you could arrange that for me, I'll be at your meeting site tomorrow at 12, you should all go back to your homes, there's nothing more you can do here" I said sternly ending the conversation. They all nodded, some of them shifted back and ran off, others walked off in groups talking excitedly.

Just then two ambulances pulled up and I prayed to God that it had arrived in time to save my best friend. The two guys jumped out of each one and ran towards us, "He's in the house, he's been shot in the chest, the other three are barely injured" I said still pis$ed that I actually let them live, they breezed past me into the house. I turned and wrapped my arm around Brook pulling her close to me pressing my face into her hair breathing in her beautiful scent. "I love you shortie" I whispered, silently thanking God that she was safe, how the hell we survived that I don't know.

She pulled back to look at me, "Are you really Alpha of this pack too?" she asked shocked, I nodded and cupped her face in my hands kissing her nose.

"I don't want to be, I'll let them fight for it, I can step down and let them chose their own Alpha through a competition" I said shrugging. There was no way I would have this pack too, I wouldn't do that to Brook, not three packs, I didn't even want one, I was thinking I would step down as Alpha of Bane's Creak and just run my fathers pack with Scott in a year or so, well if he survived.

"Don't worry shortie, in a month or so I'll step down as Alpha of Bane's Creak, and then it'll just be you and me for a year or so before I take over from my father" I said smiling at the thought of us being able to do whatever the hell we wanted. Maybe we'd wait until she finished school or maybe she'd even want to finish college, my father could wait that long. Her breath caught in her throat, her eyes filled with tears, what did I say?

"I don't want you to step down Jay, that was Dom's pack, he.....he asked you to t....take it, he wanted...." she said trailing off crying and hugging me tightly.

I groaned, damn it I didn't think about her Dad, she'd just watched her father get murdered and now I was talking about shunning his pack. Nice one Jay, really well done! "Shortie, it was just an idea, I'm sorry, I don't want to upset you, I won't step down if you don't want me to" I said quietly. I hated to see her cry, I wiped her tears with my thumbs. "I'm sorry about Dom, he was a really great guy" I whispered holding her tight.

She nodded "Yeah, at least he got to meet you, approve of my choice" she said teasingly pretending she was fine.

I nodded "Yeah" I said kissing her forehead, she obviously wasn't ready to deal with this right now, maybe later when we were on our own she'd talk to me.

The paramedics came out carrying Scott on a stretcher, Paul was walking helplessly behind, "Is he gonna be ok?" I asked desperately, the paramedics looked at me sadly and I felt sick.

"He's lost a lot of blood, the bullets still inside, it's touch and go, he'll need surgery" one of them said as they carried him to the ambulance.

"This is all my fault, there were two guys outside when we got here, I sent Scott in to help you, I shouldn't have let him go in alone" Paul said sadly.

I gripped his shoulder, "It's not your fault, this is that assholes fault, he's the one who shot him, Scott saved my life" I said honestly. If he hadn't come in when he did I would be dead and that would have left Brook either on her own with Trey, or dead. Paul nodded looking at his son getting loaded into the ambulance, I could tell he was proud. "Go with him, I'll be there as soon as I can, I just need to sort out the three guys in there" I said nodding back into the house.

"What are you gonna do about them Jay?" Paul asked curiously.

"I'll see what they want to do, they surrendered, well two of them did anyway, maybe they'll want to leave once they're healed, if they go back on their decision I'll have to kill them" I said shrugging. Paul nodded and turned to run to the ambulance, Beth walked out and hugged Brook tightly, she looked tired and so sad, Dom had meant a lot to her, that was probably a lot for her to deal with.

"Christian, come and watch Brook for me" I called, he came out straight away looking at them sadly. I kissed Brook on the forehead, "You ok Beth?" I asked wrapping an arm around her shoulders, she nodded and hugged me back.

"I'll be fine, go sort out what you need to" she said looking at me knowingly.

I smiled "Stay here shortie, I'll be a couple of minutes" I said squeezing her hand gently.

When I went in to the house I made sure to close the door behind me. the two paramedics from the other ambulance were working on the guy with the broken back. He still hadn't shifted to his human form, that was probably a good move, let the healing process take over. "I need to speak to them in private" I said sternly.

The paramedics looked at me a little shocked, "We're still working on him, and the other guys shoulder still needs treatment" one of them said.

"Your treatment might be unnecessary if I don't like what they say, I don't want to waste your time, I'll just be a few minutes" I said opening the door and nodding for them to leave. They looked at each other then stood up and left, the guy with the twisted leg started scooting away from me pressing against the wall looking terrified. Ok well he's not a threat.

I looked at the other two, "I need to know your ranks, and I need to know what you want to happen, I'm Alpha of the Trident's now, I have no problem with killing you if I feel that any of my pack are in danger" I said looking at each one in turn.

The two that had shifted back were shaking their heads fiercely, "My name's Michael, I'm.....well I was, Alpha's fifth" the one with the injured shoulder said, I nodded and looked at the other guy.

"Lee, I'm Alpha's seventh and that's Jerry he's low rank" he said nodding to the wolf who was whimpering on the ground near him.

"Right, and what's going to happen now?" I asked curious as to what they wanted. The guy called Michael looked at me confused.

"What do you mean? I thought you came here to kill all the high rankers? That you wanted this pack, that's why you're here" he said frowning. I laughed, that's what Trey told them?

"Your Alpha told you we wanted your pack?" I asked smiling, wow he really was a wimp, couldn't even fight his own battles. Michael nodded looking even more confused.

"Your Alpha lied to you, he threatened to kill my mate and me, he started all of this, it had nothing to do with your pack, all I wanted was Trey" I said honestly.

They both looked at me shocked, "He said it was a coo, that you were leading it and that you wanted to kill all the high rankers and replace us with your own" he said grimacing.

I shook my head, "That's not how it happened, so with that in mind, the fact that you felt you were in danger, is that why you chose to fight?" I asked, watching intently for their reactions.

They both nodded, "If we'd have known it was just Trey we would have stepped aside, he's not a good Alpha" Michael said looking at me apologetically.

I nodded "I think you need to leave the pack, go find somewhere else, I won't harm you unless you make me" I said warningly. They both nodded looking at me gratefully, I nodded towards the wolf on the floor, "If he's a low ranker why was he fighting?" I asked curiously.

"He wanted promotion, he does a lot of odd jobs and stuff for Trey" Lee said.

"Right, well I'm going to the hospital, you can stay here until you heal then leave and don't come back, if you do anything I don't like I swear I will hunt you down and rip your head off, is that understood?" I growled. They both nodded gratefully, I pulled the door open and nodded for the paramedics to come back in, "You can treat them, if they need to go to hospital take them, if not then they're leaving as soon as they can" I said.

I turned back to look at Dom tied to the chair the pool of blood under his chair was starting to darken and congeal slightly. I walked over and untied his arm restraints, he was a really good guy, he didn't deserve to die like that. Brook was right, he asked me to take his pack, he wanted me to keep it in his family so I would, I wouldn't step down. Looks like I'll have two packs after all, now I just needed to get rid of the Tridents!

"Will you have someone come and look after Alpha Logan?" I asked one of the paramedics, he nodded and I patted him on the shoulder gratefully as I walked out without a second glance to the three that surrendered. They weren't a threat, they were lied to and controlled by Trey the same as the rest of this damn pack.

I wrapped my arm around Brook, "Come on then shortie lets go get your leg and neck looked at ok?" I said smiling at her beautiful angels face as I led her and her mother over to the Scott's car, I looked back and noticed two dead people on the front grass. "Christian, ask the paramedics to take care of the two that you and Paul killed and have the taken to the morgue or something" I said quietly not wanting Brook or her mother to hear. He nodded and ran back to the house, I got in the car and held Brook's hand tightly waiting for him to come back so we could go to the hospital. I had a horrible feeling Scott wasn't going to make it.

Brook ended up having stitches on her leg but her neck was already healing slightly so they left it to close itself. We were now sitting outside the operating theatre, Scott had been rushed in as apparently the bullet had ripped through one of his lungs and they couldn't control the bleeding. Brook was sitting next to me quietly, she hadn't spoken much, I noticed her head fall forward where she kept dozing off. I smiled, "Come here short-ie" I said pulling her onto my lap and tucking her head into my neck rocking her gently, she kissed the side of my neck.

"Love you" she mumbled sleepily making my heart beat faster, I closed my eyes, I will never get used to those words coming out of her mouth.

An hour later they wheeled him out, "We've got the bullet out and repaired the damage" the Doctor said to Paul, he sighed and seemed to relax slightly, he looked like he'd aged ten years in the last couple of hours. "The damage was extensive, when he wakes up from the anaesthetic we'll try to get him to shift, if he can shift, he'll be fine" the Doctor said looking hopeful. I kissed Brook's forehead, thank God he seemed to be ok, the only one that's been lost is Dom.

Paul went into the room with Scott and Beth, I waited outside with Brook to let her sleep for a little while longer, she seemed so peaceful. Maybe she'd sleep through the worry of whether or not Scott would be able to shift, she loved Scott, if he died it would be worse that her losing Dom. After another hour Beth came out and waved me over, "He's waking up" she said looking stressed. I swallowed, oh God please let him be ok!

"Brook, wake up shortie, Scott's waking up" I said brushing her hair away from her face.

"He is? Is he ok?" she asked hopefully.

"Let's go find out, we need to get him to shift" I said easing her off of my lap and holding her tightly as we walked to his room in case she was a little wobbly still.

He was still coming round and was a little groggy, they were tying to wake him up and encourage him to shift but he wasn't responding. Beth and Paul were either side squeezing his hands calling his name, Brook burst into tears next to me squeezing herself to me tightly. The Doctor shook his head slightly, and I felt sick, Paul looked at me. "Make him shift Jay, make him!" he cried desperately, shit make him? How the hell can I make him? I could try I guess, I nodded to Brook and she let go of me wrapping her arms around her Mom both of them crying. Scott was really pale, he didn't look good.

"Scott, it's Jay, you need to shift" I said, his eyes fluttered again but nothing else, damn it! "Scott, you need to shift" I said sternly, his hand moved slightly, "If you don't shift you going to die, now shift" I said shaking him slightly. Come on Scott please! He opened his eyes and looked at me, he was trying, he couldn't do it, I could tell by his eyes, they were hopeless. He knew he was going to die.

I refuse to lose my best friend because of that asshole. "Scott Porter, you WILL shift right now!" I commanded using my full Alpha command, his hands started to shake, $hit he's doing it! It was almost impossible for a shifter not to submit to a full Alpha command, he was born to be a second so he had more control over his submission than other lower rankers but it would still be strong. "Shift now, I'm telling you to shift, now do it! Do it now" I commanded. He squeezed his eyes shut and a couple of seconds later exploded into his tan wolf with a small yelp. "Holy shit it worked" I cried excitedly looking at Paul who looked like he was about to pass out through stress.

Brook laughed sounding relieved and Paul grabbed me into a hug, "Thank you, oh God Jay, thank you" he said gratefully. I can't believe that worked! He was going to be fine. I breathed a sigh of relief and smiled as Brook kissed Scott on the side of his snout, she really was amazing, less than two weeks ago she didn't even know what the hell a shifter was and now here she is kissing a wolf.

I rubbed my hand down her back, "Maybe we should let him rest, he'll need plenty of sleep, we can come back in the morning" I suggested looking at Beth, she nodded and hugged Paul tightly. Brook stepped away, I looked at him, God I was so happy

I could burst. "Well done, good job and thanks for saving my life" I said grinning, he whimpered slightly. "I'll come back in the morning, rest, recover, that's an order" I said sternly before hugging Paul.

"Is it ok if I take Scott's car, I'll drop the girls home then come back to get you" I suggested.

He shook his head, "Rachel and Mel want to come to the hospital, I told them to wait at home, I'll call them, you take the car, I'll see you tomorrow, and Jay if you need me to come to the meeting with you tomorrow you let me know ok" he said smiling. I nodded, Paul was a really great guy, and such a great Dad, in a way he had been a Dad to me too, he always treated me like one of the family when I was at Scott's.

"Thanks, I'll see you in the morning" I said taking a last look at Scott who was now asleep on his side. "Come on then shortie, Beth let's go" I said nodding to the door.

I woke in the morning with my body wrapped protectively around Brook's. She was still asleep, I brushed her hair away from her face and tried my best not to look at the heeling teeth marks on her neck, he was dead now, there was no point in me getting myself worked up about it again. I still can't believe Brook shifted like that, her Dad would have been proud of her if he'd have seen that. We were both just lucky that she was able to get back, I'd follow her anywhere and be happy whatever happened, but the thought of not seeing her beautiful face or hearing her beautiful voice wasn't something I ever wanted to got through.

We hadn't spoken much since last night, by the time we got back to my house she was exhausted and barely managed to climb in the bed before she feel asleep. I loved waking up to her, it was the best thing that I could ever wish for. After an hour she stirred and pressed her face into my chest, "Mmm, I know you're awake Jayden, you better not have been watching me sleep again" she mumbled against my skin. I laughed, wow busted! She pulled back to look at me smiling teasingly.

"Sorry, couldn't help myself" I said shrugging, she laughed and shook her head as if I was being silly, she obviously wasn't over the hang-ups about her body quite yet.

She kissed my chest and I felt my wolf fighting me growling at me to take her. I sighed and wrapped my arms tighter around her, I didn't ever want to let go. "Shortie, can we talk about something?" I asked swallowing my nerves, she nodded looking at me tenderly as she ran her hand over my chest lightly making my wolf growl louder.

"I was wondering if now that everything's sorted and you've agreed to be my mate, whether you would move in with me" I said quietly, praying with every fibre of my body that she would say yes.

She looked at me a little shocked, "Um, wow that was un-expected" she said looking uncomfortable. Great, nice one Jay, she's not ready, way to go.

"It's ok, sorry I shouldn't have asked, it's too soon for you it's fine" I said trying to sound like it wasn't killing me inside thinking about not waking up with her everyday for the rest of my life. "We'll wait as long as you want, I just though that" I started but she put her hand over my mouth to stop my rambling.

"I'd love to" she said smiling happily. She'd love to? Is that a yes? Hold crap she said yes!

"You would?" I asked rolling so I hovered above her being careful to keep all of my weight off of her.

She laughed, "Hell yeah I would" she said pulling me down to kiss her. As soon as my lips touched hers, her damn hormones attacked my nose making me instantly hard. Damn it, this being mated is like I'm stuck in some permanent horny wolf state, she was gonna kill me I swear.

Chapter 25

When I finally managed to prise myself off of her glorious body we went to the hospital to visit Scott. Beth stayed at mine to pack up her stuff as they had restrictions on the number of visitors at one time, she said she would go later instead. When we walked in he was sitting up in the bed chatting to Mel, I grinned, he looked so good.

"Well you look like crap Scott, maybe you should have stayed shifted" Brook teased as she hugged him tightly making him laugh.

"Thanks Brooklyn, nice to see you too" he said shaking his head amused, Brook went over to hug Mel so I sat on the edge of his bed.

"Hey man, how are you feeling?" I asked, he smiled and nodded.

"Yeah I'm good, they said I need to shift for an hour then come back then do another hour so I don't heal too fast or something, I don't know, but I feel good actually" he said shrugging.

"Scott, thank you so much for coming in like you did, if you hadn't shown up I would have been dead and Brook probably would too, I owe you, seriously anything I can ever do for you, let me know ok?" I said honestly.

He grinned, "You don't owe me anything Jay, if that was me you would have done the same thing right?" he said shrugging as if saving mine and my mates lives were nothing.

"Yeah of course I would have but still, thanks" I said honestly, I would never be able to repay him for saving Brook. If I'd died she would either be with Trey, dead or stuck shifted.

"So Brook shifted huh? She a pretty wolf?" he asked teasingly waggling his eyebrows.

I laughed "Damn fine" I said laughing he is just too funny.

"On a serious not though, my Dad said you're Alpha of the Tridents, what's going on with that? I mean you gonna have two packs or what?" he asked curiously, hell no I wasn't.

I shook my head "Nah, I can't have two, I'm gonna let them compete for it, there'll be some guys there that want it" I said shrugging, there was no way I was having that pack too.

He nodded "Yeah, probably for the best, I mean you'll have Willow Creak soon right?" he said laughing.

"Glad my life amuses you" I said sarcastically making him laugh harder.

My phone rang and I stood up grabbing it out of my pocket, it was my father, what the hell is he gonna want? "Hello?" I said not really wanting to deal with him right now.

"Hi Jayden, I spoke to Paul early this morning about what happened yesterday with Alpha Newton" he said.

"Yeah, it's all sorted now, I just need to sort out his pack" I said frowning.

"You mind if I come to the meeting with you? I mean it would be better if there was a representative from both of the other packs in the area" he asked, I closed my eyes. I really didn't want to spend anytime with him but I guess it was better to have a repetitive from each pack there at the meeting.

"Yeah sure, I'm going there for twelve, I'll pick you up at half past eleven then ok" I suggested.

"Great see you then" he replied, I sighed and snapped my phone shut watching Brook talk and laugh with Scott and Mel, God she was so damn beautiful.

After an hour I needed to go, "Shortie, I need to go, want me to drop you home or something?" I asked grinning at the word home meaning my house that she was soon to be living in. She smiled happily too so maybe she was having the same thought about living with me.

"Can't I come with you?" she asked wrapping her arms around my waist, I shook my head fiercely, I didn't know what would happen at this meeting, I didn't think there would be any trouble but just in case I needed to know she was safely away.

"No shortie, I need to do this on my own ok?" I said kissing her forehead, she sighed and pressed her face into my chest, I tangled my fingers into her silky hair and lent down to kiss her, ignoring the blast of desire that hit me as soon as my lips touched hers.

"Ok, I'll stay here then and you can pick me up on the way through or something" she suggested looking hopeful, I smiled and nodded, she'd like to stay here and gossip with Mel some more, Scott was due to shift again for another hour so Mel wouldn't have anyone to talk to otherwise.

"Ok shortie, I love you" I said honestly looking into her beautiful hazel eyes.

She smiled "I love you too Jayden" she said going up on tiptoes to kiss me, she still wasn't tall enough so I bent my head slightly and pressed my lips to hers again, moaning slightly as my wolf growled at me wanting her right now. Wow horny wolf state again, jeez give me a break! I pulled back before I wouldn't be able to and looked at Scott.

"I'll see you in a bit then, you should shift again Scott, Mel look after my girl" I said winking at her as I turned to leave.

"Good luck Jay" Scott called as I walked out of the room, yeah good luck I was probably going to need it, they weren't really going to like what I was going to say I could tell.

I drove to my fathers house and waited for him to come out, he would have heard the car pull up so I didn't bother getting out of the car. I watched him walk up to the car seeming a little hesitant, he got in and smiled looking at me but not quite meeting my eyes as a sign of respect, damn it I swear I'll never get used to this.

"Hi" I said nodding in greeting.

"Jayden, how are you and your mate?" he asked politely, I smiled thinking of Brook.

"We're good, she's a little sad, did you know that Dominic Logan died?" I asked frowning.

He nodded "Yeah, Paul told me, I'm sorry, he was a good guy" he said.

"Yeah he was" I said quietly. We drove the rest of the way in awkward silence stopping to pick up Christian on the way.

When we pulled up at the meeting site there were cars everywhere. Damn how big is this pack? "Christian how many shifters in the Tridents?" I asked as we walked to the field.

He shrugged, "I would guess at a hundred" he said, Christ a hundred? Great this is just great, well I guess the competition will be fierce for Alpha with that many shifters there's bound to be a lot of males of age that want it.

I followed him to the top of the field to talk to the guy that was at Trey's yesterday the one that arranged the meeting. "Alpha Philips, it's good to see you, the whole pack is here" he said nodding respectfully.

I held out a hand for him to shake, "Thanks for arranging all of this, sorry I didn't ask your name yesterday" I said apologetically, I just had too much going to to worry about pleasantries when I spoke to him yesterday.

He shook my hand excitedly, "It's Alan" he said grinning.

I smiled "Well then Alan, let's get this show on the road shall we?" I asked nodding towards his pack who were watching my every move. He nodded and stepped back so I could step onto the little wooden box thing that they obviously used as a platform for meetings.

"Hi I'm Alpha Philips of Bane's Creak, as you're probably already aware your Alpha is dead as are most of your high rankers, as the rules state I killed Alpha Newton therefore I am the new Alpha of The Tridents" I said looking over the sea of faces. They all started cheering and dropped down onto one knee, I rolled my eyes. "It's fine you can stand, I need to talk through some things with you, you might want to get comfortable" I said sitting down on the wooden box. They all started whispering and sat down on the grass looking at me like I was slightly crazy.

"So I already have a pack that I have just taken over, running two packs isn't something that's going to work out for me" I said honestly. The whispering started again so I held up a hand to silence them, "What I'm suggesting I do is step down as Alpha and let you compete for it, those males that are of age who would like to compete for it would enter into a competition and the winner takes over as Alpha, obviously I'll stay on as Alpha long enough to oversee the competition so that the pack isn't left without a leader" I said looking round at the shocked and scared faces. Ok they don't look like they are going for this at all!

"So seen as we're all sitting down it'll be easy to see who would like to compete, so if you would like a shot at Alpha and are over 20 if you could stand up" I said. People started looking round at each other curious to see who stood up, but no one had moved. Shit! "If you want a shot at Alpha stand now so we can see how big the competition will be" I said sternly looking over at Alan, he was sitting on the floor next to the platform I was sat on. He shook his head firmly at me, I glanced at Christian to see him sitting down too, oh come on seriously?

"No one wants Alpha?" I asked shocked. There were murmurs of 'No' from the crowd. I glanced at my father who shrugged, damn it I don't want this pack! "Ok well as I'm stepping down as Alpha and no one wants to take over how about another suggestion, you have two pack representatives here, I'm here on behalf of my pack and my father's here on behalf of Willow Creak" I said waving a hand in my fathers direction.

"So if no one wants to take over the only suggestion I can make is that the pack splits to join the two neighbouring packs, we'll expand the territories to cover Trident territory too" I said shrugging. There was no other option, there were cries of outrage and horror from the crowd.

"No we can't split the pack" people were begging, women started crying. Oh my God!

I held up a hand to stop the noise, "You don't want this pack to split, with a show of hands, who wants this pack to stay together?" I said looking over as almost every single hand shot into the air making my heart sink.

I groaned and looked at my father for help, he moved and sat on the platform next to me. "You really can't run this pack too?" he whispered.

I shook my head "I can't do that to Brook, she's still in school, I can't have two packs right now and then there's Willow Creak too" I said feeling sick. I turned back to the crowd, "Have any of you reconsidered now and would like to stand for Alpha?" I asked hopefully, my question was met with blank stares and no movement at all. "What would happen if the pack had no Alpha?" I asked my father quietly.

He shook his head, "This pack needs a leader, after Alpha Newton they need stability otherwise they're going to go off the rails" he whispered.

"Can I chose someone and make them do it?" I asked hopefully.

He shook his head, "No they have to be willing to take it" he said matter of factly. I groaned and closed my eyes, shit this was bad, I was gonna be stuck with this pack if no one stepped up.

Suddenly I had a thought, "But if they are willing to do it I can step down and appoint someone else?" I asked hope rising in my chest.

My father nodded, "As long as there are no objections from the pack" he said looking at me curiously. Oh God please let this work!

"Ok I have another suggestion, I know of someone who would make an excellent Alpha, he's a really great guy, he's not of age for another month, he was born to be my second but he is more than capable of running a pack, his name is Scott Porter" I said looking over them slowly as that sunk in.

"If I stepped down I could appoint him as Alpha if he was willing to take it provided there was no objections from the pack" I said hopefully. I think Scott would go for this, he never wanted Alpha before but I think he probably never thought about it as he was born to be a second, he would have never thought of challenging for it. "If Scott is willing to take Alpha, would there be any objections to my recommendation?" I asked standing up so I could see better.

I glanced over to Alan he looked pleased with the idea as did everyone else, I think they would take any solution that meant they got to stay together even if I suggested a freaking child run their pack. They were all nodding enthusiastically, I grinned, shit I hope Scott went for this! "Ok by a show of hands then, all in favour of Scott Porter taking over as Alpha provided he accepts of course" I said a little sheepishly. Every single hand shot into the air, I laughed with relief.

"Ok well like I said Scott's not of age for another month so I'll remain as Alpha until that time then I'll step down, if Scott is unwilling to take Alpha then I really think we'll need to split the pack unless someone wants to step up" I said feeling better than I had felt all morning. "So I'll leave you my number and we'll meet again next week, I need to go and speak to Scott, he's actually in hospital recovering from a gun shot wound at the moment but when we meet next week I'll bring him to meet you all" I said grinning now.

"Alan do you think you could arrange another meeting for Saturday?" I asked.

He nodded "Absolutely Alpha Philips" he said happily.

"Ok guys, well I'll pass my number to Alan and we'll meet again on Saturday, I'll go and speak to Scott right now" I said heading over to Alan and giving him my number. "Thanks for arranging this for me, I appreciate it, I'll be sure to pass my recommendations onto Scott, he'll obviously need some high rankers" I said.

He grinned and nodded "Thank you Alpha Philips" he said proudly, I slapped him on the shoulder and went back to my father and Christian who were talking off to one side.

"This is ok right? Christian you don't want to compete?" I asked curiously.

He shook his head, "I'm not cut out for Alpha" he said sternly.

"Ok well I guess I had better go speak to my best friend and see if he's willing to dig me out of a pile of shit" I said laughing.

I dropped Christian back at his and drove to my fathers house, when I pulled up he didn't get out, he turned to me "Jayden, I know we've never been close and that it's my fault but I just want to go on record and say that I don't think you would have any problems running three packs, I think you'll make an excellent

Alpha and any pack would be lucky to have you" he said looking uncomfortable, I sat there in shock.

This was the longest conversation we'd probably had without it being him lecturing me or anything. I had no idea what to say so I just sat there looking at him, "I'm proud of you son" he said squeezing my shoulder before getting out of the car and walking off quickly. What the hell was that? I shook my head a little dazed and pulled out to go to the hospital praying with every bone in my body that Scott would say yes.

When I walked in he was in human form again which was awesome, Brook jumped on me as soon as I walked through the door, her damn hormones attacking me immediately as she crashed her perfect mouth to mine. I gripped her ass tightly fighting with my wolf, we would have plenty of time for that later I needed to sort out this damn pack situation. I pulled out of the kiss reluctantly making her whimper slightly, "Hey shortie" I said breathlessly, shit I needed her right now!

I pulled her tighter against me just breathing in her scent that was like nothing else in the world, "Hi, I missed you" she whispered as I nuzzled against her neck kissing around the edges of my mark teasingly being sure to not touch it. She gripped her hands in my hair, "Stop teasing me Jay, It's not fair" she mumbled, I chuckled and pulled away from her before I took her to the nearest empty hospital bed and had my way with her.

"Shortie, Mel, I need to speak to Scott, any chance we could have a couple of minutes?" I asked hopefully, I actually wanted Brook to stay but I didn't want to put any extra pressure on Scott to say yes if he didn't want to. Brook nodded and kissed me again softly before heading to the door with Mel following behind her,

I waited until the door shut before sitting in the chair next to Scott.

He was watching me curiously, he was looking tense ready to shift to help me if I was in danger by the look of his hands clenched tight. "Scott, I need to talk to you about something" I said unsure how to start.

He nodded "What do you need Jay?" he asked.

I forced a smile "Well I couldn't step down as Alpha of the Tridents as no one wanted to take over, they don't want the pack to split and join mine or my fathers packs, they want to stay together" I said running a hand through my hair nervously.

He nodded looking thoughtful, "I guess they wouldn't want to split, I can understand that, if someone asked for Willow Creak to split we wouldn't want to either" he said shrugging.

"Yeah I know, I understand but no one wanted to step up for the Alpha position, I spoke to my Father and apparently if I suggest someone to take over and the pack doesn't object then they can take Alpha without competing if they want to" I said skirting around the issue.

He nodded looking thoughtful again, "What about Pete from Bane's Creak? Or my father, he'd be a great Alpha" he said proudly.

I nodded "Yeah he would, but I already had someone in mind actually, I'm just not sure how he's gonna feel about it" I said watching his face.

He laughed "Well why the hell wouldn't he want Alpha, it's a great honour, who was you thinking of someone from Bane's Creak?" he asked curiously.

I laughed and shook my head, "No I was thinking of you actually" I said watching his face change to shock and astonishment. He didn't say anything, "Well what do you think?" I asked after a minute of him just staring at me with wide eyes.

He gulped, "Me? Seriously? But I'm not even of age" he said shaking his head frowning.

"I'll wait for you to be of age if you want it" I said trying to read his face.

"Really? You really think I could be an Alpha?" he asked quietly.

I laughed, "Scott, you could be Alpha with both hands tied behind your back, I know you were born to be second, but I have no doubt in my mind that you could do this, but only if you want to" I said firmly. He frowned looking deep in thought, "It'd be a big responsibility, you'd have to change colleges and move back here, and you've got no mate so you'd be running it on your own" I said throwing in the negatives of running a pack.

"If I took Alpha you'd help me though right? I mean I know you're new to this too but we could kind of help each other right?" he asked hopefully.

Holy shit he's gonna say yes! "Absolutely, you know I would, but you need to think this through properly, do you want to be Alpha of the Tridents?" I asked.

He swallowed loudly and nodded "Yeah ok" he said confidently. I laughed with relief, thank God for that!

"Awesome, well you'd better get yourself healed then because we're meeting them again on Saturday, I'll run it until you're of age officially but we'll start phasing you in before that, you'll need to set up a whole new high ranker system as there's literally no one so I'll let you chose all of them" I said grinning, he could basically run the pack for a month unofficially and I'll just be spokesperson.

"When are they letting you out?" I asked happily.

"Tomorrow, I just need to keep shifting in small bursts but I feel fine now" he said grinning proudly.

"Ok well I need to take my girl home, I'll come and see you tomorrow at yours and we can sort out everything Alpha Porter" I said nodded respectfully.

He grinned "That sounds fucking weird" he said laughing.

I nodded "You'll get used to it, we both will eventually, thanks for this Scott, you know you really are the best friend a guy could ask for and the Trident pack are lucky to have you" I said honestly.

He smiled "Thanks Jay" he said looking at me gratefully.

"I'll see you tomorrow, no hitting on the hot nurses while your in here" I joked as I made my way out of the door to find Brook.

I found her and Mel sitting in the corridor reading a magazine laughing about some article in there. "Hey, we're all done" I said sitting next to Brook and wrapping my arm around her shoulder.

"What was that about Jay?" she asked snuggling closer to me.

"I'll tell you leter, wanna go shortie?" I asked hopefully. I really just needed to hold her, I hadn't seen enough of her, we'd only been mated for a week and in that time so many things had happened.

I just needed to spend the day with her glued to my side, I hadn't spent enough time with her yet, mind you even if I spent every minute of everyday with this amazing beautiful girl it still wouldn't be enough. "I'm gonna go back in and see Scott, I'll see you guys tomorrow" Mel said winking at Brook as she left obviously catching on that we needed some private time.

Brook smiled at me and wrapped her arms around my neck gripping her hands into the back of my hair. "I love you so much Jayden" she said making my heart skip a beat.

"I love you too shortie, more than anything" I said honestly as I bent my head and kissed the most perfect girl in the world.

Everything was working out perfectly. I had one pack for now, my best friend was getting better every second and he was going to be Alpha which would be awesome as that means the packs would be closer and run in harmony. And I had the girl of my dreams wrapped tightly in my arms, well that's not strictly true because I don't even think I could dream up a girl as perfect as my mate.

"Let's go home shortie" I whispered.

"Absolutely Alpha Philips" she murmured flirtily making me groan as a thousand lustful thoughts ran through my brain, this girl really was gonna kill me one day.

EPILOGUE

B rook's POV

Jayden and I had been mated for three perfect years today. Jay had finally qualified as a lawyer even though he hated doing it, he hasn't done one case since he qualified. At the same time as qualifying as a lawyer he qualified as a mechanic and has set up a little business for himself which he loves. He buys run down old classic cars and fixes them up and sells them on, he does quite well for himself too, but to be honest even if he didn't earn any money at all, the smile on his face when he's talking about buying a car or something that he's done would make everything worth it.

I had finished college now too and was a book editor which had always been my dream. I loved my job and actually worked from home most of the time which was awesome as I got to see Jay every lunchtime when he came home. Not that we ever actually ate lunch in that hour mind you. The passion being mates hadn't subsided one little bit and to be honest I don't think it ever would.

Scott was Alpha of the Tridents and was doing an awesome job at it too, it was hard for him at first, he encountered a lot of problems as the pack had been running wild under Trey for so long that he had trouble reining everyone back in again. Him and Jay had managed to calm things down and they were settled now thankfully. The Tridents and Jay's two packs ran in harmony and everything was great. Jay had taken Alpha of Willow Creak from his father just over two months ago, he was an awesome Alpha, very well respected, no one ever doubted anything he said and everyone looked to him for advise and guidance and I couldn't have been prouder of him.

I stood there looking at myself in the mirror, I could feel the nerves bubbling up. There was over three hundred people out there waiting, I could hear the hum of people talking but I tried not to focus on them.

"Hey Brook, everything ok? It's about that time you know" Paul Porter said as he held out his arm to me. I gulped and straightened my dress for the hundredth time.

"Do I look ok?" I asked turning to face him.

He grinned and nodded, "You look beautiful, don't be nervous everything's fine just pretend no one else is there" he said smiling at me reassuringly as he linked my arms through his holding my hand tightly. I nodded and turned towards the door of the marquee that we had put up specifically for today.

"Oh God, is Mel out there already?" I asked feeling sick with nerves, he squeezed my hand.

"Stop panicking, Mel's exactly where she's supposed to be" he said chuckling at me, obviously finding my nerves funny.

"Thanks for doing this Paul, I really appreciate it, I just wish Dom were here" I said sadly, he looked at me proudly.

"I've always thought of you as a daughter Brook, it's my pleasure honestly, I feel like a proud father right now and I know that if Dom were still alive he would be feeling just like I am right now" he said kissing my cheek. I swallowed the lump in my throat and he led me out of the little canvas door.

As I stepped out into the field where we held our pack meetings, I noticed that it was a gorgeous warm sunny day, not too hot just perfect and seemed to match my mood. I peeked around the corner of the marquee looking up the field. All I could see was the back of people's heads sitting down on little wooden chairs in two sections with a carpet going up the middle. Each row of chairs had a bunch of red roses on leading up to the front of the field.

"So many people" I mumbled nervously.

"Of course there is, that's two packs worth of shifters and a lot from the tridents too" Paul said grinning. I gulped and nodded looking over at Mel. She looked beautiful in her red silk dress with her blonde hair all pinned up leaving some loose ringlets around her face. She grinned and pointed mouthing the words "You ready?" to me. I nodded and she walked to the corner of the marquee and waved, I heard the music start up and I felt a little shaky. What if I forgot my words? What if I passed out or something stupid and embarrassed myself in front of our packs?

"Come on then Brook, let's get you married" Paul said grinning, I smiled at the thought of being married. I had been looking forward to this for so long but now it was actually here I just wanted to run, grab Jay and jump on a plane and get married on a beach somewhere on our own. I let him tug me around the corner and I tried not to pay attention to the murmurs and cooing noises people were making as I walked up the little carpeted aisle. I kept my eyes firmly on the vicar at the end willing myself not to fall over.

I saw movement on the front row, Jayden stood up with Scott next to him and moved to stand at the front. He turned to look back at me and watch me walk to him, he was looking at me so lovingly that it made my heart ache. God I wanted to marry him so much, I started moving a little faster eager to get to him and Paul gripped my hand tighter keeping me by his side as we walked to the pace of the music. God was it this slow in rehearsals? It was taking forever to get to him!

When I finally got to the front I couldn't keep the smile off of my face, he looked so damn handsome in his black suit that I could barely suppress my lustful moan. Wow this ceremony is going to be really hard for him because my hormones are going crazy! Paul kissed my cheek and placed my hand in Jay's.

"Hi shortie" he whispered looking at me with the biggest most beautiful smile, his eyes shining with love and lust as he looked me over in my white silk dress.

"Hi soon to be husband" I whispered back, he laughed and pulled us forward slightly so we were in front of the vicar.

I tried really hard to listen to what the vicar was saying but I just couldn't concentrate. I couldn't keep my eyes off of Jayden, I watched his hair ruffle slightly in the wind, how his green eyes sparkled slightly, how the material of his suit jacket moved as he took a breath, how the proud smile on his face didn't once leave his perfect mouth. He was going to flip when I told him about my wedding gift, I couldn't wait, honestly it had been so hard keeping it secret until today, I almost couldn't do it, a few times I almost told him about it.

Jay squeezed my hand slightly and nodded his head towards the vicar slightly, I reluctantly dragged my eyes from him for the first time since I saw him and looked at the little man standing there. He was looking at me expectantly, what is he looking at me like that for? He smiled and Jay chuckled slightly next to me, "Ok you're nervous, it's fine, this happens a lot" the Vicar said smiling looking amused. Had I missed something? "Just repeat after me" he said happily, I gulped this was the bit that I was worried about. Please don't let me stumble over my words!

"I Brooklyn Logan Mills, take you Jayden Richard Philips, to be my lawful wedded husband, to have and to hold, for richer for poorer, for better and for worse, from this day forward as long as we both shall live" I repeated quietly. It didn't really matter how loud I spoke, all the damn shifters would be able to hear me anyway. Jay was beaming at me, when he said his lines he looked me right in the eyes and said his loud and clear with his damn Alpha confidence. I loved those words coming out of his mouth, it was the sexiest damn thing in the world.

He pushed a beautiful gold wedding band onto my ring finger and I knew that the words he had asked to be engraved on the inside would always stay against my skin. 'All my love forever and always' had been engraved inside my ring as per his request. After we had exchanged rings the vicar said the words that made my insides dance with happiness. "I now pronounce you husband and wife, you may kiss your bride" he said. As soon as the words left his mouth Jayden let out a victorious little growl and grabbed me kissing me with so much force that if he wasn't holding me up I would have fallen over. I wrapped my arms around his neck and kissed him back. My husband. Wow I wouldn't get used to that in a hurry.

He pulled back grinning and I realised people were clapping and cheering, but all I could see were his eyes. "I love you Mrs Philips" he whispered pulling me closer to him, I grinned, oh God I loved that.

"I love you too Jayden" I said honestly, he kissed me again and the music started back up making him groan as he pulled away from me.

"Come on then Mrs Philips, lets get the party over with so I can take you home and sort out those hormones for you" he whispered chuckling as he kissed my neck making me squirm at how close he was to his mark.

I nodded and he took hold of my hand leading us back up the aisle towards the huge marquee where there was food and a little bar and music set up ready for the reception. People were congratulating us and kissing and hugging me, everyone was shaking Jay's hand looking really pleased for us. Scott came over and hugged me, "Hey best man" I said teasingly as I straightened his cravat for him.

"Hey married woman" he replied making me laugh, that was seriously going to take some time getting used to.

"Where's Jenny?" I whispered looking around slyly, he groaned and looked around too uncomfortably.

"She's not here, Alan didn't want her to come, probably for the best I guess" he said looking relieved and slightly annoyed at the same time.

"You need to talk to him and sort this out" I whispered.

He nodded and closed his eyes, "I know, we can't keep putting it off" he said looking defeated and stressed.

Jay slapped him on the shoulder, "Alpha Porter, excuse me while I take my wife for our first dance" he said grinning happily as he took my hand. I laughed at his enthusiasm and let him lead me to the dance floor area that they had set up. He pulled me close and wrapped his arms around me and pressed his forehead to mine making everyone else disappear. I tangled my hand into his hair and guided his mouth to mine again eager for the second kiss from my new husband, I ignored the clicks from the cameras.

After about an hour I couldn't hold it anymore, I needed to give Jay his wedding gift. I smiled over at him, he was chatting to a couple of Bane's Creak, I caught his attention and waved him over. He immediately apologised to his friends and made his way over to me wrapping his arm around my waist. "What's up shortie?" he asked catching a stray hair and winding it back into my twist for me.

"I have a present for you and I want to give it to you now" I said flirtily.

He grinned and pulled me closer, "Oh really? Well I'll definitely like whatever you give me" he said raising one eyebrow suggestively.

I laughed at his train of thought, "Jay you really have a one track mind you know" I said trying to suppress my giggle at his lustful face.

He nodded "I know, I'm not going to apologise for it" he said shrugging.

I laughed, "Come on then let's go outside" I said taking his hand.

He smiled and led us through the marquee dodging through the huge crowd before anyone could stop us to offer yet more congratulations. When we got outside we walked hand in hand away from the marquee towards the trees. Jay slipped off his jacket and held it out for me to put on, Damn he is so adorable!

I stopped by a big tree and leant against it pulling him close to me, he immediately started kissing me obviously thinking I had brought him out here for some sort of outdoor early honeymoon. I giggled and pushed him back, "Jayden, stop I need to give you your gift" I said trying to sound stern.

He groaned and pulled back slightly, "Ok shortie, sorry" he said looking at me expectantly.

I could feel the excitement bubbling up inside, "Well I wanted to get you something you could keep and that you would love" I started, he nodded and pressed his body to mine lightly.

"So what did you get me Mrs Philips?" he asked teasingly as he took my hand rolling my new wedding ring around my finger.

I couldn't stop smiling, "A baby" I said watching his face, his mouth dropped open in shock as he took in what I said.

"A.....a...b-baby? Seriously?" he asked with wide eyes. I smiled and nodded. "Oh shit" he mumbled letting go of my hand to place his hand on my stomach lightly, "Really? Like a real baby? I'm gonna be a Daddy?" he asked his face getting more and more excited with each second.

"Yes like a real baby, I'm six weeks pregnant, I came off the pill a couple of months ago, I wanted to surprise you" I said laughing.

He grinned "Well I'm surprised" he said as he bent his head and kissed me gently still not taking his hand off of my stomach.

"Good surprise I hope" I whispered against his lips, he brushed his hand down the side of my face.

"The best surprise ever, thank you shortie, I love you so much and I swear I'll be the best husband and father in the world" he said looking at me like I had just given him a winning lottery ticket.

My heart was thumping in my chest at how excited and pleased he was about this. Jayden had been wanting a baby since we first mated but he never once brought up the subject, waiting patiently while I finished school then went to college, but I was ready now and I loved the little baby growing in my stomach just as much as I loved it's daddy and I could tell by his face that he felt the same.

"Oh shit, I hope it's a boy" Jay said suddenly.

I smiled "To take over as Alpha?" I asked teasingly, he shook his head and bent down and kissed my stomach softly rubbing his hands over it lightly.

"No that's not the reason, I was just thinking if we have a little girl that she's going to have me wrapped around her little finger just like her momma has, and my life will be ten times harder, plus if she looks anything like you I'll have to kill all the boys in my packs when they look her way" he said shrugging. I laughed at his serious face, he wasn't joking he was genuinely worried. "Boys are easier, if it's a little girl in there then I'm in real trouble" he said standing up and kissing me stealing my breath and making my heart beat faster.

"Thank you Mrs Philips" he said looking at me gratefully.

I smiled "You are most welcome Alpha Philips" I said kissing him again.

Everything had worked out perfectly, it was like some sort of fairytale, like I was living someone else's life. I never thought in my wildest dreams that it was possible to be as happy as I am right now, being mated to the best man in the world and expecting our first baby. Life couldn't get any better than this.